Lettie Brent Boggan
Caroline Singleton
Judy Archer
Bill Dunn
Peggy Gilmer-Ploseeler
David Creel
Philip L. Levi
Melanie Noto
P. Floyd
John M. Floyd
Patti Carr Black
Sue Stock
Marion Barnwell
Dorothy Shawhan
Michelle Graham

Mad Dogs & Moonshine

Other Stories
with a Taste of the South

Edited by Judy H. Tucker
& Lottie Brent Boggan

QUEEN'S HILL PRESS

Also from The Red Dog Writers
From the Sleeping Porch
Fireflies in Fruit Jars

Cover Illustration: Judy H. Tucker
Cover and Book Design: Marie Stauss Owen

ISBN 0-9786628-7-3
Library of Congress Cataloging-in-Publication Data

QUEEN'S HILL PRESS
Queenshill2@aol.com

Mad Dogs & Moonshine

Other Stories with a Taste of the South

Edited by Judy H. Tucker
& Lottie Brent Boggan

The Red Dog Writers

Contributors

Marion Barnwell
Patti Carr Black
Lottie Brent Boggan
David Creel
Anne Evans
John M. Floyd
Pat Floyd
Sarah Frances Hardy
Philip L. Levin
Rickey R. Mallory
Charline R. McCord
Mary Dayle McCormick
Melanie Noto
Bill Patrick
Peggy Gilmer-Piasecki
Richelle Putnam
Dorothy Shawhan
Carlene Singleton
Sue Stock
John Michael Tucker
Judy Tucker
Jacqueline F. Wheelock
Ruth White

Dedication

To the Red Dog
rescued by Pat Hall and the
Jackson Friends of the Animal Shelter,
"June Cleaver,"
who now resides with
Lottie & Willard Boggan

CONTENTS

INTRODUCTION

The Red Dog Writers welcome you to indulge in our third anthology of short stories. We offer you works of wide variety--from the comic to the tragic, and everything in between. Our writers are just as varied as the genres in which they write. Among them you can find professional writers, writing teachers, and editors; homemakers, physicians, and bankers.

The important thing is: we are all writers, serious about our art and our craft. What's the difference in art and craft? It depends on who you ask. A writing teacher once said, "I can teach you the craft; the art you are born with." The question might be stated differently: which comes first, the art or the craft? We defy you to name a successful author who does not use both. Craft is learned, art is absorbed, stirred--and studied as surely as craft is. No story can be written without both. This is not to say that the two are always there in equal measure. We believe that every child is born with art in his soul. It needs nurturing, and later it can be developed by exposure and experience and guidance.

A writer must know how to structure a piece of writing, whether it is a novel or a personal essay. He must to be able to evoke empathy, to reach the reader' s concerns and share the author's own, at the same time he should tell a structured story that the reader can follow without undue effort. Usually, all of this does not come naturally to a writer; it takes study and reading, and it takes writing and re-writing and it often calls for research--which has been made much easier with the Internet.

Mad Dogs and Moonshine is written, in the most part, for a mature reader, but it's a good text book on the short story as it offers such a wide variety of styles. It can guide the aspiring writer, and it can inspire them with the knowledge that the short story is alive and well, and has a wide readership. Let it be an example that shows you there is a place and an enthusiastic audience for your writing. Because The Red Dogs began as a writers' group, this book is, in part, published to encourage all of those who write.

Lottie Brent Boggan & Judy H. Tucker, Editors

ANGEL ON DUTY

John Floyd

Since Sheriff Charles Jones had never been fond of work—even during normal business hours—he held overtime in especially low regard. And the very last thing he needed now, elbow deep in neglected paperwork at 9:50 p.m., was a complaint from retired schoolteacher and self-professed crimefighter Angela Potts. But wouldn't you know it, here she was, looming over his desk with chin outthrust and fists planted on hips, bellowing loud enough to wake babies on the other side of town. The only things missing were blond braids and a spear and body armor.

"And a horned helmet," he murmured.

She stopped in midsentence. "What did you say?"

"Nothing. I was thinking you might need a new hat."

"What I *need*," she said, "is some cooperation, after I took the time to come over here."

Her presence here, of course, wasn't unusual at all—but her topic was. The current thorn under her saddle was neighborhood speed-demons, of all things. Angela had apparently heard from her buddy Bertha Woods that speedbumps had been installed in residential areas in the next county, and wanted to know why it hadn't been done here, where drunken hooligans roared up and down her street at all hours of the night. As an honest and law-abiding taxpayer, she informed him that she was sick and tired of living in a town with not only incompetent leaders but incompetent law enforcement, and so on and so on.

He listened to her rave awhile longer, then blew out a weary sigh.

"What can I say, Ms. Potts. Tell it to the mayor, tomorrow. I don't do speedbumps."

Angela snorted. "Trouble is, you don't do much of anything, Chunky

11

Jones. If you ask me—"

He held up a finger to interrupt her. "Come to think of it, I *will* ask you something: Why are you out and roaming around at ten o'clock at night?" He pointed the same finger, unnecessarily, at the clock on his wall.

She didn't bother looking at it. What she did was stand up even straighter, fold her arms like Mr. Clean, and study him as if he were some kind of rare and interesting bug. It reminded him of thirty years ago, when she was his fifth-grade teacher. Her penetrating gaze, then and now, made him want to crawl under his desk and hide.

But she wasn't really mad at him—he knew that by now. Hell, she probably wasn't even that upset about the speedbump issue. The simple truth was, Angela Potts just liked to complain. She also liked to aggravate him. For one thing, she always called him Chunky, an old nickname which she knew he hated. (Nicknames were abundant in small-town America, and he suspected it annoyed her that he never addressed her as "Angel" even though everyone else in town did, or even "Angela"—he insisted on calling her Ms. Potts, probably because his subconscious still considered her his schoolteacher.) Another sore spot was that she tended to correct his grammar all the time, even in front of his deputies or the mayor or whoever else happened to be in the vicinity.

Angela Potts, bless her grouchy soul, was one of a kind. Thank God.

She informed him, in a patient voice, "I am 'out and roaming around at ten o'clock at night,' as you put it, so I can be back home before twelve."

"And why's that?"

Sudden amusement twinkled in her eyes. "Don't you know what happens to angels at midnight?"

Not only did he not know, he didn't care. But it turned out not to matter anyway, because at that moment a young man with red hair and a red face and a Dixie Chicks T-shirt burst into the office.

Timothy Weeks, the disc jockey at the local radio station, stood there in the doorway, wide-eyed and panting.

"Come quick, Sheriff," he said. "Funny Sonny Jackson's robbed the law office."

*   *   *

It took less than two minutes to follow Tim Weeks across the deserted street—no speeders were in sight—to the Grayson Building and up the stairs to a long hallway. The door on the right said J. BINGHAM COLLINS, ATTORNEY AT LAW; the one on the left said WXIF RADIO. At the end of the hall was what looked like a break room. Tim and Angela and the sheriff paraded through the first door, where Becky Drennan—Bing Collins's spaced-out twentysomething assistant—sat staring at them with her mouth hanging open.

The sheriff broke the silence. "Becky, you remember Ms. Potts, right? From school?"

She snapped her mouth shut, then opened it and said, "Hi, Miss Angel."

Angela nodded but didn't reply. The sheriff knew her sharp eyes were already checking out the scene.

He took a moment too, to glance around the office. It was small and neat and functional. On one wall was the darkened doorway to the lawyer's inner sanctum; overhead, a sluggish ceiling fan shifted the warm air around. "Want to tell us what happened?"

Becky swallowed. "The cashbox," she said, tilting her bleached-blond head toward an empty shelf behind her. "It's missing. I was sitting right here at my desk when he took it."

"Sonny Jackson?"

"Yes sir."

"So you saw him?" Sheriff Jones was trying to keep his voice steady. He was still puffing a little from the climb to the second floor.

"Tim did."

All of them turned to look at Tim Weeks, whose goldfish eyes grew even wider. "I had just cued up Bon Jovi and was looking out my window," he said. "There's a streetlight outside—I saw Funny Sonny leave our building and go down the sidewalk."

"You sure it was Sonny Jackson?" the sheriff said.

"Yessir."

"But *you* didn't see him?" he asked Becky.

"I never saw anybody," she said. "I was turned the other way, like this"—she swiveled to face her computer—"typing a letter." She wiggled her fingers a little, apparently to make sure everyone understood the typing process. "Tim and I are the only ones here this time of night—him in his office, me in mine."

"Was Sonny carrying the cashbox when you saw him from the window, Tim?"

"Couldn't tell, Sheriff. But it was him all right. I came in to ask Becky what he'd been doing here, and that's when she noticed the box was gone." Tim glanced at his watch and made a sound like a strangled chicken. "'Scuse me, I gotta go do a commercial." He dashed out and across the hall to the radio station.

Sheriff Jones thought a moment. "Was your door—the one to the hallway—open or closed?" he asked Becky.

"Closed."

"And you didn't hear anybody come in?"

She held up her iPod. "I was listening to Garth," she said. At full blast, probably. Sheriff Jones, who had a teenaged niece, figured Tarzan could've driven a herd of elephants up the stairs with Cheetah screaming on his shoulder and Becky wouldn't have heard it.

Angela, quiet until now, said, "There's no A/C in here, Becky, and the fan doesn't help much—why keep your door closed, when it's this hot?"

Becky Drennan wrinkled her cute nose. "Folks smoke in the break room, during the day. I hate the smell, even after hours."

"But that room's all the way at the end of the hall, right?"

"I got a good sniffer." Becky looked at the sheriff. "Matter of fact I can smell smoke on you, right now, Sheriff."

"Wrong," he said. "I don't smoke."

"I didn't say you did. I can smell it on your clothes."

"His wife smokes," Angela explained.

"That's it, then." Becky made a face. "You might try baking soda, or vinegar."

A little irked at having two different women ordering him around when he wasn't even home, the sheriff said, "What're you doing with a cashbox anyway, in a law office?"

She frowned at him. "We're a small town, Sheriff. Some of Bing's clients don't even have a checking account."

Which made sense, he realized. "But why would Sonny Jackson—or whoever it was—take the whole box?"

"Because it was locked." Becky dug two fingers into her skintight jeans pocket and finally produced a key. She seemed to have a sudden thought then, and her eyes bugged out as wide as Tim's had been. "Think he'll have to use explosives to get it open?"

*   *   *

Further questioning produced nothing useful, which was no great surprise. After fifteen sweltering minutes Angela and the sheriff left and trudged the three blocks to Bernardo's, the Mexican restaurant where Funny Sonny Jackson worked as a waiter. It was after closing time, but the sheriff's pained expression and a badge held up to the window got them inside. When they asked the manager if Sonny was still there, they were boredly directed to his section of tables in the back of the establishment.

Funny Sonny, a usually grinning fellow (hence his nickname), seemed especially happy at first to get a break from the challenging task of emptying ashtrays and stacking chairs. When the sheriff asked him the zillion-dollar question, though, Sonny's ready smile disappeared. In fact he appeared stunned by the news of the crime. He explained that he had worked the supper shift here and had then delivered a pre-ordered container of salsa to the empty break room on the second floor of the Grayson building around 9:45, just before the time Tim Weeks had said he'd spotted Sonny leaving. But the waiter swore he hadn't entered Bingham Collins's law office.

With a call on his cell phone the sheriff dispatched Deputy Fred Prewitt to the crime scene. Ten minutes later Prewitt reported that the delivery checked out—he'd found an unopened order of Bernardo's salsa in the break-room's refrigerator, along with a bill bearing today's date, taped to the fridge door. Which did not, of course, mean Sonny was innocent—it just gave him a reason to have been inside the building. But there was as yet no real proof that he was guilty, either.

If this job were easy, the sheriff thought glumly, anyone could do it.

At Angela's whispered suggestion and against his better judgment, he made no arrest. Instead he issued a firm warning to Sonny not to leave town—he loved telling people that—and then they headed back to the sheriff's office, where Angela assumed her usual station in the chair across from the desk. She seemed almost cheerful now that there was a mystery afoot, showing no hint of the formidable Viking soprano who'd stomped into the room half an hour ago.

It occurred to the sheriff that the reason Angela had been involved in so many of his cases over the years was that she'd usually been right here, hanging around his office, when he first received word about them. *I've got a nose for trouble, Chunky*, she'd once told him. *I can smell it a mile away.* He sometimes believed she could.

"The important thing," she said to him now, as she selected a Bite-Size Baby Ruth from a jar on his desk, "is that we verified that Sonny came straight to the building from his shift at the restaurant."

Sheriff Jones put his frustration aside and tried to concentrate. Angela Potts was smarter than he was, and he knew it. When he needed her help, he was actually pleased by that fact—her quick thinking had pulled his charred hindquarters out of the fire on many occasions. Other times it was just another of the things about her that irritated him. "Why's that important?" he asked.

Instead of answering, she said, "I think you should search the WXIF office, Chunky. And Tim Weeks's car too, I saw it parked in the lot across the street. I doubt Becky Drennan's involved—she's not the brightest bulb in the chandelier, but she's not dumb enough to try something like this. Besides, if she had, she would've just taken the money, not the whole cashbox."

"So you think *Tim* stole it?"

The sheriff waited while she sampled another chocolate. "These things are great," she said, her mouth full. "I thought you were cutting back."

"I am. I only keep those for when you visit. So you think Tim Weeks—"

"Chocolate *and* peanuts. You don't know what you're missing."

He sighed and rubbed his eyes. "It's late, Ms. Potts. Bear with me. You think Tim Weeks stole the cashbox?"

"I don't know who stole it. I just know Funny Sonny didn't."

"How do you know that?"

"Trust me. Just check Tim's office and car."

He did a palms-up. "How? Judge Bailey won't okay a warrant without a reason."

"He will if you tell him it includes searching Sonny's car too. You'll be 'expediting justice'—you know, covering all the bases at once."

"Where'd you come up with that?"

"*CSI: Miami*." She paused. "Sure you don't want a Baby Ruth?"

"*CSI: Miami*?"

"Or *Law and Order*. Which one has Lieutenant Caine?"

Sheriff Jones thought he could actually feel his blood pressure spiking. "What if this doesn't work, Ms. Potts?"

"What do you mean?"

"What if we don't find anything? We'll look like a couple of fools, you and me."

"You and I," she said. Which irritated him even more.

*   *   *

An hour and a hasty search warrant later, Tim Weeks was in custody and cooling his heels in the jail next door. The cashbox had been found stashed in the trunk of his rusted Saturn, between a stack of *Entertainment Weekly* magazines and a pair of old high-topped Reeboks. When confronted with the evidence by the sheriff and both his deputies, Tim tearfully confessed to sneaking into the law office and stealing the box while Becky Drennan was merrily typing and grooving to her country music with her back turned, four feet away.

"How'd you know, Ms. Potts?" the sheriff asked again, when they were alone once more in his office. "Was it something Becky said?"

Angela smiled. "It was something she *didn't* say."

"What do you mean?"

She leaned back in her chair and lowered her head, an act which produced at least three chins. It crossed his mind that she was every bit as hefty as he was, despite his nickname.

"You of course know," she began, "that our good-for-nothing mayor continues to reject the smoke-free building ordinance."

"I of course know that," he said. Impatiently.

"And the smoking section at Bernardo's is located at the back of the restaurant, where we were awhile ago, right? I mean, that's where the tables with the ashtrays are."

"So?"

"So, we were told that that was Sonny Jackson's station tonight. He said he'd worked his shift there, before going over to the lawyer's building to deliver the order of salsa."

The sheriff sighed. "SO?"

Angela took her time, along with another Baby Ruth mini from his jar. "Think about it. If Sonny worked the smoking section during supper, then came over and entered the office where Becky was and stood right behind her to grab the cashbox, she would've smelled the smoke on his clothing—especially since she has a sensitive nose—and would've been aware, *immediately* aware, of his presence." She unwrapped the chocolate and examined it as if it were a fine diamond. "In fact, she'd have smelled him even if it weren't for the smoke on him, with or without that creaky ceiling fan of hers. I love Bernardo's, but the odor of Mexican cooking has a way of seeping into your clothes. And since Becky *didn't* smell anything strange—"

"He wasn't there," the sheriff finished.

She popped the Baby Ruth into her mouth. "Right."

"So you suspected Tim—"

"Because there was no one else to suspect," she said, chewing. "I figure what happened was, Tim saw Sonny leaving the building, and since he now had someone to accuse, snuck into Becky's office right then and snatched the box. He probably stowed it in his car, ran back up to make sure Becky had discovered it was missing, then hotfooted over here to report the crime."

Sheriff Jones nodded slowly. He found himself staring out the window at the summer night, thinking. A soft breeze riffled the pear trees lining the sidewalk. Halfway down the block, in an island of yellow light from a streetlamp, old Claude Edgemore was being hauled along by a leash attached to a dog as big as he was. Thunder grumbled in the distance.

Her version made sense, the sheriff decided. He probably wouldn't have seen it if he had a hundred years to mull it over, but Angela Potts, a.k.a. Amateur Sleuth and Pain in the Ass, had figured it out in no time.

"And now," she announced, "even though I know how much you enjoy

my companionship and I certainly know how much I enjoy your snacks"—
she licked her fingers, hoisted herself from the chair, and hitched her purse-
strap higher on her shoulder—"I have to get home."

He looked up at the clock, and she followed his gaze. "You barely made
it," he said. It was ten minutes to twelve.

She helped herself to another bite-sized chocolate for the road and
turned to the door. As she opened it he said, "I have to ask."

"Ask what?"

"A while ago, you said something like, 'Don't you know what happens
to angels at midnight?'"

"And?"

"Well, what's the answer?" he asked. "What does happen to angels at
midnight?"

She grinned, and wiggled her eyebrows. "They become devils."

He stared at the closed door for a long time after she left, thinking
about her and trying not to smile. Finally, just before leaving for home himself, he found a box of letterhead stationery and wrote up a formal request
to the mayor and aldermen. He of course knew it was a waste of time. The
board members would never install speedbumps in town—most of them
were speeders themselves.

But what the hell.

He signed the letter, dropped it in his OUT basket, and regarded the
stack of waiting paperwork for a full minute before deciding that it could
wait another day. Then he picked up his hat and paused again, his eyes on
the candy jar.

He ate three Baby Ruths on his way to the car.

UNCLE BUCK'S TRUCK

Charline R. McCord

After the funeral I spent weeks alone in the house. My assignment was clear, so sentiment would have to be pushed aside for now. I dug into cabinets, closets and drawers without hesitation, yet each time I carried a box or a trash bag outside I found myself lingering, gazing at my only real dilemma, Uncle Buck's truck. For thirty-four years he'd worn that old truck about like a big shoe, a comfortable, oversized house shoe. It had some miles on it and showed signs of wear, but it had run in the dead of winter when nothing else would and he wouldn't have sold it for a million dollars. The truck was "family."

Sitting on the carport steps, I asked myself for the thousandth time what I was going to do with it. There had been plenty of calls, and a few brave souls had even approached me at the funeral home wanting to know "how much?" Everyone knew Uncle Buck had petted and pampered it like an only child. It had been sitting up for a month now, and I noticed a covering of dust beginning to collect over the fresh green paint. I remembered the day last summer when I called him long distance and his first words were: "I put a new paint job on my truck today!" Only when I came home a month later did I discover he'd painted it himself with a brush. Claimed he didn't trust anybody else to do it right.

I walked around the 1950 Ford slowly, realizing for the first time that its slick rounded cab was like Uncle Buck's bald head, and the side mirrors protruding from each door much like his pointed ears. The front bumper and grill sort of smiled at me. It was a storybook truck, the kind of talking truck I'd read about in third grade. It was sitting here now, orphaned.

I opened the door on the driver's side and got in. A heavy, old rug covered the seat. Under it, the original upholstery was unharmed. I poked around in the tiny glove compartment and twisted the "stirring wheel" a few times. I remembered how Uncle Buck used to work the choke before he cranked her up, and I pulled on it a few times. A mustard top had been screwed over the ceiling light fixture, and he'd rigged up a metal strip on the dash with hooks to hang his keys on. Several red oil rags still hung at the base of the steering column.

Just sitting in the truck took me back in time. I lay over the steering wheel, staring at the hood ornament I'd never been able to decipher, and thought about the first time I ever saw the little truck. It was at the Greyhound bus station in Jackson, Tennessee. I was twelve that summer and thought I'd come from Laurel, Mississippi, to spend two weeks "up north" with this aunt and uncle I didn't know. When the bus pulled in, my face was pressed against the window, and I spotted an odd couple sitting in a parked green pickup. They got out and walked toward the bus, and I sent up one of my emergency one-liners: "Please Lord, don't let that be them in that stupid old green truck!" Soon we were packed in the cab of the truck and on our way to the house in the country that became my home for the next eight years.

I lifted the ignition key from the homemade rack and studied it closely. It was well-worn, but surprisingly small and delicate, more like the key to a jewelry box. I tried it in the ignition, and startled myself when the slightest turn produced a humming motor. I looked at the slick black ball on the gearshift and tried to recall the diagram that used to be there. After several clumsy maneuvers it slipped into reverse, and I found myself backing out onto the street. I approached the intersection with the uncertainty of a new driver, but the truck instinctively pulled right, onto the Miflin Road.

We soloed around the big curve by the peach orchard, and headed downhill past the gravel pit, the haunted house, and Jeter's Garage. The sun beamed through the rear window, trailing us like it always did when we made our way out toward the old homeplace—the one the three of us had shared before they got too old to manage the farm and moved in closer to town. I could already see the artesian well coming up at the corner of Ranger Road, and just past that would be the narrow bridge where the truck had performed three dramatic, but beautiful, pirouettes one snowy evening. I shifted into second and we pulled the hill by Maness' store and passed the shack where Uncle Buck used to sound the funny horn for old Joe on Saturdays. Impulsively, I hit the horn and the sound brought on a smile. The old black man was dead now, but he and Uncle Buck were like brothers. From the time I first saw him amble out to the road and climb in over the tailgate, he had already gotten too old to do any physical labor. But we picked him up in the truck and drove him to the farm every Saturday anyway. He and Uncle Buck would walk the fields, hang on the fences and study the cows and pigs, or fish for catfish in the pond down below the barn. Uncle Buck valued Joe's opinion on everything to do with raising livestock and farming, and he enjoyed his company, as well. The last few times we made a truck stop for him, he fell sound asleep before we got to the Baptist Church at the top of Pleasant Hill. It was exactly four miles from the church to the turn-off, then straight down to the white frame house at the bottom of Grove Hill.

* * *

As I eased along the vine-covered banks that told me I was close to home, Tiny came to mind. She was a stray terrier that became Uncle Buck's sidekick, and it had been hard to tell which she loved the most, Uncle Buck, or riding shotgun in the green pickup truck. She had clearance to ride with him everywhere except to work, and on those days she'd just lie in front of the fireplace and snooze. About four o'clock her little ears would shoot up. She'd raise her head, hold still for a moment, then light out for the back door yelping wildly. As soon as I could let her out, she'd tear up the hill and meet the old truck on the main highway. Sometimes Uncle Buck would pull over and let her ride in; other times she'd run alongside the truck all the way to the garage. None of us ever understood how that truck could pull her out of a deep sleep from a mile away.

In the evenings Uncle Buck and Tiny would roll in from the barn or the field, pile out of the truck and into the living room. Uncle Buck would sit in his favorite chair watching television, and from the bedroom my aunt would yell, "Buck, you haven't got that dog in my chair have you?" "NO!" he'd yell back firmly. Every once in a while she'd send me around the corner just to verify things, and I'd always report Tiny "out of sight" – meaning, of course, that she was tucked beneath the LIFE magazine Uncle Buck had draped across the chair arm.

One Saturday Tiny lay in the shrubbery all morning. She wouldn't eat. She ignored the truck. She ignored Uncle Buck. He watched her nervously, and sometime after lunch he wrapped her in a blanket, put her in the seat of the pickup, and took off to town. It was after dark when he rolled in and drove around behind the garage toward the gas tank. I waited at the window a while, but finally grew impatient and tiptoed outside. Around the corner of the garage I could see the parked truck, headlights beaming. In the midst of the bright light Uncle Buck was bent over a shovel. On the ground beside him was a simple cardboard box.

*   *   *

The frame house was in sight now, but, to my surprise, it wasn't so white anymore. Instead it was almost gray—not with new paint, but with age and the disappearance of the old. I braked the truck and pulled to a stop on the side of the road to get a closer look at things. It was apparent that the house was still occupied, but with a careless and far sadder existence than the earlier one I had known. Things were different—somehow smaller and severely encroached upon. Some type of ivy had completely sewn up the windows at the east end of the house; the tiny front stoop was overloaded with firewood that threatened to break down the front door; and a multi-colored wash hung, of all places, across the wire fencing that ran alongside the road—the same fencing that used to allow passersby to marvel at the size of Uncle Buck's prized black Angus bull as he grazed in a lush field of green. Three emaciated hunting dogs loped aimlessly about scouring the grounds with their noses, while the four-eyed stove I'd learned to cook on watched silently from its shaded resting place beside a stack of old tires under the oak tree. The shed that used to shelter the Ford pickup looked as if it had attempted to retreat from the whole cluttered scene; it had drawn backwards in fear, or maybe shock, and was clinging to the old smokehouse behind it for support. I was suddenly aware of pain in my idle hands. I glanced downward and discovered that I, too, had been clinging for support with an almost unbearable grip on the steering wheel. I let go, working my fingers in and out to renew the circulation. I eased off the brake and rolled forward, pulled the truck back onto the road and continued westward.

Soon the little Ford and I had left the blacktop, and were raising a cloud of dust behind us as we rocked along the gravel road that led to the cemetery. I turned in where the pines parted, parked in the shade, and walked softly across the manicured lawn to a central concrete bench. From here I had a clear view of both the truck and Uncle Buck's grave. The sun had dropped low in the west, and the only movement seemed to be a few ribbons rippling in the light breeze. Birds chirped softly from their roosting places in pine trees that made a complete rectangular border around the cemetery. In the center of the rectangle I sat motionless, hugging my knees. Here things had not changed; here there was order, not chaos. My eyes began to move among the rows of neatly arranged monuments, where husbands, wives, and families were grouped under one name. There was a tidiness here that life could no longer alter. One by one, I read silently down an entire row of dates and unfamiliar names. When the row played out, I found my gaze resting on the parked green pickup. I noticed it smiling at me and I quickly looked away. I'd spent half my life being ashamed to ride in that old truck, yet the truck and I were "family."

ROOKED

Lottie Boggan

"What's 'stumps'?" I ask. A snickering sound comes from across the table. "Oh, Charlotte."

I look up. Eyes narrowed, my bridge partner is studying me. My heart burns. "Trumps!" I mutter. "I mean trumps!"

My partner blows out a breath. Cupping her hands around her mouth, she leans toward our hostess. "The younger brother's definitely got it," she whispers. "Now I think Charlotte's almost as bad off as he is."

I try to give my partner the evil eye, but she faces the other way.

"Everybody thought he was just getting interesting. Until he tried to run that man down in the Jitney Jungle parking lot. And now …."

My partner cocks her head toward me. She raises her voice. "You know, they say Alzheimer's runs in families. That ought to tell us something."

"Your eyes are swinging." I point. Her eyeglasses are on a chain, dangling away from her gold sweater.

"What?"

"That's enough." The hostess taps my shoulder. "It's your turn to play."

"Well, if nobody else will do it, I'll be the goat," my bridge partner speaks, louder this time. "You're confused, Charlotte. It's interfering with everyone else's game. Why don't you go ahead and resign from the bridge club?"

"What did you say?" I stare at my partner, but she spreads her cards, studies her hand.

Lame birdie, I think.

"I'll say it again. Make it easy on everybody else. Resign."

All that's holy, I think. Wish I could murder. Clamping my eyes shut, I stick a finger on each lid, trying to push tears back into their place.

"That's enough for now," the hostess says. She puts her wax-like face next to mine. "You have to play something, Charlotte."

I touch a card, but can hardly see what I pull from my hand.

"What's the matter with you?" My partner, carrying a forkful of apple tart to her mouth, stops in mid-air. She drops her fork, clattering it onto a saucer. "Have you lost your mind?" Her bony shoulders jerk. "You trumped my good trick."

"You're all a bunch of stupid cripples!" I scream.

Lame birdie.

"Go away!" I grab the handle of my mug and throw luke-warm coffee and cream in the face of my accuser.

"What in the world?" The hostess yells as the bony-limbed woman hysterically screams for a towel.

I scoop a handful of cards into my hand, snap them shut, then raise them like a weapon. "Bang! You don't know how to play, partner."

Running for the hall closet, I grab my mink coat, and cram the bridge cards into a pocket. "I'm going home!"

Outside, I stand in the yard. But which way?

The hacking noise of a crow in a pine tree breaks the silence.

Lame birdie.

I clap a hand over my ear. The wind bites. Evil. I glance back toward the house. The lace curtain in the living room is pulled aside. Moon faces.

Home, I fret. Oh, please, home. But where?

The crow caws again. I glance up. A Rook card, I think. He looks like the silhouette on a Rook card. The kind my grandparents used to deal out around the kitchen table. I see one beady, malignant eye cocked, as if the crow warns me of something ugly.

Suddenly, my brain tells my feet what to do. I start walking, but stumble. The bird keeps up his clatter. There is menace in his call. The tones fall sharper than broken ice, chipped by a strong pick. Taunted by the prophet crow, I enshroud myself in the mink. My high heels sink into the damp ground. I begin to walk and lurch, as if one leg were shorter than the other. Memory becomes my crutch.

Lame birdie.

My mind tumbles backwards to my Mississippi childhood. I am seven, capable of creating great evil and surviving it without reproach. Along with my younger brother Hal, plus cousins Jewel and Mark, I am visiting our Kent grandparents in Summit, a place where days are bright as the cobalt hydrangeas blooming against the house. I am trying to be a good girl, worthy of Grandma Kent's attention.

"Bad girls are shunned," she warns. "You're not a boy, Charlotte. You have to act more ladylike. Didn't you pay attention in Sunday School? Will a switch straighten you out?"

"No ma'am," I say, promising to do better.

But it is hot. The weather boils my temper, prickles my skin. From my perch on the porch, I study the neighbors who sell vegetables, milk, and eggs to eke out a living for Bertie, the handicapped granddaughter who lives with them.

Bertie is a routine part of my Summit summer. Daily, Grandma Kent shuffles across the dusty road to buy from the Lows, often dragging me along with her. This day she goes alone, shunning me. Grandma returns, her apron brimming with fresh-laid eggs, their brown shells promising yolks the color of dandelions. She climbs the porch steps, still ignoring me.

"Bertie's ugly," I say. "Why does she walk funny?"

"She's God's judgment on that family," Grandma answers. "That's what Bertie is. God's dark judgment."

"But why?"

"Never you mind." Grandma puts our lunch dishes into the sink. "You children need to stay inside until it cools off a little. Polio's afoot; go into my room and rest. Just don't get too hot."

"But Grandma," I protest. "We're too old for naps. That's for babies."

"You wanna end up like those little crippled children in *Life Magazine*?"

My mind flashes to those innocents, trapped in dreadful, wheezing, iron lungs. Children stacked up like they're in mailing tubes, waiting their turn for delivery. Part of me thinks this image romantic. Just turn your head: spoon-fed. Teeth brushed and hair combed by someone else. But the bathroom, I wonder. What about that? I finally decide that children with polio never have to go to the bathroom again. And what do they do all day?

"Maybe polio kids can play cards," I say.

"What about cards?" The voice of my little brother, Hal, commands my attention.

"We won't get polio if we just play cards," I say.

We strike a compromise with Grandmother who goes to the cool sleeping porch in the back of the house to shell butterbeans, while my brother, cousins, and I sit on Grandmother's bed and play Rook.

Soon even that becomes tedious. "I don't want to play anymore," I say. Losing at cards, and out of sorts, I hide the Rook card in the pocket of my playsuit.

Quietly, I get up and ease to the front of the house. I stand at the door and look out. Damp heat, slurpier than the moist tongue of a puppy, brushes across my face. I curve my fingers around the edge of the front screen so the squeak won't be heard. I open the door, let it close, and walk, careful to stay where I can't be seen from the sleeping porch. Shuffling through grass turned by the summer heat from supple green stalks to wads of scratchy steel wool, I inch toward the edge of the yard. I have the feeling that my mother's shadow walks with me. But as I get farther away from the house, her presence fades. I'm all alone in a wide world. I pretend for a moment that I am running away. Looking over my shoulder, I listen for my mother's treble voice to say, "Come back, Charlotte."

Imagining the family looking for me forever, I feel good thinking about everyone rushing around saying, "Oh, why weren't we nicer to her?"

It will serve them right, I think.

Then comes a squawk in a tree. I look up and see a beady, malignant eye. Staring.

"Caught, caught," the bird seems to say from his sharp-beaked mouth. He makes me uncomfortable. I know if anyone finds that I have slipped out, I will be in trouble. Trouble wants company, so I hurry back for the other children.

"Caught, caught," I seem to hear the bird say again.

I ease into the house. "I'm going to be a famous scientist. Like Madam Curie. And I can prove it. Come with me," I say. "Put up the cards. There's something more important we have to do. I've figured something out." I look my cousin Jewel in the eye, then grab her hand, pulling her toward the front door. "If we don't watch out, the Lows might give us polio."

I want to entice them to go with me. "Look what happened to Bertie. They might be doing magic. Let's find out."

"Let's find out," my brother Hal echoes. He takes small copycat steps as we tiptoe through the living room. I see trust in his large brown eyes and I know he will follow me anywhere. He walks with his hands pushed down into the pockets of his short pants, his belly bowled out. We cross the dirt road and stand in front of the Lows' house.

The house sits on a little rise back in the trees, like a fading photo negative held up to the light. The yard is overgrown with weeds. It is always quiet in the Lows' yard, as if even birds don't like to nest in the stunted bushes growing next to this house.

We ring the doorbell and wait. Both Mr. and Mrs. Low come to the door, faces heavily lined like soft gingersnaps, just before they crumble into small pieces.

Mr. Low doesn't have any teeth. Faded overalls, hang from his shoulders like a deflated inner tube stretched from a rope, and he wears heavy black boots that make clumping noises when he walks. Mrs. Low is a little woman. She has patches of cockleburr gray hair stuck all over her head and she wears a long dress as big as my Grandmother's tablecloth.

"Milking isn't done yet," Mr. Low says, his tone low and apologetic.

"We want to see Bertie," Jewel demands.

"I'll fetch her, Mr. Low." His wife seems relieved to get away from us.

Bertie limps out. Her grandparents slam the door behind her. A hopeful innocence shows in Bertie's face.

She wears a faded dress that looks like it might have belonged to a grown-up. The hem sags in uneven waves. Blinking her eyes rapidly, Bertie looks happy and excited.

Jewel pulls a small apple from her pocket, acting as if she were going to give it to Bertie, then pulls it away. "Come and get it," Jewel smiles. Her dark eyes slant; tight brown braids bind her head.

Laughing in high cackles, we jump off the porch. Bertie limps after us. Her legs are thin and crooked, like earthworms.

Jewel puts the apple back in her pocket.

"Do you want to play sling statue?" Mark asks.

"She can't," I say. "She's a cripple."

"I can, I can," Bertie pleads, but she looks frightened.

"I'll sling Bertie first," I say. "But I won't let go. It'll be okay."

I grab Bertie, whirl her in a fast spin. Suddenly, I release her small hand. She flings her arms as if trying to grab hold of something, then huddles on the ground. I shiver with delight. "She can't even get up," I say disgustedly. Delicate torment. "Let's just us play. Something without Bertie. Let's play tag."

"I can." She stands up slowly. "I can play."

"Catch us," we call to each other. "Catch us."

"Lame like Bertie," we singsong. "Lame like Bertie."

Trying to keep up with us, Bertie swings one leg and drags the other.

"Run like a bird, run like a bird," we chorus. "Tag and you're it -- you have to marry Bertie."

"Bertie, Bertie, two by four," I holler, "limping through her own front door."

"We don't want your polio," Mark hollers. The muscles in his small sturdy body bunch as he stops, picks up a stick from beneath a dead tree and tosses the twig back toward the house. "Take that. We don't want your polio," he yells again. Although small, the swing of his arms and the sail of the brittle wood makes him look powerful. His hair stands up in wild spikes.

I don't want to be outdone. "Her cow doesn't really give milk," I taunt. "It gives polio. Look at her."

We all laugh.

Although I have thrown only words, Bertie gives a cry like a hurt animal who has been hit with a heavy stone. She falls and curls into a ball.

A lump hangs like thick feathers in my throat. The berries and cream from lunch have soured. I must spit them out. But still I manage an imitation of Bertie's walk as we scurry toward the street and our grandparents' house.

My mind fast forwards fifty years. I am a grown woman, swathed in mink, standing in my neighbor's yard on a cold winter day.

Lame birdie.

I push my hands down into the warm pockets of my coat and stretch the fur across my breasts. I feel the bridge cards, their slick cardboard. I catch my breath sharply. My heart burns -- it pounds. Have I carried the Rook card with me all these years?

UNASKED QUESTIONS

Jacqueline Wheelock

What I remember most about that day in the late fifties is the walk through the sandpit, the desert-feel of a merciless sun in mid July. Home was not far away now, just through the pit a little ways and up its south bank to the shade of live oaks, still harboring a few of last season's acorns in their root crannies. Mama would be waiting. Waiting to hear (without having to ask) what today's white woman paid, what she did not pay, what she did not say.

Soon after climbing out of the pit and stepping across the threshold into the cool dark kitchen, I felt the unasked questions coming from behind Mama's serene, though slightly palsied, mask: Did today's woman not say thanks? Did she notice that you were a bright girl? Did she speak interesting things of her own life and children?

"Not today, Mama," I answered wordlessly. "She only said, 'Be sure to move them mattresses.'"

"Did she not give you a good lunch?" the unasked questions continued.

"Not today, Mama. She only said—over and over she said—'Jest clean the winders and the walls.'"

Now, backing my memory up to the morning, hours before the sandpit walk, I recall the familiar novelty of the scene as the white man drove us into his yard. These were new white folks, but really not new at all, for I had been here before, on other roads on different mornings with the summer sun shining on other faded mailboxes. These were not the kind of white folks that offered steady work in air conditioned houses. This was sporadic "day work" coming down from the working class, the class who drove up to our house in their Joad-like clunkers and announced to Mama, "Cindy Bell, my wife needs to "use" one of your girls for a couple o' days next week."

These were the ones who had to bite back "nigger" at every rise of their tongues and every turn of their minds, just to keep an uneasy peace while the work was being done. But $2.50 was $2.50 more than I had. So when the new boss lady's husband drove up at 7:00 in the morning to pick me up for the first of a two-day job, I knew to take my place as a colored girl— to crawl into the back seat of a car, itself seemingly condemned to a slow, tortuous death. But I also knew not to be surprised at the small weathered house, no larger than my own, set close to the constant swoosh! of the cars on the highway into town.

The house had been cool at 7:30, fans humming promises that I knew they could not keep against the relentless march of the daily Mississippi sun—nothing like the sweet controlled air of the gentry for whom I most often worked. But "that's okay," I thought. "$2.50 is $2.50, and I want to go to college one day."

My boss lady for the day seemed somewhat ill at ease, but behind the unpolished effort to assume the role of the elite was a sure focus. She immediately started to drive me, not out of an innate meanness, it seems to me in retrospection, but more out of a sense of desperation to make her self-perceived Queenness for Two Days count for all it was worth. After all, even through the misted eyes of adolescence, it was plain to me that her husband's living was not a wealthy one, probably not even a comfortable one from the looks of the cheap precarious iron bedsteads and the yellow pine furniture. And I can imagine that her husband, out of a whimsical sense of nobility, had peeled off a ten and said, "Do what you want with it. Getcha some help like them rich beach women do all the time, if you've a mind to." But I could stand being "used" for a couple of days. I had done day work before; I knew the look, the smell, the difference between the kitchens of the rich and the pantries of the working class (though at the time I had no idea of the nominal label), so I thought I knew what to expect.

Hardly ever looking at my face, she directed me to clean the windows and walls, a fair day's work for an adult male, overwhelming for a young female. And she instructed me to sun the mattress. And sweep. And mop, and "while you're restin', fold up the clothes." By noon the motion of the blades of the fans had been reduced to an annoying buzz, beating hopelessly at the hot air like stunned dragonflies. I was hungry. I was frightened.

I wanted to go home, drink Kool-Aid or go to the colored settlement's snack store and buy a six-cent Barq's Root Beer. After all, I was still just a child.

Two o'clock came and I was still cleaning windows. No mention of lunch that I can recall. Certainly, no mention of home. Three o'clock, more of the same. Then under the sudden influence of a drive inside me, of which I was not really aware, I caught her away in some other room of the small house, and I struck out, without her permission and without pay, for the three-mile trip home.

There was a certain freedom for me in that scorching walk. Though I had not the nerve to ask her to take me home when the time came, impulse and independence pushed me out of the house onto the hot, sandy shoulders of the asphalt. Then a turn east onto the side road leading to the Negro settlement, and finally back south through acres of abandoned sandpit behind my father's property, no longer providing sand for dump trucks to expand the county highway system. I had never even heard of a sunstroke, so any symptoms I might have had of heat exhaustion were overridden by my ignorance and determination to get to the shade of our yard. I must have been a heart-piercing sight to my mama when I entered the old house.

As usual, Mama didn't ask her questions. She simply looked at my thirteen-year-old face slick with sweat, my recently pressed hair pulling back into its natural state, and said, "Supper will be ready in a while. You can rest now." She said nothing to me about tomorrow. I assumed I would go again when the man came for me. And I knew he would come.

Mama's unasked questions hung in the air beneath the low ceiling of our home all afternoon, but I was too young and too tired to think of anything except being in the shade of that old unpainted clapboard house. Like the lady's house from which I had escaped, ours didn't have air conditioning. But the dozen or so oaks always made sure that, in our home, the sun never took too much authority, nor became too proud in its daily visits.

The next morning I lay half asleep in the front bedroom next to the porch, waiting for Mama to tell me it was time to get up and get ready for work, when I heard her voice from the porch speaking to the white man seated in his faded car.

"No, sir," she said in no uncertain terms, "she ain't goin' today. She won't be goin' back a'tall."

Mama's unasked questions of love and concern that stood undying in her eyes, even as she sent each of us out to learn how to earn a living, remained between her and me throughout her lifetime. And even now, they cling to me like a freshly-washed blanket. But her unspoken answer to the question that the white man must have wanted to ask that morning is far clearer to me today than it was in my thirteenth year:

"You want to 'use' one of my girls? Bring her back to me the way you took her."

STARRY NIGHT

Anne Evans

Mama and Daddy were on a tear again, so I slipped out of the house. It was cold and clear, a week before Christmas. I figured I'd take a walk towards the square, check out the lights and wreaths and the lit up Santa Claus on top of the department store whose electronic wave looked more like a karate chop. All the way there I imagined hightailing it to the highway, thumbing down to New Orleans, splitting town for good. But I'm chicken, so instead I hoped to run into my cousin, Les.

Les was sixteen and cool. He spent a lot of time hanging out downtown ever since the tornado ripped the roof off of his and Aunt Le Le's house. Aunt Le Le moved in with the trucker she'd been dating, and Les stayed there sometimes, and sometimes he stayed with us, and sometimes I don't know where he stayed. But I always felt better when he was around. He could always find something to do. He was even more distracting than TV.

Sure enough I found him on the square near the Confederate statue. I could tell it was him because almost nobody is that tall and skinny, and his curls always spilled like tangled yellow yarn over the collar of his jean jacket, no matter how hard he tried to tuck them under. When I got closer I saw that he was carving his initials, L. B., into the statue's chalky back.

"You got a square?" he asked.

"Nope," I said.

He nodded, finished carving, and handed me the knife. I chiseled out S. for Sadie, but couldn't finish the B. for Burns because a cop car buzzed around the square. I pocketed the knife, and we crossed the street behind the courthouse, heading down to Arlis' pool hall. The smoke in the pool hall fuzzed around the hanging lights, and a twangy country number played on the jukebox. Because it was nearly empty, Arlis let us play a game for free.

Arlis let Les order a beer. Les reached into his pocket, but instead of money he pulled out a pair of silver earrings shaped like stars.

"You can have it," Arlis said, nodding at the beer, "but you gotta take the trash to the dumpster for me."

"Sure thing," Les said, then he handed the earrings to me, "here Sadie, I found these, do you want them?"

I stuck the earrings in my ears. Les was always giving me stuff he found in stores.

"They look good," he said.

"Thanks," I said, fingering their starry shape against my lobes.

We played a few games. Les gave me a few sips of beer and a few drags off the cigarette he bummed, which made my head feel light and cheery, but when that feeling passed I only felt worse. My stomach growled and I wondered if Les could get Arlis to give us some of the chips behind the bar. Once when I was real hungry on the way to school, and Les knew it even though I didn't tell him, he lifted some powdered donuts from the 7-11 for me.

"Your folks home tonight?" Les asked.

"Yeah," I said. I was tempted to tell him about the banging around the kitchen, but it made me feel tired just thinking about it.

"You think I could stay there tonight?"

"Sure," I said. The idea of returning to the house with Les eased my mind. "You know Mama and me want you to stay there every night. Mama worries when you don't. She says Le Le thinks you're big enough to take care of yourself, but she doesn't agree and thinks Le Le's just being selfish 'cause she hasn't had a man in so long."

Les's brown eyes looked tight in their sockets – like he was staring down a tornado.

"I'm sorry, Les, I didn't mean to say all that."

"I can take care of myself. I don't need nobody. You know I only stay at your house to make sure they're treating you right." His left hand clutched the pool table, and the right choked the pool stick. All ten knuckles were white.

"You know that's why I stay there, right?" He gave me a stare that froze me to the quick.

"Yeah, Les, I know."

"Things are better when I'm there, aren't they?"

"Yeah." They still drank a lot when he was there, but rarely was it the knocking and slamming around the kitchen kind of drunk.

"I'm not going to be here much longer, you know. You better appreciate it."

"Where you going?"

"L.A." I knew the answer before he said it. He'd always talked about working in the movies.

"When?"

"Soon. I hate this town. Something bad's gonna happen if I stay here. Everywhere I go there's some meanness or some hole. Feel like this town is a hole in the earth just like a black hole is a meanness in the sky."

"I hate this town, too," I said and kicked the dirty tile floor. I was looking down, so I didn't see the cue stick coming, but sure felt it: a sharp jab in the side just below my ribs. I stumbled against the pool table.

"Hey, asshole," Les said. "Watch what you're doing, you just hit my cousin."

"She shouldn't even be in here," the man said, then he bent to take his shot. But Les didn't let it go. He grabbed him by the shoulder and spun him around. The man was as tall as Les, but way bigger, broad and meaty. He glared at Les. His lips curled back like a sick dog. He was missing a top left tooth.

"I think you oughta apologize to her," Les said thumbing at me.

"Fuck off," the man said and turned back to his game. Les grabbed his shoulder again and the man threw down his cue stick and shoved Les back against the table where I leaned. Les stood up and brushed himself off.

"I guess you owe us both an apology now," Les said and smiled. I winced. He was really pressing his luck. I tensed up, ready to flee. The man studied us. His eyes were narrow and hard, two slits, but then a flicker of light caught in the corner and opened them up. He laughed. Bore that gap in his mouth.

"You've got some spunk, kid," the man said. "I like that." He looked at me and said. "Sorry, little lady. Hope I didn't hurt you none."

"Thanks," Les said to the man, then he turned to me, "you wanna get outta here?"

"Yeah," I said.

I followed him out. We crossed the street to look in the movie store, even though we didn't have money to rent one.

Les walked up to the counter and asked to see the blue book. I hid in the back by the romantic comedies, watching through the tape boxes.

"You got ID?" the clerk with moppy dark hair asked pushing up his little glasses.

"No," Les said.

"You gotta be eighteen to rent blue book movies." The clerk folded his arms across his chest and rocked back on his heels.

"You think I don't know that?" Les asked and leaned over the counter.

I edged closer and peeked at them from behind a Meg Ryan movie. Les stared down at the short video clerk. They locked gazes for a moment, and then the clerk shook his moppy head, grabbed the book, and slammed it down on the counter.

Les flipped through it saying the names of the movies in a loud voice, exaggerating the enunciation of each word, "Hmm. Let's see here *Naughty Nurse, Head of the Class, Forrest Hump, Porn on the Fourth of July, Goldie Rocks and the Three Heirs*. Give me a break, you got anything better than these? A little less cheese?"

"That's all we got."

"Come on Sadie, let's go."

I followed him out of the store and heard the clerk mumble, "Fucking redneck little shits," behind us.

"I'm gonna direct my own movie one day, not a porn, but a real movie, a great movie," Les said once we were outside. "I'm gonna call all the shots. Nothing fake or cheesy. Just real life, real emotions."

"It'll be a masterpiece," I said.

"Damn straight!"

We rounded the corner, and Les handed me a box of chocolate covered peanuts.

"You hungry?" he asked.

"Not really," I said.

"Well, I hate peanuts, I just got them 'cause I know you like them."

"All right," I said trying not to tear into them too quickly. I leaned my head back and popped three in my mouth. I sucked on them till all the chocolate melted off and then crunched down on the nuts. I ate half the box as slowly as possible and tucked the rest in the long pocket of my jean jacket for later. I sucked my tongue until I couldn't taste chocolate anymore. I was hungrier than ever.

We walked through the neighborhood near the square with the big houses and the wide yards. This year everybody had those lights that looked like icicles dangling from the roof. A Christmas tree stared out at us from every front window.

"I bet there's a fire lit up in each of those houses," I said.

"Yeah, but they ain't no good."

"Watcha mean?"

"I've been in one of those houses. Had a fake fire. Gas jets blow on these fake logs so it looks like a fire, but it isn't. Nothing burns. Just get the same fake fire every time. You turn a knob and it comes on."

"You're shittin' me." I studied the houses on the right, then on the left. It gave me a lonesome feeling, all of a sudden, how everything was decorated exactly the same.

"Nope. You know Alice Winston, from school?"

"Yeah." Everyone knew Alice Winston, even the Junior High kids all knew her by sight. She was famous for driving a red, Mustang convertible and for being homecoming queen and for looking all the time like she was on TV and nothing could touch her.

"She lives there," he pointed to the house on the corner. "I've been in there. She showed me the fucked up fireplace. She also showed me her room. She's got a bathroom in her room with a bathtub that's a Jacuzzi."

"No shit?"

"No shit. All kinds of weird shit in that house. Some good, some bad."

"How come she let you in the house?"

"What do you mean how come?"

"She's a snob."

"Let me tell you something now, so you won't be surprised when it starts happening to you. If you got something somebody wants, it doesn't matter what crowd you're in. People may not see you together, but you can still be together."

"Oh," I said. I figured he was talking about sex. "What do you have that Alice Winston wants?" I asked.

"Isn't it obvious?" He said and flexed his muscles like a wrestler on TV.

"You're as skinny as a bean pole," I said and laughed.

"It's not the bod," he said real serious, tucking down his hair.

"What is it then?"

"Chicks like her, they don't get enough excitement. She wants to know about what she doesn't know about, which is me. She wants to live my life."

"She's crazy. I wouldn't live your life for a million dollars."

"Yeah, well I sure as hell wouldn't live yours," he said. Then he came at me, picked me up, and swung me over his shoulder like a slaughtered pig.

"I got an idea," he said, setting me down.

"What?"

"Let's go to the KFC."

"Cool," I said, because that might mean we'd get something to eat. Les had a friend who worked there who had hooked us up before.

We started walking towards the Wal-Mart parking lot. It took a long time to walk there, even with the shortcut through the Jr. College campus. All the way I imagined hot, crispy fried chicken. Then I quit and tried to imagine Les with Alice Winston. I tried to imagine what it was they said to one another, and if they kissed in that thirsty way people did on TV.

In the distance I could see the red glow of the KFC sign and the purple of the Taco Bell.

"Thank the Lord!" I said, wishing I hadn't for fear Les would know how hungry I truly was.

We walked into the brightly-lit KFC, and the smell smacked me like a salt wave. My mouth watered and my eyes stung and started to water, too. I felt dizzy. I grabbed the elbow of Les's jacket to steady myself.

"You all right?" he asked.

"Fine," I said, but he was looking at me with that stare of his, so I added, "just tired; I couldn't sleep last night. Daddy was up late blaring the TV."

Les's friend wasn't there. Instead, Jacob Steel stood behind the counter. I knew Jacob from my neighborhood. He'd been arrested for too many DUIs, and the job was part of his juvenile rehabilitation program. Everyone knew his mama was hooked on Oxycotin.

"You're looking for a hand out, aren't ya?" Jacob said.

"Naw," Les said, "just looking for my friend."

"You should apply for a job, get you a free meal every night. Looks like you could use one," Jacob pointed at us, like we were pinned up on the wall for pin the tail on the donkey.

"I get plenty to eat," Les said.

"Uh-huh, I'm taking home a bucket tonight," Jacob said, "Ain't that right, Eddie?"

Eddie, a large dopey guy with brown hair hanging in his eyes, repeated from the next register, "a whole bucket."

"Are you gonna have any beer with that feast?" Les asked.

"Whole lotta beer," Jacob said.

"Lotsa beer," Eddie echoed.

"What about whiskey?" Les asked and leaned over the counter.

"Maybe some of that, too," Jacob said.

"Whiskey," Eddie repeated.

"Shut up, Eddie," Jacob said.

"Yeah, well if you run out, me and Sadie'll be at my old house. We got a stash there."

"Where'd you get whiskey from?" Jacob's face kinda twitched.

"I got my ways," Les answered. "Well, see ya."

"See ya."

"Come on, Sadie," Les said to me.

I followed him across the parking lot, behind Wal-Mart, across a barren cotton field, and through some woods. We picked up twigs and fallen branches along the way for a fire.

"You really got whiskey?" I asked, halfway there.

"A little bit."

"I thought you hated that guy."

"I do."

"So why'd you invite him to come over?"

He didn't answer for a long while.

"Alice Winston's coming over," he said, crunching down on a branch to split it.

"No shit?"

"Wait till he sees her, huh?" He bent to pick up the pieces.

I laughed because it seemed expected. Then when I got to thinking about it, I understood. It would make Jacob Steel real mad to know that Les hung out with Alice Winston. Then I started imagining what Les and Alice did in that old three-room house with the roof blown off. I saw a real fire lit, and their shadows wrestling on the walls.

When we got there Alice Winston's red Mustang was parked in the gravel driveway. Les pushed open the door and called out her name. No one answered. He lit his lighter and walked into the bare room. "Hey, Alice?" he called again, a sweetness in his voice, like when he comforted me for some sadness.

"Maybe she's out stargazing," he said.

"You can stargaze in here," I said.

"Yeah," he said and looked up at all that dazzle.

Just then Alice jumped out from the next room screaming hell for leather. I screamed, and Les jumped like a jack rabbit.

She laughed like an old crazy lady. "I got you! I got you, you son of a bitch! I got you!"

Les laughed, grabbed her, and picked her up, then spun her around, "I was just faking to give old Sadie a scare."

Alice was giggling like a goddamn maniac, she was so proud of herself. I figured, knowing Les, he had played similar tricks on her.

We sat on the floor of what used to be the family room and started a fire. Luckily, the chimney had withstood the tornado. Alice Winston had whiskey with her and pot. I'd smoked pot once before but hadn't felt any different. This time I inhaled deeply, and it felt like I burned a hole clean through my chest. I coughed like crazy and Les broke up laughing, but Alice Winston patted me on the back and said, "that's all right hon, just don't breathe so much in next time."

I had a little bit more and then I got a lot of distance on things – a lot of perspective. In art class we learned how to draw from perspective by sitting on one end of the hallway and drawing the opposite door real small and drawing everything gradually bigger the closer it got to you. I thought I was hearing like that. The voices seemed small and far away at first, and as I concentrated they loomed bigger and louder and clearer, until I had a revelation like fireworks bursting in my head.

The TV frame fell off of Alice, and she no longer looked like a snob, but someone more plain and complicated all at once. I saw how she leered at the fire in a hungry way and laughed at Les like she couldn't get enough of him. She seemed a lot like me. I looked at Les and knew that if he ever did really leave I'd have a hole inside me like feeling hungry forever. And then I smelled fried chicken.

"He's here," I said.

"What?" Les said.

"Jacob. I smell chicken."

Jacob and Eddie came in without knocking as if no roof meant no door either. They were all thumps and bumps and laughter, but they drew up quiet when they saw Alice Winston sitting there with us.

"Hey, man." Les nodded at them.

"What's up?" Jacob said.

"Y'all know Alice?" Les said cool as hell.

They nodded.

"Alice, this is Jacob and Eddie," Les said pointing to each one.

"Hey," she said in that tone that made people like Jacob think she was a real snob. That tone was working all over his face.

I didn't see the chicken, but the smell was fierce. I wondered if they had eaten it all before they came, and if the smell was only the smell of it on their breath and clothes. The whiskey bottle was about a quarter full, and I watched Jacob watching it. Alice took a pull and handed it to Les who drank and handed it to me. I drank and handed it to Jacob. He drank off pretty much the rest and then handed the last sip to Eddie who said, "shit," and drank it.

Nobody said anything for a while and then Jacob sorta started in on Alice Winston.

"So Alice, this ain't the kinda place you're used to is it?" he asked.

"How would you know?"

"I've never seen you on this side of town before."

"Maybe you haven't been looking," she said and stared at him like he was the most ignorant person she had ever seen.

I wondered if Les was going to ask him about the chicken, but he just smiled into the fire. Meanwhile the smell was getting so powerful I almost couldn't stand it. I felt like it was crawling through my skin, a live thing that had burrowed its way in there like ringworm.

Jacob started to drop hints about more whiskey.

"Y'all must have a pretty good buzz on by now," Jacob said.

"Pretty good," Les said.

"Hell, look at her eyes," Jacob pointed to Alice. We all leaned in to look at her green eyes. They had a soft watery look like late sunlight on a muddy river.

"I could drink all y'all under the table if I wanted to," Alice said.

"I'd like to see you try. Come on. I'll take you right now," Jacob said.

"Yeah, like to see you try," Eddie said.

"I would if," Alice began, but Les interrupted her.

"If I told you where the rest of the whiskey is?" he asked.

She cut her eyes at him, then said, "yeah."

"Well, where the hell is it?" Jacob said, "let's get this party started."

"How bad do you want it?" Les asked.

"What? Fuck, man, what are you trying to prove?"

Les shrugged. He was calling all the shots.

"Shit, I didn't eat all the chicken. I left it on that table in there." Jacob tossed his head in the direction of the kitchen.

"I didn't ask you about the chicken," Les said.

"Hell. I didn't ask you about the whisky."

"You did too," I said, "You just did ask him. I heard you."

"I heard you, too," said Alice.

"Yeah, me too," said Eddie.

"That's cause you tricked me into it."

"Nobody tricked nobody," Alice said. "You're just a drunk like your daddy."

"At least I have a daddy," Jacob said, which was true, neither Alice nor Les had a real daddy. Alice's daddy was really her step-daddy, and we never knew Les's daddy.

"It's in the back room, in the closet," Les said.

Jacob shoved his big butt off the ground and stomped into the back room. Eddie thundered after him.

"Get in there and get you some chicken," Les said. He winked.

You better believe that's what I did. I grabbed a leg and tore right into it like nobody's business. Even though it was cold, it was the best fried chicken I'd ever had. Les came in and ate a piece and asked Alice if she wanted one, but she said "no thanks." I figured Alice never really went hungry like that unless she wanted to.

"Where the hell is it?" Jacob called from the back of the house.

"Up on that shelf in the closet," Les called back. His voice flew over the walls through the bare starlit sky.

"I don't see it."

"Maybe it fell."

It was quiet for a while, and I started in on a thigh.

"Fuck man, it ain't here," Jacob called.

"You aren't looking hard enough," Les called back, then looked at me and started to laugh.

I laughed, too, and Alice asked, "You don't really have whiskey back there do you?"

Les shook his head.

"You just want to show him up, and I'm part of it, aren't I?" Alice accused.

Les put down his chicken and opened his mouth as if to deny or explain, but he never got the chance, because just then Jacob crowded the doorway mad as fire.

"Quit fucking around," he said, "I want some goddamn whiskey."

Les and I clutched chicken. Grease smeared our faces. I had just started to feel that satisfied relief when there he stood – eyes bulging, mouth open, panting. I stared. It was the same look my daddy got when he didn't have enough to get him drunk enough to feel better. Then everything swelled real big and close in my mind. I could see Mama holding Daddy off with the frying pan. I wished with all my heart that Les really did have some whiskey and would give it to Jacob right away.

Jacob was red and his hands kept closing into fists and opening again. He was leaning over like he was waiting for the gun to go off at the beginning of a race. I felt hot all over and backed up against the cabinet near

Alice Winston. Quick as a jackrabbit, Jacob, Eddie, and Les were all running around the table. I remembered I had Les's knife in my pocket, and I wondered if Les remembered, but Les was busy trying to get around the table. I reached into my pocket and looked at Alice. Her eyes had a shiny, glittery look.

Then Les jumped on top of the table and kicked chicken at Eddie and Jacob until they got him. They got him not like on TV when you see the neat angle and clear blow and crisp turn. Instead they got him with knuckles and elbows and knees and shoulders and noises – crunches and smacks and knocks and grinds. Blood sprayed on everyone so you couldn't tell who was hurt.

I groped for the knife. I knew I was going to get it, but I didn't know what I was going to do once I had it. I knew that Eddie was bigger than Jacob, but Eddie didn't do things unless Jacob did them, so it was better to go after Jacob. I knew that Les couldn't fight. He could con and steal and run, but fighting was another thing altogether. And I knew that I was damn good at running, but I wasn't running. I was standing still. A voice was screaming the sharpest scream I'd ever heard, and my chest hurt and shook. I shook from the inside out, and realized the scream I heard came out of my own shaking chest. When it stopped I could hear better than I had ever heard in my entire life. I could hear the footfall of a spider on its web in the corner.

They all stared at me. Their faces zoomed towards me through the long hallway of perspective, small and faraway and then big and close, and I knew that this was nothing like TV. Jacob yelled, "Shut the fuck up!"

But I had already shut up. I was burning up and held the knife in my left hand which was stupid because I write with my right, but there it was in my left. I pointed it at Jacob and said, "Leave him alone."

He left Les alone, unleashing his hand and nodding at Eddie. He took a few slow steps toward me and yelled, "You gonna make me, you little bitch?"

I backed against the cabinet and felt the drawer handle jab into my back.

"Yep," I said and the knife shook; its point shiny and glinting in the glowy light.

"Cut it out, Sadie," Les said, but I couldn't cut it out. The knife was out there, and I couldn't bring it back.

"You want to cut me?" Jacob said and stepped closer. I could see the stubble and a zit on his chin. He smiled like this was fun. I brought my right hand up and steadied the knife, grasping tightly with both hands.

Then Les lunged from behind Jacob. I couldn't move. They went down, but then back up just as fast, Les on Jacob's back. I still had the knife out, and when they came up, Jacob came up right under the knife, and for a second the knife lodged itself in the tough tissue between ear and head. It was a wild, long second – so quiet that the blood throbbed in my ears. I pushed down with all my might, and sliced his ear clean off. The pink ear bounced on the tile and rolled a little. It was like I was Peter in the Garden. I knew it was bad, but it felt mighty good. Eddie pointed and covered his mouth like an old lady, Alice Winston laughed a shrill, sudden laugh, and Jacob hollered like a mating cat. His hand came up to the bloody side of his head and then down. He looked at the bloody hand and hollered again, shaking the hand as if to fling it away from him.

We all watched him, frozen and trancelike, like he was a hole sucking us toward him, toward a place that no longer followed the usual rules of gravity and light. Then Les broke the trance. He reached down and grabbed the loose ear and cradled it in his shirt like a lost baby. He told Alice she'd have to take them to the emergency room and then put a hand on Jacob's shoulder to steady him. He did it calm as hell, as if Jacob and Eddie hadn't just been beating the crap out of him. Jacob quieted down under his touch. He looked about as vulnerable as a newborn. Like he didn't know how to use his limbs yet and he couldn't see ten inches before his face. It made me feel like the meanest thing alive when seconds before I felt like he was the meanest thing alive. I couldn't make head nor tails of the contradiction. It was as if the furniture was hanging from the ceiling, not clinging to the floor. I threw down the knife and ran.

I ran and ran and thought don't look back. "Sadie!" I heard Les call behind me, but I kept running. The cold wind whipped my face and snuck down the neck of my jean jacket. I cupped my hands around my own ears, feeling them, their peculiar hardness, not rigid like white bone, but pliant like green leaves. I crossed the stripped cotton field and thought don't look back, if you don't look back you won't get stuck teetering on that dark edge. Instead I looked down – leftover bolls sprinkled that dark earth like manna. Then I looked up – the milky sky swirled over glittery stars.

I ran and ran and then I did it. Even though I was thinking don't look back, and I was thinking run, run, run until you aren't in this town anymore, run until you see the ocean or a promised land, if you don't look back you won't get stuck, don't be like Lot's wife, don't become a pillar of salt, even though I was thinking all of those things, I turned and looked back at that starry hungry night, and when I did, it was like I had pushed the mute button on the world. Everything hushed.

But my legs still churned. My arms pumped.

MOVING THE FINISH LINE

Melanie Noto

"They give him two days."

"That's all?" Rosa's ice blue eyes widened, the motion flattening her wrinkles and taking a good five years off her face. She made an odd clucking sound low in her throat. "Beatrice must be a basket case."

"She's in his room. Knitting."

"You don't say?" Rosa shifted her purse under her arm and plopped down beside Emily on the low waiting room couch. "She always did like to knit."

"Started with a scarf," Lynnette said with a smirk. Her bobbed salon-colored hair swished as she tossed down a devotional guide. "It grew into an afghan."

"Now she has a bedspread." Emily wearily put down her magazine and looked at Lynnette. She, Rosa, and Emily had been friends for years, stretching back to when their boys were toddlers together at Ms. Marie's Pre-School in 1971. Beatrice and Robert had endured their share of problems, mostly caused by Robert's roving eye. Now, he was dying—and Beatrice was knitting herself into a corner.

Rosa settled back against the stained blue cushions. "Knitting calms her nerves."

"I think she's trying to forget." Emily had seen the pain in Beatrice's eyes over the years. She tried to hide it, but it was always there. Pain, along with a healthy dose of anger. "Or maybe…she's knitting him a burial shroud."

"Oh, now that would be a hoot." Lynette laughed. "Her yarn's bright orange."

"Beatrice has always been fond of loud colors, probably because Robert hates them." Rosa lifted her nose and pulled a romance novel out of her purse. "Mind if I read? Takes my mind off his poor soul."

"Poor Robert?" Emily scoffed. "You can't mean that. He brought the heart attack on himself, what with his wild lifestyle."

Rosa stared at her.

"Well. I hate to end this party, but I've got to go." Lynnette bounced to her feet. For sixty-five, she had a helluva lot of energy. Emily envied her. "Ed's expecting me to cook breakfast for supper."

"You two have that every Saturday night, don't you?" Emily smiled. Those two had a picture-perfect marriage. "You have for years, even when the kids were home."

"Oh, yes. It's a Wise family tradition."

"Well, for heaven's sake—don't let Robert's impending death cause you to dispense with your precious family traditions." Rosa pulled out a cigarette and a pencil thin lighter. Her mottled fingers shook.

Emily's eyebrows flew up. "You can't smoke in here."

"That's right." Lynnette frowned down at her. "This is a hospital. And I resent your remark about my family. Everyone grieves in his or her own way. Sticking with tradition eases my mind."

"Oh, please." Rosa rolled her eyes. "And I suppose you'll tell me next that Beatrice is pouring her grief into that atrocious orange monstrosity she's knitting."

"That's right." Lynnette lifted her chin. "She is."

Emily tightened her lips. "She's knitting to keep from crying."

"I don't blame her." Lynette put her fists on her hips. "Her life with him has been holy hell."

"Yes, it has." Beatrice's snapped words carried over the whir of the air conditioner. "And it will continue to be, as long as he's still breathing."

"Beatrice!" Lynnette pressed a hand over her heart. "Oh my. How is he?"

"Hanging on by a thread, damn him."

Rosa's face turned red. She crossed her legs and glared down at her book as if suddenly infuriated by the unfolding story.

Emily scooted to the edge of her seat. "Do they give him any hope?"

"He's had an experimental drug." Beatrice pursed her lips. "It's touch and go, thanks to his weak heart valves. Surgery's out of the question. So, who knows?"

Lynette tapped her foot. "I think he'll live."

"If he does, we'll be making some changes at our house."

"Doctor's orders?" Emily wondered what the doctor might ask of Robert. A new diet? Maybe an exercise routine?

Beatrice shook her head. "No. Robert cheated on me—again. I've put up with his philandering for years, but it's going to stop once and for all. I'm gonna see to it."

Rosa buried her face deeper into her book.

Lynette's mouth dropped open, and she sidled closer to Beatrice. "Oh my God! I've heard rumors—but I had no idea it was true. Do you have proof?"

"Why, yes. I know everything." Her wide nostril's flared. "Except the brazen hussy's name."

Lynette lifted her gray eyebrows.

Emily snapped her mouth shut. She wasn't telling what she knew.

"Enough about my scheming husband's extracurricular activities." Beatrice wiped her bloodshot eyes. "I need more yarn."

"I'll bring you some," Lynette said. "Is tomorrow soon enough?"

"No." Beatrice made a fist. "I need it tonight, if I'm gonna outlast him."

"This isn't a race, you know." Rosa's jerked her head up. "Your husband's on his death bed."

"Since when are you so concerned about Robert?" Lynette eyed her strangely.

Rosa shoved her book into her purse. "Since no one else is."

"Bah. He may be on his death bed, but I'm the one having to endure everything." Beatrice curled her lip into a sneer. "With him, it's always a race. First to the finish line. Always has to win, no matter the cost. The swankiest house. The classiest cars. The best vacation. And now, the youngest floozy."

"She's young?" Lynette leaned close. "How young?"

"Younger. I don't know." Beatrice threw up her hands. "Fast. It's how he's lived his life, up till now. All at once, with death looming on the horizon, he's suddenly the Tortoise, not the Hare."

"I should think you'd have compassion for your own husband," Rosa chimed in.

"He cheated on me, damn you." Beatrice snapped. "My compassion only goes so far. And it certainly doesn't apply to the bitch that brought on his heart attack."

She turned on the heel of her orthopedic shoes and marched off down the hall.

"Whoa," Lynette said, her dark eyes blinking. "She's one angry woman."

"Wouldn't you be?" Emily rose beside her. "What if you found out Ed was cheating on you?"

"My lazy Ed? Cheat?" Lynette laughed sharply and brought a well-manicured hand to her mouth. "Oh, please. He doesn't have the balls. Never did."

"I think it's a sin." Rosa tucked her purse under her arm and pushed herself off the couch. Her knees popped.

Emily widened her eyes. Rosa was the youngest in the bunch, yet she had the worst arthritis. She surmised it was because Rosa always tried to act like a schoolgirl, always flirting with men and flaunting it in front of Hank, her beleaguered husband. The man was either a saint or totally blind to forgive her escapades. Especially her latest. Robert Burnett.

*   *   *

Beatrice looked down at Robert with contempt in her eyes.

Cheating bastard. Once, a year after their marriage, she had forgiven him. That had been the first time, when she'd discovered him in bed with his chirpy blond secretary. What a scene that had been. The bitch had screamed, Beatrice had cried, and Robert had sworn he'd never stray again.

Ha. That same scenario had played itself out over and over again throughout the years, until she was sure she was so numb she could no longer be hurt. Unfortunately, she had been wrong. Just last month she'd learn he had left the straight and narrow path for another mindless fling. This time, with someone from the church. If only she could find out whom it had been.

Her bitterness boiled over, and she wrapped her hand around the oxygen tube leading to Robert's nose. With just one long, vigorous squeeze—

The door burst inward, and Sue, Robert's young, pencil thin nurse popped in carrying an IV bag of clear fluids. She paused just inside the door, like she was surprised to see Beatrice near Robert. She looked from them, to the giant afghan piled on the chair in the corner, and back to meet Beatrice's eyes. "Well, well, Mrs. Burnett. Have you finally finished your knitting project?"

"Oh, no." Beatrice turned so Sue couldn't see her release the oxygen tube and slowly lowered her hand to her side. She pasted a stiff smile on her face. "I still have to complete the border."

"Wow. That's one big afghan."

"It's for Robert," she said, and suddenly she knew exactly what she'd do with that awful orange monstrosity. She'd knitted it to calm her frazzled nerves. And now—

The nurse smiled and stepped up to Robert's IV pole. "That's just so sweet. I know he'll appreciate it."

"Oh, I doubt that," Beatrice murmured to herself, moving away. She picked up the bulky afghan, sat down in her chair, and picked up her knitting needles. They gleamed like tiny swords in the meager light from the window.

The nurse bustled around for a few more minutes, examining Robert's IV and checking his oxygen, then she left and a CNA came in to take his vitals.

Beatrice spoke to the man, but didn't try to make conversation. She was too busy planning. Her mind whirred as her fingers whipped along the border of the afghan. *Orange.* She hated orange. The good thing was, so did Robert.

Her mouth curved in a sly smile. It was simple poetic justice—like having him dying, tucked away in that lonely hospital bed with her at his side, rather than frolicking in bed with one of his many floozies after racing to some pricey Caribbean resort. He'd done that from time to time. She was sure of it.

Bastard. Her icy fingers flew. She would fix him.

If only Lynette would bring her some more bright orange yarn.

* * *

Emily didn't know what to say to Rosa. The other woman perched on the opposite side of the table in Mercy General's revamped cafeteria, devouring a piece of peach pie like she didn't have a care in the world. Beside her was her latest read titled *Sex on Wheels*, another of those racy romances she chain read.

Watching Rosa's surgically smoothed jowls stretch unnaturally as she chewed the pie's less-then-flaky crust, Emily's appetite fled. She set down her fork. Anger filled her as she thought of what Rosa had done.

Unable to keep quiet a moment longer, she leaned over the table. "I know it was you with Robert that night."

"Excuse me?" Rosa looked up from her plate in surprise.

Emily set her mouth and plowed on. She had to confront the witch once and for all. "You heard me. I know you were with him when he had his heart attack."

"You know nothing of the sort." The other woman gripped her fork with white knuckled fingers. "I was at home that night. Alone."

"Don't bother to lie. I saw your car down the block from Robert and Beatrice's place, where you always parked when she was gone and you spent time with Robert."

"I did no such thing."

"Give me a break, Rosa!" Emily's voice rose. She was furious with herself for having kept quiet so long. "I've known about your affair since day one. I went to see Beatrice the day you came back to town, and I saw you and Robert kissing in the foyer. You didn't know I was on the front porch, but I was, and I watched him lead you to the back of the house—to their bedroom. You are despicable. Simply despicable!"

"Oh my. You think...oh dear. I would never—" Rosa pressed her free hand to her throat in a theatrical attempt at innocence, something she hadn't known since she was thirteen. "You know me better than that, Emily. You're my best friend."

"Some friend. You stole Tommy Livingston from me back in junior high school, and you're still stealing men. Only now, they're married." Emily shook her head. Once a slut, always a slut. She edged forward to lessen the chance someone would overhear them. "You left the house that night before the ambulance got there, but I know you were with him. Your antics in bed were probably what triggered his heart attack."

"You don't know what you're talking about." Rosa picked up a napkin and primly wiped her mouth. "Your imagination is working over time. You do have a tendency to make up stories, you know."

"I do not. You'd better own up to this, or I'll talk to Beatrice."

"Don't you threaten me you…you…spinster!"

"Oh, please." Emily sat back and laughed. "That's the best you can do? I'm glad I never married. If I had, you probably would have stolen my husband, too. Poor Hank. He didn't know what he was getting himself into when he married you, did he?"

"Oh!" Rosa shoved her chair back so hard it hit the table behind her. She muttered a curse, rocketed to her feet, and snatched up her tray. "I don't have to sit here and listen to your insults. Consider yourself my *ex-friend*."

"That's fine by me, you two-timing *hussy*."

Emily crossed her arms. She was acting like a child, and she knew it. Yet she couldn't help herself. Part of her still ached for the attention of that boy Rosa had stolen from her back in eighth grade. That incident had shattered her self-confidence and she'd never fully recovered. Damn Rosa for being so pretty and such a practiced flirt. Married women shouldn't act that way.

She wiped her eyes and stood up. Maybe she should have that little talk with Beatrice tonight. That would fix Rosa's little red wagon once and for all.

Her heart pounding, she dropped off her tray and headed back upstairs. To her relief, Rosa wasn't in the waiting room. Maybe she'd gone home.

Emily gripped her purse and started down the hall toward Robert's room. A nurse walked toward her. Gathering her nerve, Emily stopped her.

"Excuse me, ma'am. I'd like to visit Robert Daniels in 5076, if it's all right."

"Of course it is, as long as his other visitor is leaving." The nurse bobbed her blond head. "His visitors are limited to two at a time, and his wife is in the room. Feel free to ask her when you may go in."

"His other visitor?"

"I don't know her name, but she's in with Mrs. Burnett right now."

"Thank you. I'll stop by." Emily glared at the door to Robert's room. It had to be Rosa. The woman had a pair of shiny brass balls.

The nurse headed for the nurses station in her noiseless white shoes and Emily marched straight to Robert's door. Fury skittered over her skin like a thousand tiny rodent's paws.

She pushed open the door, and the sharp odor of antiseptic rolled over her in a sickening wave. Her eyes watered. She paused to let her vision adjust to the minimal light, and she stepped inside. Sure enough, Rosa stood next to Beatrice, who sat rigidly her chair in front of the window. Knitting. That damned afghan had to be twenty feet long by now.

Emily shut the door and crept inside. The place reminded her of a tomb, except for the annoying heart monitor beside Robert's bed beeping out its steady rhythm. It set her teeth on edge. The poor man's eyes were closed, and he had an oxygen tube in his nose. His IV pole gleamed like a sterling silver gallows beside his head.

Rosa's blue eyes narrowed. "You're not supposed to be in here," she hissed. "The note on the door says only two visitors at a time."

"The nurse said you were on your way out," Emily said sweetly. Her gaze fell on Beatrice. "How are you, dear? Do you need anything?"

"Only that damned orange yarn Lynette is bringing, and for you two to stop yammering." She looked up at Rosa. "Are you still here?"

"Well, I never." Rosa stuck her nose in the air. "I was hoping to sit with you and keep you company this evening. But I guess I won't now."

"There's no need for you to stay, dear." A mean smile curled the corners of Beatrice's thin lips. "Emily's here. She'll stay with me. You should go home and spend some quality time with Hank."

"Posh," Rosa snapped. "No time with that man had any quality to it."

"Shame on you." Emily fixed her with a knowing stare. "You're talking about your *husband*. He's bound to feel neglected if you stay here much longer."

"You know nothing about my marriage. What I've put up with—"

"What you've put up with?" Emily raised her eyebrows. "What about Hank? The man has to be a saint to have put up with you for nearly thirty-five years."

"Emily, that's enough." Beatrice released a long sigh. "Rosa, get the hell out of here. I need to talk to Emily. Alone."

"Fine." Rosa glared at Emily for another moment before dropping her fiery gaze to Beatrice. "I'll be praying for both of you."

With a toss of her gray head, she stormed out.

Emily wasn't sure if Rosa meant she was praying for her and Beatrice, or for Beatrice and Robert. Either way, she couldn't help but doubt her former friend's connection with the good Lord. He tended to frown upon adultery.

"I must have touched a nerve," Beatrice said.

Emily waited until the door closed all the way before she answered her. "You did. She doesn't want me talking to you."

"I suppose there's a logical explanation for that."

"Oh, there's an explanation all right." Emily wondered how much to tell her. "I'm just not sure you want to hear it."

"Rosa's always operated on a different plane from the rest of us." Beatrice shook her head. "She and I have never seen eye to eye on anything."

"Have you noticed anything strange about her lately?"

"Nothing really odd." She furrowed her brow. "Why? What's she done?"

"I hate to tell you this—" Emily looked down at her hands. "But she's the one."

"I'm not sure I want to hear this." Beatrice cocked her head. "Go on."

"Robert was with Rosa the night he had his heart attack."

"Oh. My. God."

"I didn't want to tell you. I debated. But hell, you deserve to know. She's a slut. Always has been. Stealing men is her favorite pastime."

"Rosa and Robert?" Beatrice looked as if she'd been pole axed.

Emily nodded.

"He's cheated for years, you know." She started babbling. "I didn't say anything, because it didn't matter. I haven't shared his bed in years. I was afraid of what I might catch. That man slept with anything he could get his pecker into. I just never figured he would sleep with Rosa."

Emily covered her mouth. Sixty-five years old, and the unexpected mention of a man's privates still made her blush. Probably because Beatrice was talking about Robert's privates and Rosa in the same sentence. Emily did not want that picture etched into her mind. Her cheeks grew hot.

"It's the truth," Beatrice said, her knitting needles clacking together like ill fitting false teeth. "The man has the morals of a weasel in heat."

"I don't blame you for being sarcastic. You've just had a major shock."

"Yes, I have." Her knitting needles halted their frantic movements, and she fixed Emily with a sad stare. "You know, before our marriage, Robert promised to be faithful. Well! That lasted all of one month. I should have known he'd stray with one of my friends, eventually."

"I had no idea."

"Most people didn't. I kept it hidden. Thought I'd conquered the hurt." A familiar ache began in the vicinity of her heart. She shook her head. "But, no. Turns out I was dead wrong. Again."

"I'm so sorry."

"This one cuts me to the bone," Tears stung Beatrice's eyes as she pictured her husband with her former best friend. The image made her nauseous. "He slept with Rosa. Oh my God." She mopped moisture from her face.

"She's a man stealer."

"You can say that again." Beatrice took a deep breath and peered down at the growing pile of orange on her lap. Orange, like sunshine. A commodity she'd seen too little of lately. Sunshine was for happiness, not grief, anger, and shame.

A familiar children's taunt echoed inside her mind. *Robert and Rosa, sitting in a tree. K-i-s-s-i-n-g* Those foolish words dispelled her sadness, and an angry blue flame fired to life inside her chest. A flame so hot it seared her heart.

She wished Emily would leave, so she could put her plan in motion.

It was time.

Beatrice balled up the afghan and rose with it in her arms. She dumped it in the chair behind her and stuck the needles in the pocket of her smock. "I need to be alone."

"Are you sure?" Emily came to her feet. "I don't mind staying."

"I'm positive." Beatrice deliberately kept her eyes off Robert, who kept breathing thanks to that damned tube in his nose.

Emily picked up her purse. "Fine. You know how to reach me if you need me."

"That's right. I do. And I won't hesitate to call."

"Make sure you let me know if something happens." Emily put her hand on Beatrice's arm and gave it a squeeze. "I'll check on you in the morning."

"I'd appreciate it." Beatrice patted her hand. "You've been so good to me."

"You're a good friend." Emily dropped her hand. "Try to get some rest, okay?"

"I'll do my best." Beatrice plastered a fake smile on her face. "Thank you for everything."

"You're most welcome." Emily smiled. "Oh, and don't forget—Lynette should be back soon with your yarn."

Damn. Beatrice had forgotten. She'd have to work fast.

She tried to mask her annoyance as she walked Emily to the door. Once it whooshed shut behind her friend, she turned and faced her husband, who lay still as death in that hospital bed. The nurse would be in soon. Time was short.

She crept across the cream colored tiles to stand at Robert's side. His eyes were closed and wrinkles bunched around his mouth like a series of tiny parentheses. His jowls trembled with every labored breath. Damn him. He looked so *old*.

"The race is nearly over," she whispered. "You cheating bastard."

She pulled several tissues from the box by the bed and carefully wiped the oxygen tube where she'd squeezed it before the nurse came in. Then she fisted the tube in her right hand and pressed it closed with her thumb—protected by the tissues, of course. The heart monitor kept up its steady beat.

Robert's mouth fell open. The monitor faltered as he gasped for air. Then it started again, its beeps erratic.

Beatrice tightened her hold on the tube. Her nerves skittered, and she became aware of Robert, twitching. A wheezing sound came from his chest. Cool air spewed from the vents overhead. She shivered.

The beeps grew farther apart. Robert's face grew slack.

Footsteps sounded outside the door.

Beatrice pulled out one of her knitting needles and stabbed the tube near the wall.

The door flew open.

She released the tube and stuck the needle in her pocket. Turning away from the bed, she wiped her eyes with the tissues.

"Nurse, thank God. He stopped breathing. I-I didn't know what to do."

"Move, please." The nurse eyed the monitor and checked the tubes. A frown marred her brow. "I don't understand this."

Oddly satisfied by the nurse's confusion, Beatrice backed away. Her heart pounded. She hoped the nurse wouldn't discover that the tube had been cut.

All at once, the monitor's shrill beeps coalesced into one long, aggravating squeal. Robert didn't move.

"He's coding," the nurse announced. She picked up the phone and called for help. Then she began chest compressions, awkwardly pushing on his thick chest. "Come on, Mr. Burnett. Come on. Damn it."

Please stop! Beatrice longed to shout. *Just let the bastard go.*

She tiptoed around the bed just as a bevy of hospital personnel hit the door. One nurse dragged in a defibrillator. A doctor loped in and grabbed the paddles. They surrounded Robert and began poking and prodding. His hospital gown was ripped open.

"Clear!" the doctor shouted.

Everyone edged backwards as he rubbed the paddles together, and then pressed them to Robert's bare chest. Electricity jolted through his body, and his back arched off the bed. The squeal blipped briefly, but kept up its annoying cry.

Robert fell back on the bed. Unmoving.

Beatrice choked back her glee.

The doctor upped the amperage and yelled, "Clear!"

He shocked Robert again. No luck. His face reddened and he tried a third time, but Robert simply flopped back on the bed, his pale body already growing cold.

The doctor glanced at Robert's nurse, and then up at the clock on the wall.

"Time of death," he said with a resigned sigh. "Eleven twenty-two."

Beatrice pressed her hands together and prayed for forgiveness.

The nurse turned to her. "I'm so sorry, Mrs. Burnett."

"You did what you could," Beatrice said, creeping toward Robert. She forced a waver into her voice. "Oh, my poor, poor dear."

The nurses and CNA's slipped from the room one by one. The defibrillator disappeared. Finally, only Beatrice and the doctor remained.

"His heart was in such bad shape after that heart attack," the doctor said.

"I know," she said. "You showed me pictures from his CAT scan. I'd hoped he'd get better, but it must have been his time."

"I thought he was strong enough to allow his heart to heal."

"Apparently not." Beatrice stared down at her husband's slack face. His cheeks had an eerie gray tint, and his eyes were closed, thank God. The odor of death surrounded him. Nausea bubbled up her throat. She wanted the doctor to leave.

He walked over and took her hand. She didn't meet his eyes. She couldn't. Tears filled her vision.

"Do you need some time alone with your husband?"

"Y-yes, please," she murmured, wiping moisture from her lashes. "If you don't mind. I'd like to say goodbye."

"Of course." He squeezed her hand, and then turned toward the door. "I'll send someone in shortly to prepare his body. You might want to gather his things."

"I will. Thank you." She trained her gaze on his broad back as he angled for the door. Once he was gone, she took a deep breath.

Robert was dead. Finally. She braced herself, expecting to be pummeled by grief, but all she felt was a startling surge of relief—tempered by a tiny thread of guilt that wound its way around her heart. She was a murderer.

No. Robert had been dying. She had merely moved the finish line.

She walked over to her chair and picked up the ugly orange afghan. Her hands were steady as she tossed it over Robert's prone form and tucked it tightly around him.

The door burst open and Lynette plunged inside carrying three skeins of bright orange yarn. "Oh my God. They told me Robert's gone."

"Yes, my dear Lynette." Beatrice pulled the end of the giant afghan over her husband's face. "He is. And as you can see, I have no more use for the yarn."

"No problem. I'll call Rosa," Lynette said. "And Emily. I'm sure they'll want to know. Especially Rosa. She was so upset about Robert's heart attack."

"You do that," Beatrice said, shooing her friend away at the mention of Rosa's name. "Go on now. I need some time alone with him. Surely you understand."

"Oh, of course I do." Lynnette's pink cheeks clashed with the bright yarn in her arms. She turned and slipped out the door.

Beatrice turned back to her husband's shrouded body.

"The race is over now, Robert," she whispered. "I won."

She reached into her pocket and touched the knitting needles. They were cool against her warm fingertips. "And guess who's next?" she asked.

Her words hung in the air. She smiled. "That's right, my dear. *Rosa.* The husband stealer."

TREAT BOX

Sarah Frances Hardy

Something happens to Darvius that makes him feel mean all over every single day. This meanness gets deep down into the back of his eyeballs. You can see it there rolling around in his head.

Miz Leake is real sweet to him even when he swings his fists at her and calls her all these words my momma told me never to say. She just holds onto him until he can't hit her anymore, and sometimes he makes these real soft animal noises and then you know he'll be okay for a little while. Then he'll start being mean all over again.

One time, he brought a lighter to school and another time he brought a bottle of pills that he said he found on his kitchen table. Miz Leake was s'posed to tell the principal, but I don't think she ever did. She didn't want Darvius to have to go to that special school where they send all the other mean kids.

Some of the parents were upset about Darvius being in our class. They didn't want him around us with our clean clothes and hair and yelling out all those bad words. Miz Leake made all those parents feel bad about thinking that way, I think. Besides, all of us kids know how it is to feel mean some of the time. And, man, it would be tough to feel like that every day of your life. Think about it--you wake up feeling stinky, low-down mean and maybe you wanna hit somebody, but the only person around is you because your momma's passed out on the couch because of those pills so you just hit the next person you see who happens to be the little kid on your bus. So, your day starts out and you're already in trouble because of the bus.

Darvius is the blackest boy I know and I can still see the dark bruises rising up out of his checkered shirt. He wears that checkered shirt every single day--even when Miz Leake sends him home with a bag of clothes from the clothes closet in the front hall of our building. She sends him home with clothes all the time, but all he ever wants to wear is that checkered shirt. It has a high collar, so you know he's hiding more of those bruises underneath. If you ever ask him who it was that was beating up on him all the time, he just puts his head down between his legs and makes noises like those whales we always have to watch on those science shows in the library. It's the worst noise you ever heard, I can promise you. Miz Leake has to take him outside until he calms down and stops making those noises, because sometimes when he makes those noises he tries to hurt whoever is next to him.

Well, here is what happened one week. Darvius had never gotten to get a treat from the treat box like the rest of us. You have to be good all week long to get something from the treat box, and Darvius always had checkmarks by his name for doing things like hitting, kicking, yelling out-- and one time, he set all his papers on fire with that lighter. We all had to go outside and sit until the smoke cleared out of our room. The office tried to call his momma to come and get him that day, but I heard Miz Leake tell another teacher that his phone had been disconnected.

But, this day was a special day--special in a good way, not special in a call-the-fire-department kind of way. Darvius didn't have a single mark by his name, and you know what? It was Friday. Miz Leake was about to bust, she was so proud of Darvius, and she made a big deal out of saving his name for last so he could spend as long as he wanted getting his treat out of the box.

As soon as Miz Leake announced Darvius's name, you could see his gappy white teeth all capped in silver smiling so big. He strutted right up to the front of the room and picked out a pair of googly eyed glasses that he could take home all for his very own. He was smiling so big and Miz Leake was so proud, well, we all just started clapping right then and there. Darvius sat down in his seat and started tapping his head on the table like he always does when he is real happy.

I don't know who started it, maybe it was Bella, but one of us went over and gave Darvius our treat--our very own treat that we had earned from the treat box. Just set it right down in front of him on the table. Then we all did it. We got in a line and we each gave Darvius our treats until he had a pile that was bigger than Christmas right in front of him. Miz Leake started crying so hard that we finally had to stop clapping because we knew if we kept on, she'd never stop.

Then the next Monday, Darvius didn't come to school at all. And, he didn't come the next day. Or the next. Now this wasn't so strange because Darvius had to get himself to the bus stop everyday all by himself on account of his momma being passed out on the couch, and if he missed the bus, well you know his momma wouldn't be taking him to school. But, Miz Leake was real upset because Darvius had been doing so good. She kept calling that disconnected number and finally decided that she would try to find Darvius's house herself. But the principal told Miz Leake, she couldn't go out to that house, someone from the office had to go. Things like that always broke Miz Leake's heart because she knew Darvius would be scared of anybody but her.

Now, I'm a real good listener, and I have a special interest in Darvius because I am the only person in class who can sit by him. He kicked everybody else. So, of course, I listened as hard as I could when somebody from the office came to our room to talk to Miz Leake about Darvius disappearing into thin air. I overheard words like deplorable and inhuman and abusive and gross and jail and drugs and neglect and gone. Gone. That was the word that made Miz Leake cry. And man, those tears weren't like the ones she cried when Darvius got to get a treat out of the treat box. Those treat box tears were proud tears. These tears were the real kind that come from all the bad stuff that shouldn't happen. Now, it's almost the end of the school year and I don't guess Miz Leake was ever able to track down Darvius and find out what happened.

And, maybe that's just as well. I'd hate to see the kind of tears she'd cry if she ever found him again.

STRANGERS IN A STRANGE LAND

Judy H. Tucker

Where am I? Gemma wondered as the sound of voices penetrated her dream. A high, excited child's chatter and a woman answering. Just a murmur, the woman's voice.

Where am I? Only half awake, Gemma looked around the room at white plaster walls, white ceiling, dark oak floor, white linens, white curtains at the narrow window. A sickening, sweet, heavy odor. Other places, other rooms floated past her mind's eye, until at last, she had inventoried the possibilities, and then she knew where she was and why. There was quiet for a moment as the two people, woman and child, passed under her window, then she heard the clanking of the chains of the swing. She moaned and rolled over in bed.

Outside she heard a truck strain as it went up the side of the mountain. She sat up, throwing off the sheets, already limp and damp in the morning heat. Trying to bring herself up out of the murky deep of sleep, she looked at the clock beside her bed. Eleven a.m.. Except for the soft buzz of the oscillating fan on the dresser, the house was quiet.

Except for the clank of the chain of the swing, the world outside was quiet. Except for the heavy, sick smell, the world was clean. Except for the fog in her brain, she was alive.

Only the floor was cool to her bare feet. She pulled a white cotton wrapper over her white cotton gown and pulled the belt around her waist. Then the heat of her own body almost smothered her. She pulled off the robe and yanked the gown over her head and then put the robe on again over her naked body. She coiled her heavy, dark hair off her damp neck and twisted it into a knot on the back of her head and secured it with a comb from the dresser. She walked across the room, out the door, through the hall, and like some sort of apparition, she floated down the steep stairs, unlocked the front door, all three locks, and stepped outside.

Her house sat on a flat shelf halfway down the mountain. Behind the house the mountain rose, rocky, steep; in front of the house the yard fell away in a sheer drop of forty feet to the street where her small car was parked, off the pavement, hugging the side of the mountain. She stood now on the front stoop of the house looking out over the valley below. Panels of flat, yellow clouds obscured the view. Through the sulfurous clouds, she could barely make out the red rooftops on the street below; beyond the clouds that hung close to the river, she could see the peaks of the mountains on the other side of the valley.

A strange woman stood in her side-yard pushing the child on the swing. Her face was pitted with signs of rough days--acne scars and sun damaged with thick skin and deep furrows--hard-bitten. "I hope you don't mind us using your swing set."

"No," Gemma said. "I don't mind. We don't use it." She backed up against the low retaining wall that ran along the side of the mountain and sat down. Her toes played in the loose gravel.

There was silence until she said, "What is today?"

"The eleventh," the woman answered. "The eleventh of August."

"No, I mean the day of the week."

"Oh, it's Wednesday. Still the eleventh of August. Dog days."

"It's bad today," Gemma said.

The woman knew what she meant. "Not as bad as I've seen it," the woman said.

"It gets worse?"

"It can. You must be new. I've seen it so bad you had to use your head-lights on Capital Street at twelve o'clock noon. How long have you been here?"

"Three weeks. You live here?" Gemma asked, indicating the houses that ran around and up the side of the mountain.

"No, I baby-sit Baby."

"Well, you're welcome to use this swing set. I don't—we don't have any

72

children. So feel free. Any time."

"I'm out of work right now, between jobs," the woman explained, "and Baby's mother needed a sitter, so we're just helping each other out."

"That's good for both of you."

The conversation died. Gemma pushed some pebbles around with her feet, and then felt uncomfortable in her own yard. It didn't feel like her house, her yard yet, and these two strangers coming uninvited didn't help any. "If you'll excuse me. . .stay as long as you like." She got up and went into the house and put on a pot of coffee for herself.

Her husband Walter came home on Friday at noon. She picked him up at the airport which was the flattened-off top of a mountain on the other side of the river. Only small jets could land there because the runways were too short but they, whoever they were, had plans to build another airport out in the flats beyond town. This was, after all, the state capital.

They embraced and kissed. They were newly weds, Gemma and Walter.

She was dressing for an evening of bridge with the other engineers and their wives. It's what they did on Saturday nights.

"You're wearing that dress?" he asked her.

"Why not? It's just a bridge game." She smoothed the denim skirt down over her thighs and examined herself in the mirror over the dresser.

"But that dress? It's so—plain."

"It's just the Lawsons, for goodness sake."

"Everybody from the team will be there," Walter said. He'd put on fresh Dockers and a new Hawaiian shirt he'd picked up at the airport in Honolulu.

"Well then what? You show me." Her voice was sharp. "What should I wear?" She pulled the dress over her shoulders and threw it on the bed.

He caught no hint that he had angered her. He picked up the dress and put it on a hanger and stuck it back in the closet. "Why not wear this? You look good in green."

"Why not?" she said with a tight mouth. She pulled the dress off the padded velvet hanger and unzipped it and let it puddle on the floor and stepped into it. She pulled it up and stuck her arms in the full sleeves and turned for him to zip her up.

"Now," he said. He put his hands on her shoulders and turned her around and stood back and looked at her approvingly. "When you shuffle the cards, the fabric will fall just so. You have beautiful hands. Don't you like this dress better?"

"Infinitely," she replied.

Later that night as they lay in bed in the house on the side of the mountain, he said, "Why did you bid two no trump over my one heart?"

"To show that I had stoppers in the other suits." She yawned and moved closer to him.

"But two no trump was a jump. You didn't have the points to jump. Why did you do that?"

"I just wasn't thinking," she said and drew back from him a little. "I was thinking of other things." She put a finger on his shoulder and traced it down his arm to his wrist.

"We made the bid. So what?" she said.

"That's not the point. I have to be able to depend on your bidding."

"Well, the fabric on my sleeve fell nicely," she said, moving closer to him.

"You were the prettiest wife there." He reached for her.

On Sunday he played golf while she got his laundry ready for the next week when he and the rest of his team of engineers would fly off the mountain. His company was searching the globe, mostly third-world countries where they would be most welcome, for a sight on which to build an industrial plant. The Clean Air Act of 1965 had just passed in Congress and the chemical giants saw the handwriting on the wall. The new plant they were planning would manufacture a herbicide that would eventually rid the world of a certain vine that choked the life out of soy beans in Egypt.

"Why don't you find a commercial use for the vine and then the Egyptians would grow it instead of soy beans?" she had asked over the bridge table. Her partner, one of the team, had smiled indulgently and his knee rubbed against hers under the table.

"Then, where would we make the money to keep you in trinkets?" asked Walter who was playing West.

The wives in the room giggled. The men slapped their thighs and laughed.

And then on Monday the plane flew off over the mountains on its way across the ocean, and she was left in her bed alone, asleep, smothered, auto-intoxicated. The rattle of the swing in the yard woke her. She yawned and stretched and padded down the stairs and out on the stoop. A storm had moved through the valley the night before and the sky was a clear blue, though there lingered a residue of odor, a little like the smell of paint thinner, and on this clear day she could locate each of the chemical plants, including Carbide, because with the smog gone, she could see the individual plume of exhaust each plant sent into the air up and down the river. Soon it would fill the valley and she would have that choking feeling again.

*   *   *

The woman pushed the little girl on the swing. They came every day now. The child jumped off the swing to chase a butterfly. The woman backed up against the retaining wall and sat down.

"Stay here," said Gemma. "I'm going inside to get a cup of coffee. I can't seem to wake up. Do you take cream or sugar?"

"Black," the woman answered.

The girl retreated to the kitchen and returned with a tray holding two cups of coffee. The steam wafted up into the air where it mingled with the elements. She sat the tray down on the retaining wall and pushed it toward the woman.

"What did you do?" Gemma asked as she picked up the dainty cup from her wedding china. "What job, I mean."

"I was a truck driver."

"A truck driver. Yes?"

"My husband and I drove cross country. We were a team. Many's the night we pulled out a bedroll and slept under the stars in the desert. Nevada. Near the Badlands."

"Clean air, I'll bet."

"Pure. I miss it."

"Why'd you quit?"

"He quit me. Up and left me at a truck stop in Waco and I never saw his face again. It was his truck. I caught a ride back east with another trucker."

"I went to school in Waco. Baylor." Gemma examined the woman's face. It was hard. A hard creased face with many hard miles on it surrounded by no nonsense dirty blonde hair, pushed back, cropped. Hair for a long-haul. "Do you live around here?"

"I rent a trailer at the foot of Spring Hill Mountain."

"It's pretty out there. Can you smell it out there? The chemical plants, I mean?"

"If the wind is from the east you can. Y'all with Carbide?"

Gemma did not miss the 'y'all with Carbide.' She supposed she was, as much as her husband. She looked up at the sky, already dimming as the smog from the plants spread out in the wind high up over the river. Everybody on the mountain worked for Carbide. The higher up in the company you were, the higher you lived on the mountain, which was the reason, as a new hire, her husband bought the little house near the foot of the mountain.

"You won't be down here long. They move up real fast at Carbide."

"You can't see the stars like you can in the desert, can you?" Gemma said to the woman.

"No, you can't. I miss laying out in the desert."

"Under the stars," Gemma said.

"Anywhere." The woman cracked her knuckles. "Anywhere beside a man."

Gemma looked at the ground and took a sip of her cooling coffee.

The child ran back. "I want some kool-ade," she said.

*   *   *

On Tuesday the weather grew sullen; a low pressure cell stuck over the valley holding in the heat as well as the fumes from the chemical plants. The girl woke up to the sounds of the chains of the swing and the groaning of the milk truck going up the mountain. There was a bitter taste in her mouth. She had the thought suddenly that one morning she would not wake up, that the whole valley would go to sleep at night, and suffocate, and never even know that they had died. How long would it take the outside world to discover that she was dead? Death Valley, she thought as she stumbled down the stairs, and then naturally she thought of the woman, the truck driver, sleeping out under the desert stars beside a man.

"Where'd you come from?" Gemma said, starting right in on the woman.

"Pittsburgh. My daddy worked in the steel mills."

"My goodness," Gemma said. "That's not far. You haven't come far from home. Is that where you met your husband?"

"No, I met him on the west coast. I went out there to visit my sister when her husband was in the Navy."

"Criss-crossing the country for some man," Gemma said. "Don't we all do that?"

"I did it the last time two years ago. Two years."

"Two years, you've been back?"

"Two years since he dumped me. My how I miss it."

"Traveling cross-country. Sleeping under the stars?"

"Sleeping with a man," the woman said. "I used to go to one of the tonks down by the river on the edge of town, danced with men. I wanted 'em so bad the wetness ran down my leg."

Gemma was uncomfortable with the drift of the conversation. She got up and walked across the yard. She rubbed her sticky hot arms, and imagined the mountain covered with snow. "Do people ski in these mountains?"

"Only the locals. The plant people—they go to Sugar Loaf."

*   *   *

Saturday mid-day, one of the team members brought her husband home from the airport. Exhausted from jet lag, he lay across the bed and went to sleep while Gemma unpacked his bag and did his laundry. At three o'clock the next morning he woke up and pressed himself against her back. Gemma bit her lip and turned over to face him. She woke up the next morning with a migraine just as the sun peeked through the smog. She took a Demoral and put a pillow over her head to keep the light away.

* * *

The woman and child continued to come and the swing continued to creak in the mornings and wake Gemma out of her long, restless sleep. She was at once repelled and compelled by the woman. Her feelings of unease, and a little resentment of the woman's presence, lay flat up against her need for human contact. The wives of the other team members were up and busy getting children off to school, cleaning house, shopping and gossiping among themselves who were more senior and had ties from years past.

Each time they visited, the conversation with the woman eventually veered into her personal life, at which time, Gemma began to back away and edge toward the stoop on the front of her house. Yet again and again she went down the stairs and out the door in her nightclothes, and shyly wiped the sleep from her eyes, and said hello to the woman and child.

"I used to go to this tonk on the edge of town toward Hartsville."

Gemma tried to imagine the 'tonk.' She'd been to one once with a gang of friends in the Mississippi Delta. Just to see what it was all about, to experience the blues. There'd been a mixed crowd, mixed in every way: young and old; black and white; blue collar and some college kids; drunk and semi-sober. It was the first time she'd drank till she was totally oblivious. She'd sat in the booth between two guys and downed the vodka and Seven-Up, not even knowing what she was drinking. Time collapsed around her.

"I picked up a man," the woman continued. "He took me outside and pushed me up against his truck and I came before he touched me."

* * *

Walter said, "In Uganda where we were last week they circumcise baby girls."

"What?" said Mary Lawson. "You were where last week?"

"One diamond," said Gemma.

"Central Africa as well as Nepal and India," Walter said. "We're looking seriously at Bhopal." He looked at Gemma. "That's in India." He turned to Mary. "Didn't Paul tell you where he was?"

"I really don't remember," Mary answered. "What's the difference? If I had to find him I'd call the plant. They know where you are." Without a pause she bid one heart.

Walter bid two spades. Mary's partner passed.

"Besides," Mary said. "By the time they found him, what good would he do me?"

Gemma bid two hearts.

Walter came up out of his chair. "You can't bid two hearts. I jumped. I bid two spades!" he said. "Why don't you pay attention?"

"I'm sorry," Gemma said. "I guess I mean three hearts."

"You guess! You guess? What kind of bid is that?"

"Three hearts," said Gemma. Tears blurred her vision.

"If I was to die," Mary said, "they'd have to bury me before he could get home."

"They could wait, Mary," Walter said. "They could ice you down till he got back."

Mary Lawson seemed to slump deeper into her chair.

Walter said, "Four no trump. Pay attention now. That's Blackwood."

* * *

The woman and the little girl came again on Monday morning while Gemma slept. She woke to the usual sounds and the usual miasma. She lay in bed a long time before getting up and going, like a zombie, downstairs and out the door.

After the general fumbling conversation, the woman said, "Would you watch Baby for me a little while this afternoon until her mother gets home. I need to leave early."

Gemma hesitated, thinking of all the reasons she shouldn't--there being no reason she could not. She thought of the lonely hours of the long day, especially the late afternoon, waiting for time to eat her meager meal, turn on the news. She knew she should be looking for a job to help her pass the time, but she had no energy for that and Walter liked for her to be at home, should he pop in between his travels. And so she told the woman she would watch Baby that afternoon. "What are you doing?" she asked, not that she cared. It was just an attempt to keep a conversation going. "I hope there's nothing wrong."

"No, no," the woman assured her there was nothing wrong. "I'm just going up on the mountain. Sort of like a date."

"Up on the mountain?"

"I'm going to meet somebody up on the mountain."

"Oh well, by all means," Gemma said. "I'll be glad to watch Baby. What time does her mother get home?"

"Six," the woman said. "I'll call her and make sure she knows where Baby is and see if she can get here early. You won't have to feed her. I'll bring her a snack."

"Sure. It's okay." Gemma paused—fumbled. "Who—who are you seeing up on the mountain?" She knew it was rude, none of her business, but her curiosity was aroused and besides this acquaintance with the woman broke all the rules. She looked over the woman's shoulder, farther up the mountain where the air was almost clear, the houses bigger, the atmosphere more rarified in every respect.

"It's someone I see from time to time," the woman said. She seemed to hesitate, as if suddenly there were limits on their topics of conversation.

"Someone?" Gemma pried. She no longer cared if she was being rude. What did it matter in this weird world? The woman had imposed herself on Gemma from the beginning.

"A man."

"A man on top of the mountain? What do you do up there? Is he a doctor of some kind?"

"No." The woman sighed. "But my doctor arranged our meetings."

"Your doctor?"

The woman looked away. For once, after all the confidences she had shared, she seemed ashamed. She sucked in her breath and continued: "I told my doctor about my problem—needing men—sex. He said he had a patient who lived up on the mountain who had the same problem, and he thought we could help each other."

"But why would he…" Gemma didn't know how to say, *why would he need you? Him, high up on the mountain?*

The woman could clearly see the question hanging in the air. "He's had a stroke. He's ashamed to be seen by a woman of his kind. He's all drawn up, he drools, he leaks. But," she added, "he treats me with respect." She took a deep breath. "His house—he's very rich—it sprawls all over the mountain. Wood and stone and glass. You should see it. You have to push a number to open the gates to get in the driveway." She paused again and gazed faraway out over the valley. "He treats me very kindly. It pleasures him to please me."

Gemma followed her gaze out over the trees along the river where the water was green, or pink, or yellow, depending on the chemical discharge of the day.

"Thank you for keeping Baby. I'll owe you."

* * *

"Why do they circumcise their baby girls in Africa?" Gemma asked Walter, as they dressed for their bridge game.

"I think it's to make sure they become faithful wives."

"Well, how--?"

"It takes the pleasure out of sex, so the woman won't go looking around for it in other quarters," he said.

"But how do they do it?" she asked.

"I don't know. I'm not an authority on the subject. It's just fodder for conversation."

"Like Mary's nervous breakdown?"

"Now where'd you hear about that?" Walter demanded.

"I overheard it in the kitchen at a bridge game. They said she ran naked down the street chasing the garbage man." Gemma picked at a hangnail.

"That happened a long time ago," Walter said. "She was trying to stop smoking. The doctor told her to smoke all she wanted to, it was safer than chasing the garbage truck."

Red blood welled up on Gemma's finger. Walter pulled out his clean, white handkerchief and handed it to her.

* * *

The woman pushed the child on the swing. Gemma stood in the shadow of the fir tree.

"I have to go soon," the woman said. "I'm leaving early today."

Gemma took her place behind the swing and gave Baby a push.

"No, no," the woman said. "I'm not asking you to watch her. Her mother's coming home early. Thanks anyway."

"You're going up on the mountain?" Gemma could tell that yes, the woman was going to meet the man. Her mood was always lighter, she actually smiled on those days.

"Yes, I am."

Gemma turned away. She bit her ragged cuticle. "Someday..." she hesitated.

"Someday?" the woman repeated.

The girl pushed her chin up. She blotted her bloody finger on her gown. "Someday, will you take me with you?"

The woman stared at her. "Do you mean—you want to go up on the mountain?"

"Yes," Gemma said.

The woman was silent for a moment as if she were deciphering Gemma's meaning. The wind stirred the fir tree and the fog moved through the air like oil on water.

"You understand, don't you, I don't go up there for a regular tea party?"

Gemma smiled. "I understand all of it," she said. "I understand more than you can ever imagine."

THE TAX ASSESSOR

Patti Carr Black

Tax Assessor Homer was halfway down the block on his bicycle. The neighborhood houses were just beginning to stir with lights here and there throwing geometric shapes on the thin cap of frost. As his bike began to pull to one side, Homer dug his boots into the ice and dragged the bicycle to a halt. He saw that his front tire was almost flat. His chest buckled. I cannot get started late, he thought. Papa would never forgive me.

"You're taking on a responsibility, son. You've made a contract with your customers that you have to honor."

Homer turned his bike back toward home, trying to hold in the sobs that were rocketing against his ribcage. This was his first morning to deliver newspapers, his first job outside the chores his father gave him around the house. He was nine and conscientiousness weighted his small frame to the earth. He knew he had to get to the tool shed and find his bicycle pump. As he bumped over the big oak roots in the corner of his front yard, he heard a loud discharge. The sound startled him but he was more concerned with sneaking past the front bedroom where he knew his sisters were dressing for school. Vivian would tell on him for sure. Vivian, sitting gingerly on the just-made bed, was cross because Mama was making her plait Louise's hair. The December sun was already up and she still hadn't done her own braids.

"Ouch, you stupe!" Louise shouted.

"If you don't hold still," Vivian warned, "your plaits are gonna look like Sally Yates."

"Oh, if you make me look like that billikin, I'll tell Papa."

Vivian knew she would, too, and knew that Papa would take Louise's side, he always did. He even made her take Louise on dates. Last week at City Park, Freddie had gotten mad because Louise asked too many dumb

83

questions about the baseball game. At that thought, Vivian snatched harder with the brush. "Oooh-ee," Louise squealed.

"Girls," the mother called, "It's less than an hour until school … and don't forget your beds."

She stood at the stove, waiting for the wood to catch and heat the water. She had risen earlier than usual, propelled by a sense of disquiet. She and her husband had argued again. Ever since the election he had been querulous. Last night, as they lay side by side, the space between them charged with the effort of self-control, the mother said, "You're too hard on him, Walter. You expect too much. He tries so hard to please you and he never can seem to."

Walter bristled at her frequent plaints about Homer. "I'll not have him grow up to be some irresponsible pantywaist. Homer needs to learn how to stand on his own two feet. He cannot chew gum without asking me how to do it."

The quarrel heated up when the girls were discussed. The mother pleaded her case. "You don't realize what you're doing, Walter. You are making Vivian's life miserable. She can't even keep a beau because of your constant surveillance and your strict rules. Vivian's growing up now, you've just got to make up your mind to be more lenient… and Louise, too… trust them more.

"Oh, hogwash." Walter flopped to his side, away from her. She stared at his back a long time, remembering the young bookkeeper who had won over her parents with his reasoned speech and rectitude. During the years of marriage, now as many as she had lived before she met him, they had suffered the death of their firstborn and the triumph of his first election as county tax assessor. When she was seventeen, he seemed transcendent. But through the years she had watched him wrap his rectitude, like a cord, tighter and tighter around himself until he seemed bound by precepts so demanding they were strangling him, and now maybe her, too, and Vivian and Louise and Homer.

The loud report brought her attention back to the clean, spare kitchen. Vivian called out, "What was that, Mama?"

"Must be the new flivver down the street," Mama called back. She worried briefly about Homer's riding his bike now that Webb City had several automobiles in the streets. Even Mr. Clover, right in the neighborhood, had bought one.

The father, Walter, had come fully awake when his wife left their bed. He lay perfectly still, his head nestled in the pillow that his aunt had made him long ago. The whirring in his head had not subsided. Every morning now he awoke with the terrible memory that something unacceptable had happened to him. When his mind cleared to the present, it came to him again, like a hatchet plunged deep into his chest: the election; he had failed in his reelection. Things had been said against him that the electorate, his own neighbors, apparently believed. His honor had been questioned. The pain of it held itself in his body like an unremitting welding torch. He closed his eyes tight and listened to the sounds of the house---his wife in the kitchen moving metal against metal; the shrill voices of Louise and Vivian fussing again. Then he remembered that today was the day. He got up and dressed methodically. Buttoning his clean, starched shirt and deciding against a tie, he snapped suspenders over his shoulders and fastened the fly of his best Sunday pants. He squatted down, reached carefully under the bed for his lock box, and pulled out the pearl-handled Colt .22 that Uncle Bo had left him. Stepping into the back hall, he walked quietly through the empty sleeping porch and out into the yard where matching rose trellises made a gateway through the privet hedge. He walked down the path to the tool shed gleaming silver in the sun, closed the door, put the gun to his head, and fired.

* * *

It was sixty years before anyone in the family discussed that moment, which was suspended in their separate minds like Mama's necklace of mustard seed, floating loose in a tiny globe, never touching anything. The forward motion of their lives was signified by the passage of years and the subsequence of events, but their spirits seemed fixed in time. Vivian married a cotton farmer and raised three children in a Delta town large enough to have two gins and a Chinese grocery. Louise caught herself a husband while visiting Vivian one summer and settled in the house next door, depending on Vivian for all things except the production of her single offspring.

The two families, living side by side, were curiously passionless. Like a set of magnet bars they alternately attracted and repelled each other through proximity, without intention. Homer spent his life being transferred from one Southern city to another by a company that retired him before he realized he had grown old. Vivian and Louise measured the time between his visits in decades and assigned his absence and his bachelorhood to his penuriousness.

"Do you think Homer's coming this Christmas?" Louise would ask. Vivian always replied, "Not unless they are offering free bus tickets from Savannah." Or Richmond or Montgomery or Jacksonville, wherever Homer was that year.

Their children grew up with little curiosity about their uncle or their forebears. When occasionally a child inquired about the grandfather's death, Vivian and Louise repeated their litany: "Papa was always a careful man, but he was cleaning his gun and it went off."

After Louise's child grew up and moved away and her husband died, Louise seldom took her waking eyes off the television screen. Her conversations were filled with news of Jessica, Angela, Mark and other daytime characters whose reality gradually obliterated her own. Nevertheless, when Louise died, Vivian grieved. She suffered the loss of disapproval in her life. Vivian lived on in the cotton town with two of her children and their children nearby. The same sense of family detachment pervaded the subsequent generations. Her daughter and son, and occasionally a grandchild, took turns with duty checks by her house. Otherwise, Vivian amused herself with the Woman's Missionary Union on Wednesdays and bridge club on Fridays. Church on Sunday was less a communion with God than communion with people, Vivian searching for new bridge partners to replace those who were dying off like a procession. When Homer telephoned on her seventy-seventh birthday to say he was coming to spend Christmas, her spirits lifted for the first time that winter. He arrived with a dog named Wormy and bridgework in his mouth that he snapped together without ceasing. The three-day visit stretched long as each struggled with the irritation of the other's presence.

Finally, on the last night of his stay, Vivian spoke her mind. "Homer, you ought to be ashamed of yourself for not helping out on Mama's tombstone." She was able to bring up her old grievance only after a third glass of eggnog.

"You didn't tell me anything about it, Sister, until after you'd done it. Mama'd been dead fifty years and you made the decision to buy a grave-stone then tried to bill me for my third. Hell, no, you didn't even ask me."

Vivian looked at Homer over the rim of her holly beer cup and thought again to herself, Homer's so stingy he probably bought those teeth from the undertaker.

She said aloud, "I knew if I asked you, you'd think of all the reasons why we shouldn't spend money on it---or anything else for that matter."

Homer, opening his fourth beer, jerked the pop top and threw it on the table. "I don't know why you say such a thing, Sister. I've worked hard all my life to try to save a little money…"

Vivian waved her hand through his words, interrupting with a whoop. "Worked hard? Understated! My God, Homer, you've been a slave to your-self your whole life long. Three jobs at a time since you were in grammar school. You've retired three times and you keep finding another job. What for? What's it for? You've never had a life. You've never had any anything, because you won't spend a dime."

Homer winced as her voice shrilled. She heard herself and hushed. For several minutes the only sound was the whirr of the plastic color wheel which splintered the metallic Christmas tree into blues and greens and magentas.

"Anyway," Vivian continued, "when Louise finally drove me to Laurel to visit the cemetery, there was Papa's grave marker that Mama had sac-rificed to buy looking so fine, and there was her grave with nothing but a rickety metal marker so rusty you couldn't read. I told Louise right then that whatever it cost, we had to get Mama a stone."

Wormy scratched and thumped, Homer sucked his beer and clacked his teeth. Louise began to snuffle. "Mama. Our sad, poor Mama. She never, never got over Papa's death. Blamed herself," Vivian hesitated, "and I'll go to my grave blaming myself."

"Blaming yourself?" Homer's voice was incredulous.

Vivian nodded.

"That's claptrap," he said. "What do you mean, you blame yourself? It was an accident."

"Well, you know how Papa was. I know it was me bothered him. I was too wild. I didn't want to mind him. The night before he died I had a fit about his rules. I think he was distracted with thoughts about that, not paying attention..." her voice trailed off.

"Sister, you're crazy! Papa was cleaning his gun and it went off. It's that simple." For Homer the words were an incantation. He used them to conjure up a tableau that he could superimpose, meld with, and blur over a vividly remembered image.

Vivian got up to dip herself another dollop of eggnog before she continued. "You know what that hellion, Louise, used to always say? She always said that she was Papa's favorite."

Vivian paused.

"And then, I think about our little brother up and dying right when he was born. That must of still been on Papa's mind from time to time. Or maybe he was distracted by the humiliation of losing that last election Goddamn claptrap! It was an accident," Homer shouted. "Anyway, they've proved now that cause and effect don't even exist. It's quantum physics, Sister."

Vivian dropped her spoon in surprise. "You don't make a lick of sense, Homer."

The television set, without sound, unfurled the American flag and filled the screen with snow. It was Vivian's invariable curfew and she weaved huffily off to bed. Homer pulled the rocking chair to the window, eased his bony frame into it and stared out at the trapezoid made by the living room light on the frost-covered lawn. He felt again the chill and heard again the crunch of his bicycle tires as he pushed home sixty Decembers ago. He shoved open the door to the tool shed. He saw Papa on the dirt floor sprawled at an odd angle, like a life-size rag doll that had been tossed. He approached slowly, mesmerized by the strangeness of what he saw, and knelt beside his father.

Papa's eyes fluttered once, twice, and Homer, confused by the dark russet color under Papa's head, bent toward him.

He heard the labored suspiration and Papa's last words, "Get out of here, Homer, I don't need you."

Homer picked up his bicycle pump, then stumbled out of the tool shed and toward the house, relieved that he did not have to tell Papa that he had let his tire go flat. Vivian and Louise were almost ready for school. His mother turned in surprise to see him back from his rounds so quickly.

"It's Papa, Momma, come quick," Homer sobbed.

He would never, ever, tell them that Papa wanted to die.

DELTA COLORS

Mary Dayle McCormick

Roberta Lea scurried about her kitchen, wiping toast crumbs and milk drops from the counter, putting away the breakfast dishes. When she paused for a last swallow of coffee, a glimpse of kelly green on the coat rack made her gasp as if it were a cashmere ghost.

The hall clock struck eight. It was time to pick up her last best friend.

Edie stood in the driveway like a model in a cigarette ad, uncharacteristically punctual. She slid into Roberta Lea's front seat, smoldering Salem and a cut crystal tumbler in one hand, slamming the door and blurted, "Mornin', hon. Hey, that's the green sweater Ladye gave you last Christmas to make you set off that red hair of yours. She gave me this bracelet, remember?" Edie leaned back and shook the silver bangle on her wrist, flinging ash to the floor. She sighed and said, "Wonder what she would've given us this year."

Roberta Lea stared at her passenger through fluttering eyelids. "Good morning. Yes. And I have no idea. What's the beverage?"

"Scotch on the rocks in Waterford. It's my new signature quirk, my homage to the silver flask Ladye always carried." Edie rattled her ice, taking a drag from her cigarette. "Want some? Loosen you up. Smoothes the edges."

"Right," Roberta Lea said, turning her attention to putting the car in reverse. "No, thank you, and please crack your window. You know how I am about smoke in the car."

"I still can't believe it," Edie said, rolling down her window an inch as they backed out the driveway. "People our age don't just drop dead like that. Hell, people our age aren't supposed to die at all unless they're in a war or wreck or something." She patted her highlighted mane and sipped from her glass. "She's the first one."

"Who's the first what?"

"Ladye. She's the first one in our class to die."

Before she could stop herself, Roberta Lea said, "Nora Jean Barrett."

"Huh?"

"Nora Jean Barrett," Roberta Lea repeated, resigning herself to whatever prattle would probably follow all the way from town to Ladye's house at the foot of the Mississippi River levee.

"Yeah, that's right. The girl in ninth grade with the boyfriend in the Marines. I forgot about Nora Jean killing herself. We didn't see her," Edie said as Roberta Lea fought the tightening in her jaws with deep, slow breaths. Edie gazed into her glass, spinning ice cubes with her finger, "I can't imagine shooting myself in the head, of all places. I mean, what's the point if people can't look at you and weep?" She licked her finger and looked up. "So Ladye will be the first person our age we see dead."

"Do you think we could change topics, or maybe observe a little silence?"

"Sure." Edie put her cigarette out and reached for the radio panel, fidgeting with stations, filling the car with flashes of talk, music and static until Roberta Lea said, "Please stop."

Edie slumped back in her seat. "I've cried myself out, at least for this morning. You cried yet?"

Roberta Lea shook her head. "I cannot fall apart. There's too much to get through right now."

"I'm not saying have a nervous breakdown." Edie leaned across the armrest. "Look at me, Berta Lea. Just let go a little."

Roberta Lea sat rigid, gripping the wheel. "I'm driving," she said, and peered down the straight two-lane highway that pierced the encompassing Delta fields, so perfectly horizontal.

Praying she'd survive the morning without tentacles wrapping around her skull, Roberta Lea's thoughts wandered to her husband's study last night when her most recent migraine began. James was sitting at his desk finishing arrangements he'd begun during business hours at his law office – decisions about Ladye that couldn't wait for her husband Curtis to return and, most likely, sober up. James told her, "Sweetheart, I'll need you out at Belle Haven to get clothes for the body. The funeral home wants them by eleven. Hozie should be around the house to let you in."

Roberta Lea listened to him with the air knocked from her lungs, her eyes blinking so rapidly she felt dizzy. That was when the tunnel vision started.

James yawned and rose from his desk. "I have to be at a bond hearing in Vicksburg in the morning. Get Edie to go with you." He lightly grasped her shoulders and cast the smile that had reassured her since they were teenagers. "You're stronger than you think. You can do this."

Roberta Lea's five foot frame stiffened. "Well, of course I can, James. I'm not an idiot."

Those staccato words had surprised her almost as much as him, but he flashed that smile again and said, "I never implied you were incompetent, but you'll have to admit, you're pretty emotional right now. I'd take you myself but this couldn't have come at a worse time."

"I'm sure Ladye didn't plan to inconvenience you." As she stormed off for the ice bag and her prescription, James called out, "What's the matter, now? I didn't mean it like that. You know that's not how I meant it."

Edie said, "Are you planning on participating in this conversation, or do I have to do all the talking?"

Roberta Lea's fingers were numb grasping the steering wheel.

"After all these years," Edie shrugged, "I still don't know whether you're self-disciplined, introverted, or just weird." She lit another Salem and aimed the smoke at the window. "At least it's sunny. I hate a rainy burial. Remember how it was when we buried Ladye's baby? And Curtis running off because he couldn't stand waiting for that pitiful little thing to die. Can you believe it's been ten years since that baby – ?"

"Eleven," Roberta Lea said.

"Now the redneck coward's run off again. I hate him. Why couldn't it have been him?"

Roberta Lea squinted at the highway and concentrated on anything but Edie's voice. She thought about how short-lived autumn color is in the Mississippi Delta and how the flat land would soon wear a colorless winter shroud. Already, surrounding fields were bare except for stalks, and the roadside was littered with dirty cotton drifts and spilled soybean trails from the harvest.

Edie said, "With all that frou-frou engraving, Ladye's sterling flask was a real work of art."

"Pardon me?"

"I guess it's an orphaned heirloom, now."

"Of all her beautiful things, why in the world do you keep bringing up that flask?"

"It was such a part of her. She took it everywhere. I was just thinking about what'll happen to it. "

Roberta Lea glared at Edie as if witnessing a desecration.

"Don't you cut your eyes at me like that, Berta Lea. I'm not saying I want it. Is that what you're thinking?"

"I'm not thinking anything."

"Of course you are. You're always thinking." Edie took a gulp from her glass and a deep drag from her cigarette.

Along the rest of the highway to Belle Haven Plantation, Roberta Lea studied the alignment of her hood ornament with the blacktop's center line as Edie sipped and smoked. The hazy woods crawling along the horizon, the deep blue autumn sky, the side roads and ramshackle houses they'd passed throughout their lives – all was made invisible by a fog of bewilderment.

Edie stubbed out her cigarette in the ashtray and drummed long scarlet fingernails on the door. "It's been exactly twenty-four hours. Her birthday was before ours, so this will be the second day it's been just the two of us – not the three of us "

Roberta Lea clenched her jaws, suddenly aware it was time to slow for the turn-off. She steered from the highway onto the county road, Edie saying, "I'd go nuts if I had to drive almost half an hour each way to pick up a stick of butter. Why she lived in this old barn out here when her daddy would've built her a nice modern house in town is beyond me."

"Brown's little commissary has always been just down the road."

"You know what I mean." Edie tipped up her glass to drain it as they crossed the bayou bridge. "Anyway, I hope to God none of Curtis's redneck family comes down from the hills for this funeral."

"His people haven't shown for anything before."

"They've never been related to a rich widower before."

"Is that all you can think about, right now – Ladye's estate?"

"No, Berta Lea. And what has possessed you to suddenly contradict everything I say?"

Roberta Lea ignored Edie as they entered the plantation gates and the car churned gravel in the winding driveway. Beyond a stand of hollies the home Ladye's great-grandfather built came into view. It stood on what had been virgin timberland he'd cleared all the way to the river. Perched atop a tall brick foundation, the big white house with its towering green hip roof and deep encompassing verandas seemed suspended between land and air among oaks and magnolias.

Edie said, "I don't see any sign of Hozie's heap. At least Curtis's truck isn't around either."

"I'm sure Hozie's here. James told me he'd be here."

"Saint James the Greater."

"I've asked you not to mock my husband that way."

Edie rolled her eyes and slurped scotch-flavored ice as they parked in the *porte-cochère*. Wordlessly, heels tapping on enameled wood, they climbed the half flight to the veranda and walked midway around the house to the *entrée formelle*. Roberta Lea didn't push the ancient buzzer Ladye loathed hearing, but used the brass knocker. They waited, listening for Hozie's ragged footsteps to vibrate the door glass. They heard only Belle Haven's customary faint creaks and groans.

Edie tried the door knob, saying, "Have you ever noticed how this place smells like a great big ole cedar chest? Even out here on the porch. I detest the way a cedar chest smells. Reminds me of my grandmother's house."

They walked to the back porch, beating and jerking on the latched door. It held tight. Returning to the veranda, they tapped on each wavy-paned window, calling, "Anybody home? Hozie? You in there?"

Roberta Lea looked at her watch and felt panic creeping into her scalp. She imagined James saying, "Okay, we'll switch to the backup plan," and visualized Ladye in a pink satin funeral home shroud, her beautiful lifeless face frozen in horrified embarrassment.

Hands on hips, Edie said, "It's obvious Hozie isn't here. If we bust out this side light next to the front door, we can reach the handle and – "

"Oh, no. We can't do that. This is her great-granddaddy's original beveled French glass. We can't break the glass."

"You still believe that French B.S.?"

"Couldn't we open a window and get in?"

"I'm not tearing up my clothes and ruining my nails to crawl in there. And that's providing we could jimmy one of these painted-up sills. Otherwise, we're back to breaking glass."

"There must be something else we can do," Roberta Lea said, kneading her hands in her sweater pockets.

"Sure," Edie nodded, "we can high-tail it back to town and buy a size twelve polyester shirtwaist at Pat's Fashion Stop. Or I could pull something from my own closets, even though I don't have anything that'll go around her unless we slit it up the back. Your stuff is way too petite, of course."

Roberta Lea's eyelids quivered as she visualized Ladye in some matronly frock from Pat's or a backless dress from Edie's discards – outdated because Edie would never part with anything in style.

"So, Berta Lea? What's it fixing to be?"

Roberta Lea's head dropped. "The beveled glass," she rasped, and retreated from the porch to the front steps.

Edie stepped past Roberta Lea, down to the front walk and loosened a brick edging the azalea bed, taking care not to chip her manicure. "This oughta do it."

Roberta Lea cowered, her eyes scrunched to slits, palms cupped over ears, as Edie marched up the steps and crossed the porch, drawing back her hand with the brick, aiming, readying for the pitch.

The front door swung open.

Curtis stood before them, poised like a barefoot wrestler, half empty gallon of Wild Turkey in one fist and cigar in the other. His baggy khaki shirt and pants were crumpled and stained, his three days' beard a frosty mask, his eyes as red as his nose and cheeks.

Edie eased the brick behind her back.

"What y'all want?" Curtis thundered.

In her high heels Edie towered above him. She spoke melodically, as if to a feeble-minded child, "We're here on Ladye's behalf, Curtis. We wouldn't dream of bothering you at a time like this, but we need to come in and get her clothes. You know she'd want to be dressed really nicely, don't you? So, you step aside, now, and we'll – "

"Y'all ain't taking nothing of Miz Ladye's."

"We know how you feel," Edie cooed and nodded, "but this has to be done. We're simply trying to – "

"Like hell. Y'all don't know a gotdamn thang." He crossed the threshold toward Edie, snarling, "Ain't nobody touching nothing."

Edie would later explain what happened next as Roberta Lea "just snapping." Roberta Lea would remember it as more of a spontaneous fusion reaction.

She bounded up the steps and lunged across the porch, waving her fists and yelling, "You damn crazy redneck. I put up with your crap eleven years for Ladye's sake, but she's gone now and I'm done putting up with it." She screamed into his face, "I'm going to her east closet and I'm getting her favorite outfit. So, by God you get outta my way, Curtis Wells. Ladye's meeting her maker in a blaze of glory – she's wearing red Chanel!"

Curtis remained motionless, except for his mouth dropping, and Edie crumpled to her knees as the darkness of the front hall absorbed all but Roberta Lea's voice: "Dammit, Edie, are you coming in here to help me accessorize or what?"

REUNION

Rickey R. Mallory

Jo sipped at the too-sweet punch as she let her gaze roam around the room. She'd forgotten how large the Henderson family was. Her mother's family had always been prolific and prone to excessive amounts of southern hospitality.

In the forty-two minutes she'd been here, she'd been invited to have dinner with three aunts and two first cousins, been told by four relatives of varying degrees that she had a place to stay whenever she wanted to come to Sellville, and had said at least twenty-five times that yes, she was Maude's daughter, and yes, it had been a long time.

She had to get out of here. Surely forty-two minutes was long enough to satisfy even her mother's definition of attending a family reunion.

As she set the cup down, a hand grasped her arm. She turned and found herself enveloped in hard, warm arms. A familiar voice rumbled in her ear.

"Jo, it's good to see you."

"Tommy. I can't believe you're here." She hadn't expected to see Tommy. He'd always hated these things as much as she had.

She was surprised to find herself tongue-tied and bashful, avoiding his gaze as he pushed back and held her at arm's length. She would have liked to have been given time to prepare for seeing him, to practice what to say.

"You look great," he said. "Haven't changed a bit."

"Oh, yes I have," she said ruefully, smoothing the front of her hip-length sweater. She knew she carried ten, maybe twelve pounds more on her long-legged frame than she had the last time she'd seen him. How long had it been? Twenty-five years? Thrusting the thought away, she gave him the once-over while he scrutinized her.

"You haven't, though," she said. That was a lie, too. His face wasn't the smooth, handsome face of twenty-five years ago, although his eyes were the same devastating blue. He hadn't gained any weight, maybe even lost some, but his kind of lanky, graceful frame could vary twenty pounds or more without looking either skinny or fat.

She remembered something her mother had told her. "I was sorry to hear about Janet."

A shadow crossed his face and he shrugged. "Yeah. It was pretty bad there at the end. I'm just glad she didn't linger any longer than she did."

"Are you doing okay?"

He nodded. "Sure. It's been over a year. Patty's still taking it hard, though."

Jo had to think a minute. "Patty. Your daughter. Is she here?"

"Over there, with all the other kids."

Jo looked, and sure enough, she saw a pretty teenager with the same bright blue eyes. "I see her. My God, she's gorgeous. How'd you do that?"

"She's my love, Jo. She's a lot like her mother."

Jo smiled, wishing she could get over the stinging regret that occasionally hit her when people talked about their children. Brendan hadn't wanted any, and that had been that. "Introduce me, Tommy. Introduce your kissin' cousin to your daughter."

"Hah," Tommy laughed. "Kissing cousins. I haven't heard that term in a long time. Is there really such a thing?"

Jo shrugged. "That's what my mother and your mother always said. Kissing cousins were best friend's children. Come on. I want to meet your daughter."

"There's plenty of time for you to meet her," he said, the quiet, determined tone of his voice drawing her gaze back to his. "You and I have a lot to talk about."

Jo blinked and looked away. A hollow sense of trepidation settled under her diaphragm. She didn't want to talk. She glanced at her watch. Fifty-seven minutes. Her mother would have been ecstatic.

"You heard about Mother," she said.

He nodded, never taking his eyes off her.

"She's the only reason I'm here. She came every single year."

"Yeah. I kind of figured you'd be here this year."

She smiled in spite of herself. "You did?" He'd always known her better than anybody.

"Well, you know how dramatic she could be. It was her 'last wish' that I come this year in her place."

"Somebody told me you were divorced."

Tommy's eyes were getting bluer, as they always had when he was cooking up some scheme. She tugged on the hem of her sweater, and gauged the distance to the door, like a bank robber planning a getaway.

"Two years ago. If I didn't know better, I'd say that's what killed Mother. Heaven forbid there be D-I-V-O-R-C-E in the Henderson family."

She glanced toward the door again, trying to think of a good conversation-ender. What was the matter with her tonight? Usually she could stop any conversation cold, whether she meant to or not. It was a particular talent of hers that served her at times.

"Jo, you're doing it again."

At the familiar words she cut her eyes back to his face and saw his smirk. Suddenly, all the memories she'd been fighting came flooding back.

Memories of bright summer days, riding around in his shiny red Mustang, being cynical and irreverent, listening to *Suite: Judy Blue Eyes* and wondering why they couldn't find anyone in the entire town who sold marijuana.

Memories of hot, sticky nights when they would sneak off to the park to smoke cigarettes and wonder some more about why they couldn't get their hands on any marijuana.

"Doing what again?" she asked in a voice that almost shook, because she knew exactly what he meant.

The smirk stayed in place, but it softened just a bit -- almost enough to be called a smile. "You know good-and-damn-well what.. Acting tough, trying to pretend it doesn't hurt."

Tommy had always known her, always seen through her façade, even while he helped her to perpetrate it. She dropped her gaze to her shoes.

"Hey, come on, Jo. The guy must have been a bastard or an idiot. Otherwise you'd still be married. Right?"

"Right, I guess," she said, feeling the prick of tears behind her eyes and compressing her lips to keep them from trembling.

"Listen, we need to talk." Tommy took her arm and leaned over to whisper in her ear. "You can't get a drink at a Henderson reunion. Let's split this place."

Jo wanted to pull her arm out of his grasp, wanted to stop the feelings his touch engendered, but somewhere between one breath and the next, she lost all her willpower.

"But I haven't spoken to Aunt Maizie," she said, hardening her voice with a desperate determination, "and Mother would kill me if I don't introduce myself to the preacher."

"Forget them. Let's go." He cocked a brow toward the door.

She'd never been able to resist his charm. His pranks had gotten her into trouble at least once every summer.

"Thank God we never found any grass." she muttered as he held the door open and they stepped out of the air-conditioned church into the hot summer night.

"Oh, yeah?"

She looked up at him, her mouth open. "You didn't--"

His eyes danced with mischief.

"And you never gave me any?"

"Hey, Jo. Give me some credit, will you? You were two years younger than me. I'd have been thrown under the jail if I'd given drugs to a kid."

"Watch who you're calling kid, kid," she bantered, then stopped when she saw it.

Just as red, just as shiny. A sixty-five Mustang convertible. The most beautiful car ever built.

"Oh my God, you still have it?" Now her eyes were stinging again, and this time no amount of lip compressing or blinking would stop the tears. She brushed them away quickly, embarrassed to be so sentimental, she who hated sentimentality for this very reason. All it was good for was messing up makeup and making her feel like an idiot.

She sniffed. "This can't be the same car?"

"Sure it is. I could never part with her. She's my baby."

More memories drifted through Jo's mind, like the clouds that drifted over the moon above. She blinked one more time and furtively wiped her face.

"Let's go, then," she said, climbing into the vintage car and carefully tucking her skirt under her so it wouldn't get caught in the door.

"You don't fool me, Jo," Tommy said as he pulled out of the parking lot. "Never did. I saw you wiping those tears away."

He shook his head. "Crying over a car. You always were the mushiest person I ever knew."

"I was not," she said indignantly, watching him drive. He had the most beautiful hands, and they caressed the steering wheel like a lover. He had always driven like that, she remembered. Lovingly, carefully.

"Sure you were. You were a pushover. That's why you always acted tough. It was just a cover."

"What makes you so smart all of a sudden?" she tossed back at him, studying his profile in the darkness. The classic aquiline nose, the determined chin, were all just as she remembered them. She decided the lines in his face just added character. He'd been too handsome twenty-five years ago.

He glanced over at her, his eyes glittering in the reflected light from the street lamps. "I was always smart."

They drove in silence for a few minutes. Jo ran her hand over the seat. How many times had she sat in this car while Tommy drove? How many wonderful, precious memories could she call up if she were just willing to deal with them? The odor of gardenias, the feel of worn vinyl under her fingers, the sound of his voice rumbling against her ear.

"What do you drink these days?" he asked. "Beer?"

She shook her head. "Lord, no. I can thank beer for these ten extra pounds," she said wryly, patting her stomach. "Besides, I'm not much in the mood for a drink tonight."

"Me either, and you look just fine. I like those ten pounds."

"Yeah, right."

They fell silent again, Tommy driving carefully if not slowly, while Jo tried desperately to keep the memories from overwhelming her. Especially the later ones.

"So how old is Patty?" she said lightly. Kids were always a safe subject, no matter whether they were a joy to their parents or a disappointment. They still generated safe conversation.

Tommy smiled as he maneuvered a turn. "Sixteen. Amazing, isn't it." He glanced at her. "I remember when you were sixteen, and now I've got a daughter that age."

So much for safe subjects.

Please don't, she wanted to beg. *Don't dredge up the memories.* She didn't want to wallow in sentimentality. He was right. She was the mushiest person she knew too, and sometimes the hollow feeling got so strong it was almost unbearable. So she steeled herself against it and tried to act tough, because tough was a lot easier than mushy for someone with no skin.

She pulled her gaze away from his profile and looked out at the dark landscape. "Where are we going?" she asked with a sinking suspicion she'd already figured out the answer.

Tommy didn't answer, just turned the car to the right and drove down a familiar road to a familiar parking lot. There were a few more street lamps than there had been twenty-five years ago, but he drove to one end where the lights were out. Someone had probably shot them out with a pellet gun. That's what they used to do.

"Tommy--" she started as he turned off the engine, but he held up one hand.

"Sh-h-h," he whispered. "Let's just sit here for a minute."

Jo sat rigid, berating herself for letting her mother's dramatics force her to come to the reunion, for letting Tommy talk her into leaving, for not protesting now and demanding he take her back to the church. He'd always been able to get her to do anything, and she'd always been the one that got into trouble.

As she watched him out of the corner of her eye, she doubted seriously that anything had changed in twenty-five years. He would still have some crazy idea, and she'd still be the one regretting it afterwards.

"Do you remember this?" he said quietly, sliding his gaze over her face in the darkness.

"Sure," she said lightly. "We spent many an evening here, smoking cigarettes and watching the kids in the other cars."

"Yeah."

Jo cleared her throat nervously. "Tommy--"

"Remember the last time?"

Her heart slammed against her chest like a racquet ball against the wall. "No, Tommy, I don't," she said harshly. "Look, I need to be getting back."

"Back where? Come on, Jo. A few memories aren't going to hurt. I swear. We need to talk about this."

"That's just it, Tommy. I don't want to talk about it. I shouldn't have come."

"Still the same old Jo, aren't you? Still trying to be tough." He turned slightly in his seat and took her hand. "But I know you, Jo. I remember everything. What do you remember?"

Jo sighed and squeezed her eyes shut. His hand was warm on hers, engulfing it as always. His thumb played lightly over her knuckles, and she remembered that too.

She remembered too much. Her head was full of memories. Bursting with them.

"I remember the heat, like tonight," she said softly, not wanting to talk, but compelled by his presence, his charm.

She could be sixteen tonight. She could be silly, and vulnerable, and madly in love with her kissing cousin who wasn't her cousin at all. "I remember the smell of gardenias and dirt. I remember--"

"What?" Tommy was still caressing her knuckles. She could feel his bright, burning gaze on her, even though she didn't take her eyes off his hand.

"I remember magic."

Magic. They had always spent the summers together. Ever since she could remember. Tommy and Jo. It was just something they did, like getting up in the morning, or brushing their teeth. They stayed together all summer.

And as they'd grown up, as Tommy had gotten taller than her and filled out his lanky frame, Jo had developed the most incredible crush on him. But, tough as usual, she'd ignored the feelings as much as she possibly could, and just enjoyed being with him like always, like best buddies.

Until that last night.

By the time Jo realized Tommy had moved, he'd let go of her hand and was getting out of the car.

"Tommy, no," she whispered. He came around and opened her door for her and held his hand out. Wishing she were anywhere but here, she let him pull her out of the car.

As they walked toward the bleachers, Jo's mind was awhirl with memories. The sudden realization that he was looking at her, really looking at her for the first time. The incredible flash deep within her when he'd put his fingers on her chin and his warm, firm lips had touched hers. The mixture of fear and excitement as he'd led her over to the soft grass behind the bleachers.

Tommy took her hand as they walked, and when they reached the very spot where he'd lain down beside her all those years ago, he turned to her. "So what do you remember?"

Jo's heart still pounded in her chest, stealing her breath. She looked up at him and saw the cocky, handsome eighteen year old he'd been back then. They had never spoken since that night.

It had been the last summer she'd come to Sellville, the last time she had seen him.

And that had been just fine with her. It had been a dreadful mistake, what they'd almost done. She had been so embarrassed, so humiliated, and he had been so angry.

"I remember what you said," she whispered, looking at his mouth, at his chin, all the familiar planes of his face. "You were so mad. You said 'you are just a little girl, aren't you? You shouldn't tease, Jo. You're not tough enough to handle the consequences.'"

Tommy smiled. "I said all that?"

She nodded, pulling her gaze away from his face and staring somewhere around the third button on his shirt, still embarrassed after all this time. "I'm sorry."

"Sorry?" He put a finger under her chin and lifted her head until she was forced to look at him. "No, Jo. I'm the one who's sorry. You were my responsibility, and I let you down. You were too young."

She nodded again, feeling the pressure of his fingers against her chin. His gaze traveled to her mouth, which she knew was trembling. She compressed her lips, but suddenly his were touching hers and she couldn't make her mouth obey her brain.

Her lips relaxed, her mouth opened to his kiss, and her hands reached up to pull his head down. His kiss deepened and more memories flooded Jo's brain. This time they were good memories, welcome memories.

Memories of magic. As she kissed him, Jo relived the magical moments twenty-five years ago before her fear and confusion had stopped them.

When had she felt that way since? As soon as she asked herself the question, she knew the answer.

Never.

No one since had ever stirred her the way Tommy had. No one, not even her husband, had made her insides quiver and her limbs weak like this. How could she have forgotten it? How had she lived without it?

Tommy lifted his head, his eyes questioning, his face softening into a wary smile. "Are you old enough now, Jo?" he whispered, his mouth so near her ear she could feel his lips move.

"What are you doing?" she gasped.

"Finishing what we started," he whispered, his lips moving to her mouth, moving like moth wings on hers. He looked at her again and she lost herself in his eyes. "Or starting something that maybe we should have started a long time ago."

"Tommy," she gasped, her heart pounding and her pulse roaring in her ears. "I can't do this! I didn't shave my legs."

He lifted his head, his mouth open, and stared at her, frozen, for a moment, then threw back his head and laughed.

"God, I'd forgotten how incorrigible you are," he said when he could finally speak. "I'm doomed. Am I going to have to spend the rest of my life listening to you try to be tough?"

Before she could even digest what he'd said, he took her hand and led her back toward the car. "You win, Jo. You always could bring me back to earth. Maybe it is time you met my daughter."

Jo stared at him as he deposited her back in the red Mustang. His voice echoed in her head.

Am I going to have to spend the rest of my life

--rest of my life--

Her heart was still pounding. The blood was still roaring in her ears. And she felt like a sixteen year old in love for the very first time.

SANS FAMILLE

Ruth White

I don't think my Aunt Lorena ever intended for the spare bedroom to be off limits to us kids, but we interpreted it that way, never daring to enter unless bidden. After all, it was right next door to the pantry, which was kept locked for a reason. An entire summer had been spent canning and preserving the season's harvest that in a previous time had to see the family through the winter. Hers was a farmhouse, and as such, completely devoid of pretentiousness. Still, it never occurred to me as a child that its walls and floors of unfinished planks were anything less than beautiful, and I knew without a doubt that the spare bedroom would some day reveal wonderful treasures.

This simple country house charmed us with its mystique. During those hot summer nights of our visits, we slept with all the windows open, serenaded by tree frogs and cicadas, and I could feel the dawn even before it arrived. In the winter, we gathered around the fireplace in the living room. My Uncle Ty, in his green velvet chair with the swirls, sat closest to the fire because, after all, it was his job to put more logs on. After the day's chores, we settled in, and stories were told and retold until eventually the grownups said their good nights and encouraged us kids to do the same. Until we got too old, my mother would let us change into our pajamas right there in front of the fire, then dash for the unheated bedroom, where we slipped beneath a mountain of quilts to sleep the cold night through.

Had it not been for the kitchen, we may have lain in that warm bed forever, but the kitchen, well the kitchen was magic. Always the first one up in the mornings, Lorena called whenever breakfast was ready. One by one, we'd gather courage to leave those warm beds, dash for the bathroom and its heater across the hallway, change clothes, then join the rest of the family in the kitchen.

The kitchen was really one big room separated by a chin-high counter, where the dishes were stored, and it remained the soul of the house. On the right, Lorena performed her cooking miracles, and on the other side, we ate at the oilcloth- covered table and sat in the sturdy oak chairs with cowhide bottoms. It was in that kitchen that my aunt produced her famous cathead biscuits served with mayhaw jelly made from berries she scooped off the river, velvety grits slathered in hand-churned butter, and eggs the color of the first wave of jonquils in spring. I think it was also there that I first fell in love with the idea of cooking.

While the kitchen served as the center of our family's life together, the spare bedroom lured only me. So it was that on the summer day when I'd garnered permission to enter, I did so with a sense of awe. For long seconds, I remained standing in the doorway while I surveyed the simple room. Its only occupants were an iron bed covered by a chenille spread of pink and blue, a pedal sewing machine whose drawers contained my grandmother s glasses and spools of thread made from unraveled flour sacks, a dark, heavy dresser with a wavy mirror, and shelves and shelves of books. The furniture held little interest at the time, but the books beckoned with the promise of unheard stories.

Craning my neck, I sought out the titles in gold and black, lured on by faraway places and strange-sounding names. Only later would I discover that some of these books held a monetary value some might say outweighed their worth in terms of wisdom and wit. On that day, however, I didn't care. I'd finally gotten up the nerve to ask to enter the room and to read one of those books. I could not be deterred.

The first one I chose hardly fit my ten or eleven years, but enticed by its black and white drawings and its smooth leather binding, I took the book to the back porch, situated myself in a wooden rocker, and began to read. I stumbled on some of the unfamiliar words, but the story spoke for itself. Soon I understood that a poor boy named Oliver had no family, that he suffered mistreatment unheard of to me, and that his England bore little resemblance to my aunt's farm in Mississippi. I continued to read, on and on, picking out the master's words as he wound his tale. Before afternoon turned into dusk, I had fallen entirely under Dickens's spell.

The allure of the spare bedroom never left me. Throughout my summer stays at the old house, I turned more and more to that room for entertainment and learned names I'd never known before. William Faulkner, Flannery O'Connor, Eudora Welty. Their stories enticed and their characters leapt from the pages with all the familiarity of the countryside around me. I'd seen people like that, and I'd heard them talk. Although I didn't always capture the full meaning of what I'd read, I couldn't stop. I read and read until one day, nothing remained. In dismay, I went to my aunt.

"Do you have any more of those books?"

She gave me her signature half-smile and opened the door of the closet.

Instead of the musty clothes I expected, I witnessed a closet filled with stacks of cardboard boxes.

"See what you can find in these," she said, my greedy hand already reaching for a magazine from the topmost box.

"McCalls," I read aloud. "Is this a good magazine?"

"I think so," she said, turning to leave the room. "They have stories in them."

Again I was in heaven. For two wonderful weeks that summer, I reveled in stories written for older ladies, ladies who knew something about married life and, yes, sex.

Eventually, though, I grew up, the summertime visits turned to memories, and things that happen to all of us if we live long enough happened to me as well. Thus, when as an adult I entered the spare bedroom for what would be the final time, I wondered how much more I could lose. With my parents, aunts and uncles, including my Uncle Ty, and even a husband already gone, I felt every bit the battle-weary veteran, and I wondered why my aunt had chosen me for such a heinous job.

I didn't mind helping her, but the house was hot and musty from years of being closed up, and, truth be told, I didn't want to face a past so filled with ghosts. A cousin had come to finish cleaning out the pantry, leaving me with only the spare bedroom. Already the iron bed and sewing machine rested in an upstairs bedroom of my home, albeit minus the chenille spread now too faded and dirty to redeem. The dresser with the wavy mirror had gone home with another cousin, and my brother would organize the upcoming sale of the property. All in all, I felt as if we were selling bare remnants of a family. My heart, broken so many times before, faced yet one more obstacle, and I didn't know if I could get through the day.

The treasured volumes of my childhood had been sold to a book dealer in Atlanta. What remained were the leftovers, the stragglers that nobody wanted. Although they amounted to no more than a couple of dozen volumes, I didn't want to throw them away without first looking at them. I gathered them into neat stacks and sat down cross-legged beside them on the floor. The first one I picked up proved to be an early twentieth century grammar book, and aside from a lock of hair, contained nothing of interest. I moved on to the second.

Written partly in a distinctive hand and partly in printed text, this book intrigued me more. My father's youngest brother apparently had used this one in his veterinary studies, and I thumbed through it thinking about his sad life. He'd earned a degree just in time to enlist in the Navy and see duty in the most horrible battles of the Pacific. Once a stellar talent in his field, he turned to alcohol to forget what he'd seen, and a life once so promising ended in sorrow.

The day wasn't getting any better. Still, a promise is a promise. I'd sorted through nearly the whole stack when I found a small green cloth volume entitled Hector Malot: Sans Famille. Striking me as somewhat not belonging, I looked to the inside cover. There, in his unmistakable script, was my father's name. Henry White.

My head spun with memories of a breakfast table badinage that he and I kept up until the day I married. As a dairyman, he loved cream in his coffee and couldn't understand why I preferred mine black. Thus, the ritual.

"Want some cream in your coffee, Sis?" he asked every morning, using his special name for me.

Still bleary-eyed at that hour, I tried to answer with a simple no thanks. But he would have none of that. "*Pourquoi?*" he asked each and every time.

Some mornings I wanted to scream my answer, but even in that early hour, I knew better. I respected the man, and I also knew that he'd never tolerate the lack of such. So each and every morning, I answered, "Je prefer café noire, s'il vous plait."

Of course, the day had come many times since when I would have killed to have those moments back. My father died only nine days before his retirement, before I took the opportunity to tell him how much our simple ritual meant to me.

Now I held his French textbook in my hands. I opened the book, expecting the standard conversation at the beginning, the kind that any native Frenchman would no doubt laugh his sides off at for initiating, but this little book had no such ritual. Except for a brief introduction in English, the story continued in French, which I began to decipher, words and phrases at a time.

It seemed that Sans Famille told the story of an orphan, not unlike my Oliver, whose life presents him with one tribulation after the other. The poor boy had no family and suffered enormously because of it. Only his genuine sterling character, his perseverance, and his belief in right prevailed.

I didn't have to read the rest of the story; in fact, I couldn't if I had wanted to. The text swam before my eyes as tears fell onto its yellowed pages. That little book had belonged to my father. What thoughts did he have when he'd enrolled in a French class in his tiny country high school? Did he dream of going to France? Did he envision roaming the French countryside, wineglass in hand? Did my father, the stoic, conservative Southerner that he was, picture himself atop the Eiffel Tower or watching showgirls in the Moulin Rouge?

For long moments I held the little book in my hands while I wept for knowledge that I'd never possess. When I managed to slow the tears, I turned to the final page in the book and discovered that it, too, bore his signature, with one major difference. Henry White had become Henri Blanc.

Now it was my turn, and I asked the empty room, "*Pourquoi, mon pere. Pourquoi?*"

YOU CAN'T GO BACK

Richelle Putnam

Four months after Ryan's Monte Carlo was found abandoned on I-20 near Meridian, Mississippi, Cheryl Barnes stumbled to her next door neighbor's house clutching a dead phone to her cheek. At the front door she banged and banged until Juanita Barry finally opened it. For a moment the two women stared wide-eyed at each other. Cheryl managed the first words between them. They sounded strangled and pleading.

"It's dead. How will he get through? He could be calling right now." She shook the phone, pressed the number buttons like she'd done earlier when she found the phone lying dead on her pillow. "Oh, God, I don't know what's wrong. We paid our bill, but—"

Juanita took one step onto her porch, looked around outside, and then pulled Cheryl into her house. Once hidden inside from the neighbors, Juanita pried the phone from Cheryl's hand and led her to a chair in the den.

"Sit right there, sweetie, while I fix you a cup of coffee. Go on now. Sit down. Take some deep breaths. Cheryl, please. Just relax. I'll only be a minute. Coffee's done. I just have to pour it. That's it. Lean back. Rest your eyes. Good girl."

Since Ryan's disappearance, waiting of any kind tortured Cheryl. But at least this wait was not silent like waiting for the phone to ring. This wait was loud, very loud, with Juanita going on and on about how she and her daughter, Madison, had driven to Birmingham for the after Christmas sales, how they'd hit the Galleria and The Summit and splurged at P. F. Chang's for dinner, and later topped their bargain day off with mochas from the Barnes and Noble on the hill overlooking 459.

"Here you go, sweetie," said Juanita, floating back into the room, handing Cheryl a steaming coffee mug. Juanita's short hair was layered now into a stylish new cut and her makeup gave no hint of tiring and slipping down her aging skin even this late in the day. "And how's Rainer, dear?" asked Juanita. "She's what, a junior now? Oh, just wait till she leaves for college. You'll cry for days. Why I was telling Mark just this morning how I detested this quiet house. The empty nest syndrome is everything…" Juanita's enchanting green eyes grew as big as melons. "Oh, sweetie, I meant that, well…, I'm sorry…" Her words seemed to freeze inside her mouth and she handed the phone to Cheryl. "All it needs is recharging. Put it in its cradle for the night. Then it will work fine. Just fine."

"Its…cradle?"

"Yes, Sweetie. This thing." At the table beside her recliner, Juanita picked up her cordless and its charger. "See?"

"Cradle," said Cheryl nodding at the phone she held.

Juanita pulled Cheryl to her feet. "You best go home now. Get some sleep, darling. The police know to call here if they can't get you. And I'm sure Ryan would, too. Go on now. You're plumb worn out. Want me to put that coffee in a to-go cup?"

Cheryl shook her head as she returned the cup to Juanita. Then, she rushed out the door without another word, anxious to tuck the receiver into its cradle.

Since Ryan's disappearance everything had changed, including Cheryl's home in their north Meridian West Haven neighborhood, one block east of Northwood Country Club. Once immaculately kept, the house now featured unmade beds, unopened mail, undusted furniture, and unwashed dishes. Even from the outside, the two-story stucco house seemed to grow faint and smaller each day, empty except for memories that rewound everyday like family videos where smiles seemed abundant, real, and easy to find.

At night when no life appeared to exist in the Barnes house, a light clicked on in the upstairs window on the right. Ryan's room. This was where Cheryl sat alone eating Hershey kisses and drinking black coffee. Each time, she would search through his things, as if the moment she left his room, every memory of every item disappeared and she had to relive them whenever she returned. Or maybe, just maybe, a clue would've miraculously showed up over night or sometime during the day, a clue as to why he locked himself in this room with only the company of loud, irritating music. Why his world became as small as Cheryl's was now, a twelve-by-twelve space in a thirty-five-hundred square-foot home.

On the nights Cheryl's husband, David, was home, he sipped her freshly brewed coffee, the kind that left a bitter taste that didn't wash down. He clung to the TV or the newspaper or the mug in his hand, his eyes unnaturally blank, mouth taut. Only his rising and falling chest assured Cheryl that he still breathed. This was the only time Cheryl still felt connected to her husband and she watched him from the kitchen wondering how he stood the pain from day to day, wondering if it dug into him like the claws of a caged badger. He acted so strong, but Cheryl knew his insides were folding in on him and that every morning when he looked himself in the mirror he asked the same question.

Why?

Since Ryan's disappearance, blame bounced from one parent to the other, just like it had when Ryan was there, struggling with the life he couldn't seem to live.

"You were too hard on him," she accused.

"You were too lenient."

"He needed more."

"He needed less."

Cheryl retrieved David's empty mug from his stiff fingers, took it into their kitchen that was now more jaundiced than the sunny yellow color Cheryl has chosen long before Ryan's disappearance. The brick floors were crunchy from chips and pretzels, sticky from spills that were never wiped up. Dirty dishes cluttered the countertops. A loaf of bread sat open and several slices had fallen over, one on top of the other. The end piece peeked out the cellophane opening, crumbs scattered along the outside of the bag. Beside it were an open jar of mayonnaise, a squirt bottle of yellow mustard, and wilted lettuce.

Cheryl poured David's coffee without a glance at the muddle she'd grown accustomed to. Steam from the hot coffee fogged her glasses. She removed them, placed them beside his mug. What an innocent picture they created. Wake up, the mug said. Open your eyes, her glasses said.

Some mornings Cheryl forced herself out of bed and on those mornings, the house smelled of freshly brewed coffee and bacon, like she had a maid she didn't know about. She dragged into the kitchen and the lights screamed at her to go back to bed. Her daughter, Rainer, sat at the counter buttering her toast and drinking from a cup that was more milk and sugar than coffee.

"Where's your father?" Cheryl asked, shielding her eyes.

Rainer, unable to look her mother in the eye anymore, would say, "He left over an hour ago. But how would you know that?"

Since Ryan's disappearance, Cheryl mourned the child she lost and ignored the child she still had. So Rainer did her own searching everyday, for someone who noticed that her image was not imagined, but solid and alive. Some mornings when it was still dark, Cheryl heard the backdoor click open and then quietly shut. She glanced over at the clock to discover that her daughter had been out all night doing who knows what with who knows who. Cheryl lay in the dark, eyes open, listening to Rainer creep into her room. She stayed real still listening for other sounds, outside sounds of approaching cars or footsteps outside her window, but David's snores cluttered her ears like everything else. Sometimes Cheryl would rise and sit on the side of her bed thinking that she should go to Rainer's room, talk to her. But what would she say and how she would say it? She no longer had the words or the energy.

And Ryan had hated for Cheryl to come into his room uninvited or for her to knock on his locked door. He shouted for everyone to, "Leave me alone." She remembered how David removed the doorknob of Ryan's door so he could no longer lock it and how David had yelled back, "I'll take the damn door off its hinges if I have to. This is still my house and you will respect that."

Ryan had pushed through them, charged down the stairway, out the door to his car, Cheryl calling after him, "Ryan, please. Just talk to us."

But he never did. He sunk further into himself, as if each plea from David or her were heavy boots stomping him down, down, down into himself.

Since Ryan's disappearance, Cheryl had no energy for anything but grief, her arms and legs weighing a thousand pounds, her head filled with as much mayhem as her kitchen counters. She awoke tired and went to bed exhausted. Early morning sunshine speared her eyes and fresh air only reminded her of everything stale in her life.

She wondered if this was how Ryan felt, tired of life, tired of people, tired of questions, tired of decisions. Tired. Worn down. And never really knowing why.

In Ryan's room, Cheryl leaned against the cool windowpane, noticing how each breath steamed the glass, obstructing her vision of outside. Then, when she pulled away, the misty circle faded and the outside world became clear again.

Across the street, Mark Barry's belly hung over his pants as he guided the stream of water from his hose like one miss might destroy all he had created. Next door to him, Valerie Jenkins trimmed her square boxwoods, the ones she'd planted before Ryan's disappearance. This year Valerie had removed Little Brittany's training wheels and ran alongside her bike to keep her from falling. Now, Brittany twisted her mouth just right, leaned over the handlebars, and sped up and down the street, ponytail flapping behind her. It seemed only yesterday when Rainer had brought baby Brittany over in her arms and for hours had tended her like a child-mother, Cheryl looking on in amazement at how much her daughter knew, from burping to changing diapers to rocking and cuddling until the infant's whimpers ceased and sleep came. Rainer loved to baby sit Brittany and Ryan often went over to watch TV with them until the Jenkins returned.

The Barrys moved out. The Merricks moved in. And with the Merricks came a teenage son with thick black hair and dark eyes, about the age of Ryan when he disappeared. A toddler grandson visited frequently and Cheryl would cross the street to watch both boys laugh and play. She loved how the older boy took care of the little one and she cuddled the images, sometimes all day, until Mrs. Merrick stormed out and urged her boys into the house, her glare saying to Cheryl, "Why can't you just get over it?"

After that, Cheryl watched them from Ryan's window, pulling back the drapes just enough to keep the sunlight out and yet still be able to watch without anyone seeing her.

Not two weeks after Rainer graduated high school she packed up to move to Montgomery, Alabama with best friend, Macy. There they would rent an apartment and attend Auburn University. This summer, when she and Macy weren't waiting tables at Outback, they planned to paint bright colors onto the drab white apartment walls. They had agreed on orange and lime Green, but Rainer had refused to give in to yellow. "I hate that color. It fades," she said. Cheryl knew this because sometimes she stood at Rainer's closed door and listened. She would hear things like, "She's lost it" or "I've got to get out of here" or "I can't take her anymore." But the statement that clung to Cheryl like sutures was, "This place is a cemetery and Ryan's room is the coffin that she climbs into everyday."

Unable to look at Cheryl, Rainer and David packed Rainer's things into the Mazda. David held his daughter for a long moment, opened the car door for her, but before Rainer had time to back out into the street, Cheryl had turned away and headed for the house.

Since Ryan's disappearance, Cheryl could only handle the guilt of failing one child, not two, and so she buried any regret and guilt relating to Rainer down, down, down into herself. She didn't deny her failures. She simply didn't have the energy to deal with them.

Cheryl knew David was seeing another woman, but this was another thing she didn't have the energy to face and so at night, she pushed her husband out the door so she could abscond into Ryan's room. His turquoise lava light still formed amoebic designs. Inside the bubbling twenty-five gallon aquarium seven tropical fish darted about as if nothing had ever gone wrong in this room.

Cheryl celebrated Ryan's birthday alone in his room with picture albums and a bag of Hershey kisses. She liked to place a Hershey on her tongue, allow it to melt before swallowing it down. This seemed to calm the voices inside her head that chanted: He's alive. He isn't. Is. Isn't. Is. Isn't. Is. Isn't. Flipping through each page of the picture album, she touched Ryan's face, his curly black hair, looked into his narrow brown eyes, trying to see through them, into the hidden place where he'd disappeared.

Strolling down the grocery store's long, narrow aisles, Cheryl picked out Ryan's favorites: Cream of Chicken soup, Sugar Frosted Flakes, Vienna Sausages, and Hershey kisses. She didn't care what people thought about the extra seventy pounds she carried now or the coarse gray hair that had grown into thin split-ends, past her slumped shoulders. Every time she heard a little boy cry, "Mama!" she hunted through the faces, but never found her son's.

The park was her favorite place to go where pigeons and geese gathered around the pond to be fed, their coos and honks competing with the children's laughter. Toddlers darted from swings to slides to sandboxes, their hurried feet kicking up dirt. Her favorites to watch were little boys with black wavy hair and she studied their mothers to see if they were attentive. If not, she crept closer. Squeals of delight and frustrated cries wore on the sultry air, but not on Cheryl's nerves like they used to when her children were small, when she sent them outside because they were too loud or sent them to their rooms so she could think or when she hired babysitters so she could wander mall corridors or the aisles of bookstores while sipping four-dollar lattes.

One day, leaving Walgreen's, she heard a child yell, "Ryan!" She saw the daycare center across the lot and hurried through parked cars to get closer. The little boy named Ryan ran over to a girl with freckles and orange hair. Cheryl dropped her bag, pressed her face to the fence, entwining her fingers into the metal links. She was still holding the fence when the police arrived.

David took care of everything at the station, telling them about Ryan and how Cheryl had not handled it well, and that, yes, he'd tried to get her help, but it's very difficult to get help for someone who doesn't want it. He does what he can, he really does, but he doesn't know what to do anymore. Cheryl thought her husband did a good job of retaining what little pride he had left.

In the car, icy air blew through the vents and Cheryl reached out, as if she could gather the coolness into her palms.

"I wouldn't have yelled so much," she said. "I would've listened more."

David's eyes never left the road. He drove the same way he did when he and Cheryl dated so many years ago, right hand on the steering wheel, left arm draped along the driver's window. "You can't go back, Cheryl."

She kept her eyes ahead, too, thinking of everything she would've changed, wondering if David and she could ever be good together again, their hands quick to touch rather than push away. Could they ever sleep entwined like they once had, two threads joining to form a strong, durable stitch? And even if they could go back, would they change? Could they change? David was right. You can't go back. You can never go back.

* * *

Cheryl still closes her eyes to David's lover. After all who is she to judge David for needing someone to love him back? They're still a family nonetheless. Every night, David returns to his dark house, closing his eyes to unmade beds, furniture he can write his name on, and newspapers stacked up like important papers. Cheryl accepts his pity because pity is more powerful than love. Love has no pride and is willing to let go. Pity clings like a ravenous tick. Pride refuses to say, "I failed." They go well together.

Today, Cheryl is at the new playground she found on Cleveland Avenue where mothers don't watch their children so closely, where she can sit in the sandboxes with the children, push them in swings to heaven and back, and catch them at the bottom of silvery slides that glimmer in the sunshine. Through dark sunglasses, she notices how it takes so much more effort to climb to the top of the slide, yet so little to slide to the bottom. It's always the climbing that tires you out.

She is partial to boys with black hair. She often imagines putting one in the backseat of her car and driving away to that mysterious place where no one can find you no matter how hard they look, where you disappear forever.

Cheryl's attention is drawn to an older woman reading a thick novel. Ever so often she glances over at a little boy who sits beside her on the bench, coloring in a coloring book. The woman straightens his collar and pats his shoulder.

The boy starts whining. "I got out of the lines again." He rips the page from his coloring book, places it on top of other pages stacked beside him. "I'm never coloring again."

The woman closes her book, reaches over, and takes the coloring book. "Just start over on a new page. Like this one." She flips through the coloring book. "Or this one. The more you practice, the more you'll be able to stay within the lines."

"But I'll use up all the pages."

"Then we'll get you another coloring book. And when you color all those pages, we'll get you another one."

The boy swipes his arm across his wet face and picks up his box of crayons. The woman returns the open coloring book to his lap.

"What color should I do his antennas, Mimi?"

"I like blue, don't you?"

"No. I like purple."

"Then purple it is."

Cheryl swallows hard several times, but the tears still fall. She rises quickly as if a sudden burst of energy has overwhelmed her. She runs to her car. Once inside, she adjusts the rearview mirror, removes her sunglasses, and is tempted to look at herself. But instead, she glances at the woman and the boy before backing out of the parking space.

At the large trash can at the edge of the playground, she stops, rolls down her window, and tosses the half-empty bag of Hershey kisses inside, keeping seven in her lap for the ride.

She thinks about what colors would best paint Montgomery, Alabama, what colors would best paint....

Her stomach begins to roll and ache and she opens one of the chocolate kisses, places it on her tongue. The voices in her head urge her to go back, back to the playground or back to Ryan's room, back to where she feels safe.

She remembers David's face as he drove her home that day from the police department, his hands on the wheel steering them back home. "You can't go back," he had said.

You can never go back. And so, she drives on.

THE PRICE OF PATIENCE

Dorothy Shawhan

Carla had practiced enough patience in her 35 years for three lifetimes, and she was done. She glared at Jameson across his desk when he said, "Be patient with the guy, Carla. He's a crack tech writer. I want our best people on this project. I gave you a real break when I put him on your team."

"Patience is a virtue," her mother had always preached to her back on the poultry farm outside of Gainesville, Georgia, and for too long she believed it. Now she believed that patience was a doctrine fed to young women to keep them back, keep them docile like the chickens being fattened for slaughter. Not that parents did so consciously, but the patience factor was so deeply embedded in the culture and associated with the feminine that few could resist. She never noticed her brother being extolled to be patient.

"Look," she said, trying to keep her voice calm, "he takes 10 minutes to get a sentence out. I simply don't have that kind of time. I'm sure he's a very nice man, and if he's so good, you shouldn't have any trouble assigning him to someone else."

No, patience had led her to put up with Al for eight long years, with his rages and drinking and carrying on, deferring her own education, trying to be a good wife, hoping for a change. She endured a severe beating and a broken arm before she at last came to her senses, divorced Al, returned to school to finish her degree in architecture, and took control of her own life and of her son's. Now she was on her way up with a position in one of Atlanta's top firms. For the first time she was leading a team of architects and engineers to propose a major project -- a film production center for the heart of the city. Its success meant that Atlanta might become an East Coast equivalent to L.A. in the film industry. Her firm had a late start though, and Orlando was reportedly far ahead of them.

"I can't make any team changes at this point," Jameson said.

"We don't need a writer," she said. "I'm a good writer. I'll do the documentation."

"I've heard that before," Jameson said, raring back in his chair with a snort of a laugh. "I haven't seen an architect or an engineer yet that could write their way out of a paper sack. It's like you guys speak some foreign language. We've got to have a proposal that managers like me can read and politicians can understand. That's what Jerry's so good at, translating y'all's jargon into plain English.

"I could write the supporting documents fifteen times over in the time it will take to answer that man's questions." Carla's capable hands were clasped together in her lap so tightly that her knuckles were white. She had been considered pretty when she was a girl, nice figure, shiny black hair, blue eyes, but she had become so intense in her profession that no one would have thought to use the adjective 'pretty' to describe her. 'Professional' certainly, 'attractive' maybe, but not 'pretty.'

"Lemme tell you a little story." Jameson settled even further back in his chair, his hands propped over his round stomach, and looked at her over the tops of his reading glasses. How did such a fat man get this far? Carla thought, but, of course, would never say. She, like most people, thought lots of things she'd never say.

"This warehouse owner came into a bunch of Bibles, see, and he could turn a nice profit if he could sell them for $10 apiece, and so he wanted to hire three guys to sell them for him door-to-door." Of course he would hire men, Carla thought. Of course you couldn't hire a woman to sell a Bible.

"He interviewed them first because he didn't want to send just anybody out with Bibles. Well, the first two were good-looking, clean-cut guys on summer vacation from college. They filled the bill just fine. But the third was not so satisfactory because he had this severe stutter. He could hardly get out the word B-b-b-bible." Carla felt slightly horrified, like she should walk out and report him to somebody. Was this a joke or some kind of sick parable?

"Anyway, the owner finally decided to take a chance and hire him, and the three of them stayed gone all summer, and when they got back, the first one said he had sold 100 Bibles, and he turned in $1,000. The second one had sold 300 Bibles and turned in $3,000. But the third one said he had sold 2,000 Bibles, and he ante-up'd $20,000.

'How in the world did you do that?' they all wanted to know.

'W-w-w-well,' the guy said, 'w-w-w-when they c-c-c-came to the d-d-door, I s-s-said, d-d-d-o you w-w-w-want t-t-to b-b-b-buy a B-b-b-bible, or d-d-do you w-w-w-want me t-t-to s-s-s-stand here and r-r-r-read it t-t-t-to you?'

Carla glared at Jameson. "That is not funny," she said. "I would never make fun of anyone's disability."

"You missed the point. That's not a story about a disability. That's a story about playing with the hand that's dealt you. And winning. Capitalizing on impatience."

"Jerry doesn't stutter exactly," Carla said. "He just pauses for a long time between words."

"You don't know how hard he's worked to get to that point. When he first came on board the man stuttered. Then he learned to pause instead."

"I'm sure he's worked hard, but I have too. We're under an almost impossible deadline where every hour counts. Please, Jameson, please give me another writer."

"No. I won't do it." Jameson stood up, moving quickly for a heavy man. "Jerry stays. Try looking him straight in the eye when he talks to you. That helps." Carla knew she had been dismissed, and she left Jameson's office fuming.

Jerry Smith looked as ordinary as his name. Carla hardly realized he worked for the company until he landed on her team and came to the initial meeting. Sandy hair, blue eyes behind thick glasses, medium height and build, 40ish. He could be anybody's husband or anybody's father, except that he wasn't. Glenda, the department's secretary who entertained herself with pop psychology books and applied the theories to the employees, told Carla he was single, probably because his slow speech isolated him in these fast times. He had not been married so far as she knew, though he never talked about himself. In fact, he never talked at all except when the work required him to. The only times he missed work was when he had to take his mother to the doctor.

"I'm suspicious of adults who live with their mothers," Carla said.

"There's worse things," Glenda said, shifting her chewing gum from one side of her mouth to the other. "My mama always told me that you could tell the worth of a man by how he treated his mama."

"She better stay healthy until we get this project done. That's all I've got to say."

"She may not," Glenda said, clicking her well-polished nails on her desk. "She tends to be poorly."

"Oh, great. That's all we need, a writer who has to play nursemaid for his mama."

"Now if you were sick, you'd want Andy to see about you. How is Andy anyhow?"

Carla's face softened at the thought of Andy, her ten-year-old son. He was a handsome, sturdy boy who looked a lot like Al, but she didn't hold that against him. In fact, Al's looks were about the only thing going for him and were the reason she was attracted to him to begin with. She learned the hard way that looks don't go very far toward building a marriage. "Oh, he's good," she said. "He likes his teacher this year. They're doing this whole arts curriculum at his school, where they integrate the arts into all the subjects. He comes home with some of the most beautiful work, like illustrated poems, and graphs and charts that have a visual component. The refrigerator door is completely out of room. He may grow up and be an architect some day."

"He's a cute little fella judging from that picture on your desk," Glenda said. "You need to bring him up here sometime and let us see him."

"If we can just get through this project, maybe we'll have more time." Carla checked her watch and rushed off to see one of the engineers.

The next day before the weekly design meeting, Jerry met her outside the conference room door. "My........mother..........is....."

"Sick? I'm sorry."

"You...... see........I........must take...."

"Her to the doctor? Jerry, that's a problem. I need the whole team here each week if we are going to pull this thing off. Can't you wait until after the meeting?"

"She's......in......a ....lot of...."

"Pain? Well, go then. Whatever. But it's up to you to find out what goes on in the meeting. And I am not happy. If we're going to function as a team, all the members have to be here." Jerry's face looked like she had slapped him, and he turned abruptly and walked away.

Jameson had come up behind Carla and overheard. "Don't ever finish his sentences," he said. "That's the worst thing you can do. And you weren't looking him in the eye either."

Carla flushed with anger. "What are we running here, an architectural firm or a rehabilitation center?" The minute she said it, she was ashamed of herself. Jameson merely lifted his eyebrows and walked through the door.

For the next few months if Mrs. Smith were ill during meeting times, she was ill without her son Jerry. He did not miss another meeting. If he had questions, he asked someone else, never Carla. Yet when she saw his preliminary reports, they surprised her with their accuracy.   She couldn't help but feel a twinge that he never had to question her, yet, God knows, she didn't want to talk to him. As all the aspects of the project began to come together, however, one morning in early April Jerry e-mailed a request to meet with her about a particularly innovative and troublesome element of the design.

Carla was feeling the pressure severely this day, just two weeks before she was to present the plan to the decision-making board. She e-mailed him that she had fifteen minutes between 3:30 and 3:45 when she could see him. He was there promptly, and the two of them gathered at the large table where all the blueprints were spread. Jerry pointed toward the central core of the complex, a courtyard with fountains and elaborate landscaping.

"I don't……..see….. how….the…..roofline here…..

Don't finish his sentences and do look at him, she could hear Jameson saying. Frantic with impatience, she took several deep breaths, and let him complete his question. When he turned toward her, she looked him squarely in the eye. His eyes locked into hers as if nothing could ever persuade them to let go. Hungry eyes, she thought, and dangerous. She saw a depth of suffering in them that threatened to pull her in and that scared her. She had had enough suffering and couldn't bear to think of sharing anybody else's. She wanted to look away, run out of the room, but she couldn't, and so she answered his question, and he followed up with another one, more fluidly than she had ever heard him speak. She gradually began to relax.

Their exchange continued until the phone rang, and Carla wrenched her eyes away feeling as if she had been hypnotized. So Jameson was right, as he tended to be, and who would have thought a plain man like Jerry Smith would have such extraordinary eyes? She looked at her watch as she picked up the phone, and realized that 45 minutes had passed and she was a half hour behind schedule. She would have to move quickly to get through the day's list.

"Carla Goodman," she said briskly into the receiver. Then abruptly all the color drained from her face, and she swayed toward the desk and dropped the phone. "Oh, God," she said, "Oh, Jesus."

Jerry caught her before she fell. He supported her with one arm and reached for the phone with the other. "What?" he said, then listened intently. "Where?" Andy had been hit by a car as he came from school. His mother should come to the hospital immediately. Jerry hung up the phone, and took his car keys from his pocket. "Let's….go."

Carla would later have no memory of the trip to the hospital. She would remember a nurse in the Emergency Room telling her that Andy was still alive, that doctors were working with him, that they would report the extent of his injuries when they could. The police came and told her what little they knew. The driver had left the scene, hit and run. She would remember sitting in the waiting room for what seemed an interminable time with Jerry. She would pace a while, then sit back down, dig in her purse, then forget what she was looking for. Jerry sat quietly. "Should we….. call….his father?"

Carla looked at him dully, her eyes almost swollen shut from crying. "I haven't heard from him in four years. I don't even know where he is. Las Vegas probably. He likes to gamble."

"Oh. Isn't…… there….someone?"

"Andy is all I've got. My parents are both dead. My brother's a Marine—in Iraq. But you don't have to stay."

Jerry flushed. "That's….not what…..I meant."

"Won't your mother be worried?"

"She….she….died….February 8."

He averted his eyes from Carla's. She felt chilled and nauseated. What kind of a person was she, not to know that a colleague's mother had died? "Nobody told me," she said in strained whisper. "I am so sorry."

Jerry shrugged. "She suffered. Now….she doesn't."

A doctor bustled into the room, pulling off his surgical mask. "A broken leg, fractured ribs, broken arm, but he'll be O.K. Just gonna take a long time, lots of patience." He smiled brightly. "Mom and Dad, want to go in and see the boy?"

Jerry looked like he would be grateful if Atlanta opened up and swallowed him whole, but Carla didn't notice. She grabbed his arm and started for the door. "Come on."

Andy was a cocoon, wrapped in bandages from head to toe, like the people you see in cartoons. One leg was hoisted high in traction. Just his round little face was visible, his eyes glazed with pain and anesthesia. "Oh, baby, Oh my baby," Carla said. "Honey, I am so glad to see you." She bent and kissed his cheek.

"I thought I looked both ways," Andy said groggily.

"I'm sure you did, too," Carla said. "This is not your fault."

Jerry hung back in the door while Carla reclaimed her son. Finally she called him to the bedside and said, "Andy, this is Jerry. We work together."

"Hi," Andy said. He put out his unbroken left hand and shook Jerry's right in an awkward clasp. Then he was asleep.

A nurse came in and told Carla she would get a cot so she could stay the night. "You go on home, now," Carla said to Jerry. "I'll be fine. Just ask Glenda to bring my car from the lot when she leaves work tomorrow. She has a key. And thanks." Already she was planning how she would manage, juggling work and hospital.

"Don't…..you need……some……things from home?" Jerry asked.

Then Carla thought how good it would be wash her face, brush her teeth, get into her pajamas. "Do you mind?" she asked, fishing her apartment keys out of her purse and telling him the address of her townhouse, which was not far from the hospital. "I hate to put you out. You've done so much already. Just my toothbrush and my pj's hanging on the bathroom door." Ever since she and Andy had had to refugee to the battered women's shelter, she knew how to get by with little or nothing.

"I don't…..mind." And he was gone. Within the hour he was back, following the nurse who said, "Your husband is back," and causing Jerry to blush.

"He's not my husband," Carla said, smiling at Jerry. "He's my col-league." He handed her a small bag with anything she might need for overnight--even make-up, a change of clothes for the next day, and the book from her bedside table, *Ecology of a Cracker Childhood.* How did he know? Then she remembered. The mother. He had had plenty of experience with women and hospitals. But what really surprised her was the Subway vegetarian sandwich and bottled water that he handed her. So he had no-ticed what she ordered the times the team had worked through lunch. What an observant man.

"The hospital. It must bring back sad memories for you," Carla said as she took the sandwich and water and placed them on the table by Andy's bed.

"The eternal......return....of the same," Jerry said. Then as Carla looked blank, he added, "Nietzche," leaving her to ponder.

Andy slept a drugged sleep and Carla a restless one, scrunched onto the short, narrow hospital cot. She dreamed, among other nightmarish scenarios, that Jerry was giving the final presentation for the film center before all the decision-makers because she was with Andy at the hospital. She woke with the sheet wrapped around her neck, a cold sweat beaded on her upper lip, Andy's IV drip, dripping. With first light she was up, shower-ing, bumming coffee from the nurse's station. Andy was livelier and ate a bowl of Cheerios. Thank goodness he's left-handed. Carla hoped she would never have to be in the hospital again; she had only been once before as a patient and that was when Andy was born. They don't give you a minute's peace, poking, prodding, asking questions. The physical therapist came in and worked a bit with Andy. He was entirely too cheerful and too young-looking for Carla's taste. Besides he said rehabilitation would take at least six months and require lots of patience. After ten minutes she wanted to strangle him, but Andy, though pale with pain, did his best to please him.

Now that she knew Andy would live, she shifted into a gear resem-bling her usual—calling members of the team to be sure they were on-task, checking with the tech department on her power point presentation for the gala unveiling of the film project, sending Glenda a list of messages on her Blackberry, calling the school for Andy's assignments. The principal said that since it was so near the end of the term, Andy could finish the school year at home. The teachers would send his assignments, but she would have to see that he had a tutor.

By five o'clock, she was fit to be tied, as her mother used to say, having finished her book, written a list of all she had to do, and called everybody she could think of. Glenda brought her car by and came up to the room with a balloon-o-gram for Andy, who was watching cartoons. "Look at the brave boy," she said, giving Andy the balloons anchored by a Snickers.

"Thanks," he said. "Snickers are my favorites."

"You're welcome, Sweetie." Then to Carla, handing her the car keys, "We're sorry this happened, but don't worry about a thing. We've got it under control."

I doubt it, Carla thought.

"Jerry followed me over. He's circling the parking lot because I took the last place. Your Altima is on row D, the last one. Guess what I found out about Jerry?"

"I have no idea," Carla said.

"I was cleaning out some of the old company files," Glenda lowered her voice conspiratorially, "and saw some insurance records. He was married. Five years. His wife died of breast cancer ten years ago."

"That's terrible."

"Explains a lot," Glenda said. "I was afraid he was gay."

"My Lord."

"I take each gay guy as a personal affront to us single girls," Glenda said, adjusting the belt that circled her perfect hour glass figure.

"Have mercy," Carla said, resorting to her mother tongue as she always did when astonished at how people are.

An hour later Jerry came to the room with a bottle of white wine, brie, crackers, and, for Andy, a chocolate ice cream cone.

"Gee, thanks," Andy said, licking the soft chocolate meltings around the edge.

"How did you know I was ready to trade my soul for a glass of wine? Please, join me."

"I....can't stay." Jerry flipped up the corkscrew from his Swiss Army knife and opened the wine. Carla noticed how strong his hands were and how the muscles rippled up his arm. He must work out. He turned to face her son. "Andy.....do you....play chess?"

"No."

"Want….to learn?"

"Sure."

"Tomorrow?"

"Sure."

"You are so thoughtful," Carla said, feeling left out. "The doctor says we can go home in three days. He'll have to go to the rehabilitation center each day, Home Health will come in, and I've got to find a tutor, work out a schedule. Then I can get back to the office."

"I could….tutor…. afternoons."

"Really? What about work?" She knew it was more important for her to be at the office than for Jerry, given the nature of their jobs. And he was essentially finished with her team project. Still she couldn't imagine a man volunteering to miss work in order to tutor a kid. No ambition. She had seen that before. She thought less of him in spite of herself.

"I can….do my job….from anywhere."

"That would be wonderful, Jerry. We'll talk tomorrow."

In the next few days, Carla settled Andy back in their townhouse, managed a thousand details, and got back to the office. Jerry came each afternoon and stayed until she got home, sometimes quite late. On those evenings, he cooked dinner for him and Andy and left hers on the stove. Her big presentation came and went, and Jerry chose to stay with Andy rather than go. "But you were on the team," Carla said. "You should be there to take credit."

"Credit's no….big deal," he said. Maybe to you, Carla thought.

Andy was a remarkable quick study with chess, Jerry said, and did a good job with his lessons too.

"When we do homework, Jerry don't yell at me, Mama."

"Doesn't. And I don't yell at you, Sweetheart." But she knew she did. She would quickly lose patience and could not understand for the life of her how anybody in their right mind could voluntarily home school a child.

Two months passed before the firm received word that Atlanta had been chosen for the film center. The bosses threw a huge party with champagne and cake. Carla called home and asked Jerry to come and bring Andy, who could now maneuver like a little monkey on his crutches. When they appeared in the door, her beautiful boy and this ordinary man, she felt an unaccustomed surge of affection, and rushed to meet them afraid she was going to cry.

The next day Glenda said, "So what's with you and Jerry?"

"What do you mean?"

"People say you're stringing him on just so he'll babysit your kid." Carla was speechless at this charge.

"You're called the piranha around the office," Glenda went on. Folks just figure Jerry's caught, being eaten alive."

Carla sat down abruptly. "Well, thank you Mary Sunshine. Look, he volunteered. I never asked him to do a thing. Piranha?"

"Yeah, them flesh-eating fish down in Florida."

"I'm hurt. I really am."

"You are?" Glenda looked genuinely surprised. "I figured you'd be flattered."

"Sweet Jesus."

"I don't know why else he'd take such an interest," Glenda said. "Do you?"

"As far as you're concerned, does anybody ever do anything that's not motivated by sex?" Carla asked with righteous indignation.

Glenda thought until her forehead wrinkled into a frown. "Men don't. I know that for sure."

Carla brooded on this conversation all day and by the time she got home, she had decided to take action. The direct approach is always better, even if it hurts.

"Jerry," she said, following him to his car, "let's be clear about our relationship. I'm a damaged person, if you haven't noticed. You deserve better." She looked straight into his eyes.

"I.... could say.... the same," he said, locking his eyes into hers. "This....is not....about you." Before she could feel humiliated, he went on. "I'm...selfish, but....not like that. I've had....three....big failures. To please...my father....to teach....to have kids. Helping Andy...helps me."

Carla bit her bottom lip, tears catching in her throat. "O.K.," she said, then blurted, "Do you call me a piranha too?"

"No. I admire...you."

"Thanks," she said, turning quickly and running back into the house. She had not felt so bad since the days with Al, but she couldn't imagine what would make her feel better. Jerry was simply a good man, but she had lost the ability to recognize one.

That evening Andy chattered like he usually did about Jerry, what they had done that day, what they had planned for the next--the zoo. Usually Carla didn't pay much attention, but tonight she was interested. She almost went to the phone and called Jerry Smith up, asked him to be her friend. She wanted to take their relationship to the next level immediately. Then she remembered he had said he wasn't interested. Well, what did she care anyway? What was the matter with her?

As she paced around the den after Andy went to bed, unable to focus on anything, even her daily planner for tomorrow, she spotted a book Jerry had left. Pierre Teilhard de Chardin. What in the world? The things that man did read. She opened to the page where he had left a bookmark and where he had underlined a passage: "Above all, trust in the slow work of God." Ordinarily she would have tossed the book away in disgust at this point. Don't talk to her about God. Where was he when her marriage crashed and burned? When a hit and run driver almost killed Andy?" But now she kept reading:

> We are, quite naturally, impatient in everything to reach the end without delay. We should like to skip the intermediate stages. We are impatient of being on the way to something unknown, something new, and yet it is the law of all progress that it is made by passing through some stage of instability—And that it may take a very long time.

She sat on the sofa and read the words patiently again and again, as if she had been sent a sign.

THE OVERDOSE

Philip Levin

I studied Cheryl Stevens as she lay on the stretcher beyond the sliding glass door. She rested comfortably, her bronzed hair neatly brushed above a carefully made-up face. Lipstick ran in perfect lines, mascara accented her long lashed lids. Only crow's feet around the eyes gave away her late forties age. Wires ran from the monitors on her chest, arm, and finger to the scope in the corner. Vital sign readings were displayed there, as well as on a central monitoring station outside the locked door.

"Sixty beats a minute," Rosie, the desk clerk noted. "Not as upset as our typical suicidal patient, huh Greg?"

"Did she come in with her make-up like this?" I asked.

"Yeah, but she had to reapply it after we gave her activated charcoal. That stuff makes a mess of everything."

I reviewed the chart Rosie handed me, the brief description of Dr. Morgan's treatments, and the lab tests ordered, though the test results hadn't returned yet. A one line suicide note read, "The world will be better off without me." Dr. Morgan handled the medical part. It was my job to handle the psychological.

Passing in, I gently slid the glass door closed. I stood a moment, watching her quiet, easy breathing. "Mrs. Stevens?" I spoke softly to judge the depth of her trance. Immediately her eyes flickered, then snapped opened, dazzling blue opals evaluating me.

"Cheryl Stevens? I'm Greg Phillips, the counselor tonight."

"Nice to meet you, Greg. Please call me Cheryl." She brought her hand out from under the sheets for a gentle squeeze of my hand. It's unusual for a patient to want to call me by my first name, a warning of too easy familiarity.

"I understand you took some pills tonight?"

Mrs. Stevens nodded. "I couldn't stand living with Robert another minute. Please, don't let him back here. No telling what he's liable to say or do. Best just send him home."

"Robert? You mean your husband?"

She nodded emphatically, raising her eyebrows in a little girl pleading look, her lips a pout. "Robert's been very erratic lately. One minute he tells me he loves me, the next he's threatening to divorce me. You best put me in the hospital to protect me. Otherwise I'll probably end up taking an overdose again. You must promise to keep him away."

I nodded. "We can certainly keep him away from you for now, if that's what you prefer. Tell me what happened tonight."

I watched Mrs. Stevens' expression, her eyes closed, her brow pursed in thought.

"Promise you won't tell anyone, Greg?"

I shook my head. "I can't make that promise."

She shrugged. "I guess I have to trust you. Robert and I have been married for thirty years. At first we were very much in love, I worked while he attended law school, then he took care of me as his career blossomed. We never had time for children...at least, that's what he kept saying. I'm sure it's a story you've heard a hundred times. Husband is off at work, wife is home bored. I suppose I've been depressed about it for a long time. Tonight I prepared a delicious meal, prime rib, cooked just the way he likes it, asparagus au gratin, twice baked potatoes...the works. Then Robert called at the last minute saying he had to go to some meeting. I...I just couldn't take it anymore. My doctor had prescribed some nerve pills for me. I took them all."

I glanced at the chart. It listed an empty bottle of Xanax found at the scene, sixty pills, filled four days before. "So you tried to kill yourself?"

"Yes. That's what I just said."

"And how do you feel now? Do you still feel like hurting yourself?"

"You send me out and I'll do it again, Greg." Mrs. Stevens put her chin up, a defiant gesture that surprised me. Most people who perform situational overdose gestures like this usually say they're sorry and won't do it again.

"Did you call for help or did someone find you?" I asked.

"I woke up when the rescue squad started to roll me onto their stretcher. I guess Robert finally came home and found me."

I nodded, putting a note on the chart. Clearly she expected to be found. This "suicide attempt" continued to have a strange feel to it. "Please tell me more about why you wanted to kill yourself, Mrs. Stevens. Was it just because your husband was late for dinner?"

"I can't stand living like this, the constant worries, the mental stress, the fear. You can't imagine what it's like. Robert has to have everything perfect. If the laundry isn't stacked neatly in the drawers, exactly as he wants it, he loses control. If dinner isn't served precisely on time, he screams. Last week I slightly overcooked the steak and he threw his fork into the wall. Oh, it's fine if he's late or forgets to put something away. But everyday, in every little way, he insists that I have to be just perfect.

"I try so hard to please him, but I'm just never good enough. 'That dress doesn't work on you,' he'll say. He never takes me out for a little romance anymore. And even when he has to take me to some company function, he'll tell me exactly what I can say and who I can talk with."

"And jealous? Oh my God. Yesterday the mailman came to the door to get me to sign for a package, and Robert acted like I was trying to seduce the chump. You should have seen Bruce…that's the mailman, you should have seen Bruce turn white and run down the sidewalk when Robert came at him.

"My life has become a living hell. Tonight I couldn't stand it anymore and I emptied the bottle."

"You took sixty tablets of Xanax tonight?" I asked.

She shook her head. "Not all sixty. I might have taken a few over the last day or two."

"Fifty?"

"Well, no. I flushed some down the toilet."

"So, how many do you think you took?"

"I don't know!" she cried. "Leave me alone, Greg. I don't want to talk about it." She turned away from me.

After a moment I asked, "Twenty? Mrs. Stevens, do you think you took twenty tablets?"

With her back towards me she murmured, "Yeah. Maybe twenty. Or fifteen. Maybe only a dozen."

That's still a lot of Xanax. "When did you take them? It's three a.m. now."

She rustled under the sheet, finally turning back to me. "I'm not sure. Maybe nine o'clock after I cleaned up the kitchen."

Six hours ago? The Xanax had already run its course. "Did you take anything else? Tylenol? Other pills or drugs? Alcohol?"

She shook her head. "Just the Xanax." She pulled her arm out from under the sheet to pat her hair straight and I saw the band aid where the nurse had drawn blood. I noted that there weren't any "track marks" on her arms, that is, no sign that she injected herself with drugs. I'd know soon enough if anything else showed in her system.

"Do you have any other medical problems?" I asked.

"Yes, Greg. I suffer from Migraine headaches."

"Migraines? What do you take for them?"

"I have Percocet at home. I took one tonight. When they're real bad I come to the E.R. for a shot. I've had to do that more often lately."

I noted that on the chart, and told Mrs. Stevens that I'd be back after awhile. Leaving the cubicle, I slid the glass door closed, and turned back to the nursing station. "What do you think, Rosie?"

Rosie shrugged, her magenta scrubs adding a bright sense of surreal to the psych unit.

"Doesn't seem very suicidal to me. Did she tell you not to let her husband come back? He's waiting in the Quiet Room."

"Yes, she told me. I'll go talk with him there."

I found Mr. Stevens picking at some food while reading the Wall Street Journal. He stood when I came in, displaying his tailored business suit sporting a red tie hanging in a perfect Prince Edward's knot. With his gray tinged hair and artificial tan I placed him at a handsome fifty, maybe a few years older. I held out my hand.

"Mr. Stevens? I'm Greg Phillips, the counselor taking care of your wife."

He grasped my hand in both of his, a strong controlling grip.

"Dr. Phillips, thank you for coming to talk with me. Is Cheryl going to be all right? When can I see her?"

I succeeded in freeing my hand and directed him to sit back down. I settled into another chair at the table, placing Mrs. Stevens' clipboard beside me.

"Your wife is doing well right now. Her vital signs are stable and we're fairly confident that she'll have no ill effects from this."

"Thank heavens," he cried. "Thank you for saving her life, Doctor. When can I go back to be with her?"

"Dr. Morgan took care of the medical part. I'm just a counselor, not a doctor."

He nodded, then indicated his pie. "Excuse my eating. On the way out the door, following the rescue squad, I grabbed something."

"Don't worry about it." I picked up the chart again ready to take notes. "What happened tonight?"

Mr. Stevens' long legs brought him to a quick stand. He began pacing.

"Mr. Phillips, I don't know what to tell you. Cheryl's been very wound up lately. She keeps pleading with me to stay with her. I've been very busy at work, and she keeps calling me and checking up on me. She's developed an obsession with keeping the kitchen spotless. If I touch anything she goes crazy. She is a great cook, in fact, she had a home dinner planned for tonight. She always thinks everything has to be so perfect. She'll wash her hands several times a day. If her makeup isn't just the way she wants it, she'll cold cream it out and start all over.

"Trying to get her out of the house is almost impossible. When we do go out, she's absolutely paranoid of saying the wrong thing to the wrong person. She's constantly asking me what can she say and who should she talk to.

"Yesterday something very strange happened. The mailman came to the door to have her sign for a package and she tried to seduce him. You should have seen him blanch, then rocket down that sidewalk.

"Tell me, counselor. Is she having a nervous breakdown? Good Lord. How stupid a question is that? Of course she's having a nervous breakdown. She took a bottle of pills tonight after all. I should have seen it coming. The signs were all there."

He wrung his hands a moment, then made fists and lowered himself carefully into the chair. His version of their interactions didn't surprise me.

I supposed the truth to be somewhere in the middle.

"Tell me the circumstances of how you found Mrs. Stevens tonight, please."

His mouth twisted just a moment, then smoothed again in his chiseled handsome face.

"As I said, she had planned on us having dinner tonight…some idea she came up with without telling me. When I had to stay late at work, I called to let her know and she blew her top. I guess I was a little ticked off at her, so after my meeting I just stayed out a little. Went to a lounge for a drink. When I got home I took a shower in the downstairs bathroom, then flicked through the TV for a couple of minutes. Checking on the weather report and the overseas financial news."

He paused a moment, shaking his head. "I can't believe I wasted all that time while she was dying of an overdose upstairs. What if she had died due to my fiddling around? I'd never have forgiven myself. What would the police have thought?"

"So, what time did you finally find Mrs. Stevens?" I paged through the sheets on the chart while I waited for his answer. I found the EMS rescue sheet. "911 call received 0120."

"Hmm," Mr. Stevens muttered. "I guess about midnight. No, it must have been later than that. I watched the end of the game before retiring. It must have been a little after one o'clock. When I went upstairs I didn't think anything was wrong at first. Cheryl looked natural, lying under the covers. It took me a few minutes to notice the empty pill bottle. Then I tried to arouse her, and when I couldn't, I called 911."

I waited patiently while Mr. Stevens took out a handkerchief and dabbed at his eyes. Both he and his wife knew how to add the dramatic touches.

I asked, "When you had your argument on the phone, did you have any idea she might be thinking of hurting herself?"

Mr. Stevens rose again, this time pacing very slowly. He had his back to me when he answered. "Cheryl told me that she was getting one of her headaches and was going straight to bed. That would have been around six o'clock. I have no idea when she took the pills."

"Do you think she expected you to find her? I mean, normally after such an argument would you have gone straight home to check on her?"

Mr. Stevens had turned back to face me. "Maybe so. Sometimes she pulls stunts to try to manipulate me. I hope I'm not sounding cynical if I wonder if this was another one of those. These pills she took, Xanax, are they likely to be fatal?"

I hesitated, then shook my head. "Usually not, unless mixed with other sedatives like alcohol. But even so, a suicide gesture should never be considered trivial. People who may be acting out often accidentally succeed. This certainly is a serious call for help."

Mr. Stevens shook his head, his mouth a grim line. "Cheryl is very bright, Mr. Phillips. I'm sure she knew exactly what she was doing. Well, since she's going to be okay, I would appreciate you letting me back to talk with her."

"She's not quite ready for visitors, I'm afraid."

Mr. Stevens began pacing again. He stopped right in front of me. "Imagine how you would feel if you thought your wife had attempted suicide. Besides the personal devastation, the blow to my reputation could be incredible. I can't remember when I've been this upset. I'm so disgruntled that I broke my diet, grabbing something from the kitchen on the way out. I guess this is from the fancy dinner Cheryl cooked tonight."

I made a few notes in my chart, concerned that Mr. Stevens seemed as concerned about his reputation and his diet as about his wife's suicide gesture. "Mr. Stevens, has your wife ever attempted suicide before? No? Has she seemed particularly depressed lately, crying a lot, not sleeping well, losing weight." This time he nodded vigorously.

"Yes, Mr. Phillips. She has been crying a lot lately, and not sleeping well. Perhaps I should have expected her to do something desperate."

"To your knowledge has she been hearing voices or seeing things other people don't see?"

He shook his head. "She's not crazy, if that's what you mean. She just got a little upset tonight and took some pills." He seemed to be getting agitated. "Look, if she's doing so well, why can't I see her?"

I stood too. "I'll go check on her and send word. I'll let Mrs. Stevens know that you're here and concerned. I anticipate that she's going to be admitted, probably in isolation for tonight. She suggested that you might want to go home."

I noticed that his face looked flush and he seemed to be breathing hard.

"Mr. Stevens, perhaps it would be best if you went for some coffee. Do you have a friend or relative you can call?"

He sat down on the chair. "I'll be okay. Too much excitement." He took out something small from an inside coat pocket, but then glanced up at me, and replaced it. I wasn't sure, but it looked like a small pill bottle.

I reached the door, then turned to ask one last question. "By the way, Mr. Stevens, what's your mailman's name?"

"The mailman? How should I know? Do you know your mailman's name?"

Back in the psych unit I found Rosie watching Mrs. Stevens through the glass door.

"How's she doing?"

Rosie nodded. "Just fine. Sitting up reading a magazine. Fixed her make-up again. She doesn't act like someone who's hell-bent on suicide. What do you think? Just a lover's spat?"

"Rosie, I want you to have security keep an eye on Mr. Stevens. He's not to come back here. Also have someone tell him that his wife is doing fine but still can't have visitors."

I flipped through Mrs. Stevens' lab test results. Blood counts were normal, urine clear, heavy metal screen negative. I paused over the drug screen.

"Did you see this, Rosie?" I asked, showing her the paper.

"Yeah, negatives except positive for opiates. Didn't she say she took Percocet?"

"It's like the Sherlock Holmes mystery, don't you think? The strange thing that the dog did in the night?"

"What did the dog do?"

"Nothing."

"I don't get it."

"Neither did Watson, my dear Rosie."

I went back in with Mrs. Stevens. "How are you feeling, Mrs. Stevens?"

"Did you talk with my husband, Greg?" she asked with a smile.

I nodded. "Yes. He's very concerned for you. He'd like to see you."

Her smile vanished. "Oh of course he would. He needs to be sure his little possession is in perfect shape. You promised you wouldn't let him come back here. Am I safe? Why doesn't he just go home?"

"Are you concerned for your safety, Mrs. Stevens? Has Mr. Stevens hit you or threatened to strike you?" Physical abuse would change this picture.

She shook her head no.

"You're quite safe, Mrs. Stevens. There are two locked doors between him and you as well as security guards. There may be alternatives to your being admitted. If you're not still suicidal perhaps you could stay with a relative?"

Mrs. Stevens' perfect composure cracked for just a moment with a wide-eyed anxiety. "I'm still suicidal, Greg. I think it would be a good idea to admit me to the hospital, don't you agree?"

I nodded. "I suppose that's the safest option. Are you hungry? What time did you last eat?"

"Lunch time I guess. I cooked dinner for Robert, but when he told me he wasn't coming home I lost my appetite. I became so upset that I developed one of my headaches. Well, you know the rest. I went upstairs and downed those pills."

"That's when you wrote the suicide note?" I asked Cheryl.

She nodded. "I'm a woman of few words."

"You put all the food away before you went to bed?"

"Of course. I told you, Robert insists on a clean kitchen. Besides, he never eats late at night. Too concerned about having a perfect body. Can we talk about something else?"

I nodded. "Do you have any idea why Mr. Stevens didn't come home?"

"Well, he SAID he was at a meeting. He's always going to meetings."

"Did he tell you when to expect him home, when you could expect him to find you overdosed and rescue you?"

She glared at me and turned away. "I don't feel like talking to you anymore, Greg. You're a bore."

"I apologize. Let's change the subject. What's your mailman's name?"

"Bruce Krueger. Bruce doesn't wear a wedding ring. Maybe that's why Robert blew a fuse."

"Were you purposely trying to make Robert jealous by flirting with the mailman?"

She glared at me again, and I thought she was going to turn away again. But instead she spit on the floor. "Yes, damn it, I was. I may be over forty, but I'm still attractive to men. You know what they say about the goose and the gander, don't you Greg?"

"You mean that Mr. Stevens is having an affair?"

For a moment she stared at me defiantly, then she dropped her gaze and nodded. "Thirty years of marriage, and I've been as faithful as Odysseus' wife. I want Robert to consider what it would be like to lose me. He needs to value me, damn it!"

I left quietly, leaving her to her tears. Outside Rosie had been watching us on the monitor.

"One thing I always admire about you, Greg," Rosie said, "is your devotion to your patients. You're determined to find out why she did this, aren't you? Other counselors would just admit her and let the in-patient folks tease it out."

I nodded. "Every case is like a detective mystery, Rosie. These things never are as simple as they seem. Go ahead and get the psychiatrist on the phone." I waited while she dialed the number. I turned when I heard the security door open behind me. Bill Reeves, the security guard, was signaling for me.

"Hey Greg. You know that guy you wanted me to watch, Mr. Stevens?"

My pulse jumped as I asked, "What happened?"

"He collapsed in the waiting room. They're coding him on stretcher six."

"What?" I raced past him and around to the trauma center. A crowd of people were working on Mr. Stevens. His heart kept jumping out of rhythm, requiring shock.

"What's going on, Dr. Morgan?" I called to my friend who was running the code.

"Don't know. He grabbed his chest and collapsed. Must have had a bad heart. He had a bottle of nitroglycerin tabs in his pocket. Funny though."

"What?"

"Well, he's not acting like a typical MI. His complex is very strange looking. Could have a bundle branch block I guess. ALL CLEAR! SHOCK!" he called out.

I ran back to the crisis area.

"Cheryl!"

She looked alarmed. "Oh my God, he didn't collapse already did he?"

I stepped back. "What made you ask that?"

Mrs. Stevens tried to smooth her expression. "You're coming in to tell me Robert's sick, right? Through the glass door I saw you run out of here when that guard signaled you. And now you've run right back in here, so naturally I assumed something has happened to Robert. I know he has a bad heart after all."

"Okay. But what did you mean already?"

"I didn't say already, Greg."

"Yes, you did."

Suddenly it all came together for me.

"You poisoned him, didn't you?"

She looked frightened. "What do you mean? Of course not! He has a bad heart I told you."

"You staged this whole thing. You never took any pills. There weren't any in your system. You set up a poison meal for your husband, then staged this overdose so you'd be in the hospital when he died, giving you the perfect alibi. You didn't expect him to eat the poisoned dish you prepared until tomorrow."

She shook her head vigorously, but her eyes betrayed her.

"Mrs. Stevens, I know you did it. I'll insist they get an autopsy and they'll find the poison. You'll go to jail, maybe even the electric chair. Tell me NOW what you gave him and we can save his life."

Her face turned pasty white. Her pulse shot up to a hundred and thirty on the monitor.

"Oh my God," she sobbed. "You don't know what it was like. He was supposedly going to meetings all the time. I couldn't be good enough for him, but he sure found a new young one that he thought was. I couldn't stand it!"

"Cheryl. Tell me what was the poison."

"Wintergreen. I baked wintergreen into his favorite apple pie. I read somewhere it will kill you quickly and I figured with his heart history no one would suspect a thing."

I ran back to the trauma room.

Between breaths, I puffed out, "Dr. Morgan, it's Wintergreen."

He stared at me for a moment, then comprehension dawned. "Sodium Bicarb," he barked to the nurses. "Four amps. Stat!"

A stunned silence broken only by machine alarms enveloped the room. "Four amps?" someone asked.

"Yes," Dr. Morgan repeated. "Four amps and I mean Stat. Mainline them as fast as you can."

I don't claim to know medicine, but I trust Dr. Morgan. So do his nurses. Four ampules of clear strong base joined the dozen drugs already in his body. Over the next several minutes Mr. Stevens' vital signs stabilized. He even opened his eyes for a moment and tried to talk. Dr. Morgan sedated him and transferred him to the I.C.U.

The police took Cheryl Stevens and the leftover apple pie. Bringing that food and eating it in the Quiet Room had saved Robert Stevens' life. It was a crazy idea of hers to prepare the poison in his favorite food, counting on him not eating it until the next day. But then, I see all sorts of crazy people on my job.

FAMILY HAPPENINGS

p.floyd

One.....the body

"Keep his nubbin worn down," Aunt Dell said. "That's where his brain is. If he can see past ten feet, throw some loving on him."

"Dell, don't say such things," Mother said, opening the oven to place a peach pie inside. "Sarah and Richard will be just fine."

Hiding beside the china cabinet, I was listening to an all-important conversation. Mother and Aunt Dell were giving my older sister, Sarah, advice on how to handle her soon-to-be husband. As an eight-year old, I was learning a lot. Like, where a man's brain really was. The nubbin part and throwing loving was confusing--but exciting--and meant someday, as a girl, I would get to throw some. *Pow!*

Aunt Dell, Mother's sister, is my favorite aunt and she is always saying grown-up stuff that answers my questions. Questions Mother is reluctant to answer. It's an adventure when I stay overnight at Aunt Dell's.

Father walked into the kitchen and headed for the stove. "Something smells great," he said.

"Lunch isn't ready," Mother said. "Give me another ten minutes. After we eat, the pie will be ready."

Taking a seat at the table, he noticed me. "Is that my number one detective hiding behind the cabinet?"

"Tracy!" Mother said in a stern voice as I stepped out. "Are you sneaking around eavesdropping? Haven't I told you not to?"

"It's time she learned a few facts of life," Aunt Dell said.

"She'll learn, but not from a foul-mouth person like you," Mother answered. From the tone of Mother's voice, I knew elsewhere was the place to be and started backing toward the door.

The kitchen phone rang and Father answered it. Hanging up, he said, "I'll miss lunch. George says we've got a body over by the old shirt factory and it's definitely foul play. Stabbed. Gotta go." Mother said something about O-My-God as he left.

A shiver tingled my backbone. A body! A good-to-life body here in our town! Before anyone noticed, I was halfway across the backyard headed to Uncle Lomax's house. Experienced with murder, he would want to know we had one.

Many years ago, someone died in a bar fight up in Jackson and Uncle Lomax, Father's younger brother, was sentenced to the penitentiary at Parchman, Mississippi. Last summer, after sixteen years, he was released and the town had been wild with rumors. A killer was coming home.

When Father began to fix up the old storage house in our backyard as a place for Uncle Lomax to live, things got tense in our home. Mother said no. After much discussion, and the promise that it was only for a short time, she reluctantly agreed.

I had never met Uncle Lomax and when he arrived at our home, I was shocked at how he looked; tall and thin with white hair reaching his shoulders. His skin was as white as his hair. White on white with constantly moving blue eyes. A scar ran down the left side of his face and it was whispered an ear was missing under the long hair. That day, when Uncle Lomax looked at me, my insides turned to mush.

Two…..the plan

Racing across the yard, I hit upon a fantastic idea. If there was a murder, Uncle Lomax could help Father solve the crime! Who better than someone with experience? That would make the snooty town people realize Uncle Lomax was a good person. This is going to work out great! *Super-Pop-Pow!*

I ran up the steps of Uncle Lomax's little house and knocked. "Hello, Tee. What's up?" he said as the door swung open.

Uncle Lomax calls me Tee and it makes me feel special. Mother doesn't like the name and he only calls me that when she isn't around. I took his hand and led him to the chairs under the shade tree. He had his knife and a half-finished carving of a squirrel. Father says Uncle Lomax is a world-class carver.

"Uncle Lomax, I got some exciting news...Father has a body...murdered! It's over at the old shirt place and the man was killed with a knife... and a hatchet! Stabbed hundreds of times and then chopped to pieces! The blood must be ankle deep!"

He stopped working on the squirrel's ear and looked at me. After a moment he asked, "What else did you hear, Tee?"

"That's all, Uncle Lomax, except maybe an ax was used too." Darn, I hate it when I don't have all the facts. "I'll try to find out more, but I have a plan. You and I can help Father solve the crime and then those town people will stop telling..." Realizing what I was about to say, I blurted out, "Uncle Lomax, you know about these things."

Neither of us spoke for what seemed a long time and then, standing up, Uncle Lomax folded his knife and put it in his pocket. "The plan won't work, Tee," he said, and walked into his house.

Dang! Why wouldn't the plan work? All we had to do was catch a killer.

The afternoon slowly passed and no one at our house heard anymore about the body. After calling three of my friends, who knew nothing, Mother told me stay off the phone. The telephone was reserved for Sarah and lover boy. I tried to talk to Sarah, but she was so full of getting married, someone could have murdered the whole family and she wouldn't have noticed.

Uncle Lomax didn't come out his house all afternoon and hanging around his porch was a waste of time. I listened to the radio for news, but all I heard was stupid songs about love and someone's woman had left them. Bored to the point of going blind, I went back outside. Joel, my six-year old brother, followed me out to the shade tree and started swinging.

"Joel, what do you think a dead body looks like?" I asked.

He dropped to the ground, thrashed about, and then froze with his eyes and mouth open. Ask a moron, get a moron, I thought.

"Tracy, what happens when we get baptized?" Joel asked.

"You get wet," I said.

"Come on, Tracy, why do we get baptized?"

"To see who can survive. Most don't make it. They drown." I didn't care to have a conversation with a retard.

"They do not!"

"It's true. Boys drown more often than girls. Takes out the runts." I then remembered to be careful. Being small for his six years, nothing gets me a whippin' faster than calling Joel a runt. And, there is a big difference between a spanking and a whippin'.

"I'm not a runt!" Joel said bitterly.

"I didn't say you were. When you're baptized, you have to hold your breath for five minutes, so go practice." Stupid sat in the swing holding his breath.

"I'm not going to be baptized," Joel said, taking a deep breath. "I'll run."

"Don't. They turn the Devil Dogs loose on running sinners. You wouldn't stand a chance."

"They do not!"

"Yes, they do, Joel! The deacons keep them in underground pens and the only meat they eat is sinners like you."

"They do not! How do you know I sin?"

"Because you're stupid." Glancing once more at Uncle Lomax's house, I went to get something to drink.

Three…..dirty words

Mother came into the kitchen as I was drinking a glass of water. She teaches the fifth grade and my biggest fear is she will be my teacher when I reach that level. Fourth grade is where I will be when school starts this fall.

"Has Father called?" I asked.

"No, I'm sure he's busy. Did you bring your dirty clothes to the laundry room?"

"Yes ma'am."

Joel came into the kitchen. "Tracy called me stupid again."

After a very creative denial and comments from Mother about future action, I went out on the front porch and sat in a rocker. Where were my friends? Usually someone comes by on their bike or they call to invite me over to play. The day was a bummer, plus now I was in trouble because of Joel. Bad mood time.

What's wrong with the word stupid? Stupid is the word my friends and I are into now. Last year the word was moron and before that, it was dorky. Now the word is stupid. Everyone and everything is stupid, and we use it like oxygen. Stupid is not a bad word, like a curse word, and I've heard Mother call herself stupid when she did something unexpected. Why call yourself stupid when there are so many opportunities to call others stupid?

Lately, I've been thinking of using bad words and have selected Aunt Dell's favorite to be my first. The "S" word. I wanted to practice it a few times and then spring it on my closest friends. *Pop-Pow!* I was feeling better already.

"Tracy, come set the table," Mother said through the screen door.

My heart jumped, just thinking about using bad words with Mother around. Wait! I would think the "S" word at supper tonight and no one would know anything! *Genius! Super-Pow!*

Supper came and Father wasn't there. When asked, Mother said he had called and was running late. "Let's go ahead and eat. He may be at work a while longer."

Sarah was full of the wedding and talk flowed back and forth between her and Mother. Sarah is twelve years older than me and we get along but don't do many things together. She's too bossy. I'm glad she's happy but I don't understand why she is marrying this guy, Richard Bunns. He's always asking me stupid questions about boys.

Each time I began to focus on the "S" word, Mother would look my way and I would freeze. She can read my thoughts! After this happened twice, I lost my nerve and knew I would have to come up with another plan. Bummer.

"Tracy, what do you think?" Sarah asked as she finished some point about the wedding.

"I don't think, I know." I snapped back. *Pow! Homerun! Center Field Fence! Throw another softie in here sister and let's make it two in a row!*

Mother gave me a little of 'The Stare' but I felt good. Another chance to show my wit didn't happen as everyone ignored me for the remainer of the meal. Of course, Joel said several things they thought were funny. He's such a dork. Women will have fewer babies when the world finds out about him. Later, while helping Mother in the kitchen, she told me my attitude needed improving.

"You need to watch yourself, young lady," she said.

"I don't have a mirror," I said before thinking and when Mother grabbed my arm, I knew I had messed up. With her face as red as her hair, she told me to go to my room. She would be up in short order. Now I had done it! As Aunt Dell would say, I had really stepped in it. Bad, bad, mood time.

Upstairs in my room, I was determined to say the "S" word. As I closed my door, my heart started racing...I was finally going to do it! How should I do this...just say it out loud....

I looked at myself in the mirror and tried to get my lips to form the word. My ears were pounding and my breathing was coming fast. This is it...my mind focused on the word and I opened my month...wait... Mother may be in the hall...

I ran over to my closet, got in, and closed the door. Good, no one can hear me now. I'm free to say as many bad words as I want...I have won! This will be my secret bad word room.

When I opened my month to say the "S" word, I remembered Mother knew everything. Like, where I had hidden my drawing of Joel naked. After hiding it where Christopher Columbus couldn't have found it, she had gone straight to where I had put it. Getting ready....Wait, someone said walls have ears...

Hanging in front of me was my big winter coat. Sticking my head up into it and pulling it close, I felt faint. Now surely no one can hear me. Yes... perfect... Trembling, I whispered the word..."shit."

"Tracy," a muffled voice said.

My brain exploded with white fear. MOTHER!!!…She's in my room…
OH, GOD, NO!!!…She knows everything…Jesus, please help me…I'm
sorry…I'll never say another bad word again.

I couldn't breathe and fought my way out of the coat. Someone
coughed…FATHER!!!…She had called him…and maybe our pastor…
DEACONS!!!

Something ran down my leg and I realized I was wetting myself. Maybe
if I cried…get some pity…had never worked before…Jesus, I promise you
the "S" word is forever blocked from my mind…Please take me to heaven
now…

Facing certain death and prepared to be re-baptized as many times as
necessary, I slowly pushed open the closet door. There, sitting on the floor
playing with his toy truck, was Joel.

I picked up a shoe and beat the shit out of him.

The next morning, I woke to the sound of Father's voice. Quickly
dressing, I ran downstairs to the kitchen where he and Mother were drinking coffee.

"Hi, young lady," he said as I climbed into his lap. Father always smells
clean and fresh in the mornings.

"What's this about you fighting with Joel?"

"I don't know," I said. "He was in my room and I couldn't get him to
leave." That answer was easier than the truth and the truth was I had gotten
a whippin' after Mother pulled me off Joel.

"How's the murder investigation?" I asked. "Who was killed?"

He turned me around so I was looking him in the eye. "No more fighting or I will deal with you next time."

I know when I have crossed the line and it's time to back up. I told
him "yes, sir" and promised not to do it again. As I turned around in his
lap, Joel walked into the room. My heart gave a jump. *A Shiner!* There was
discoloration around his right eye! Go girl! With the shiner being a reminder
for days to my parents what I had done, I knew it was time to become the
caring sister.

At breakfast, the wedding was the topic of discussion and then Father finally brought up the body. From the conversation with Mother, I knew he had called in the Mississippi Highway Patrol investigation unit. They had gone over the crime scene and several items were taken to the crime lab in Jackson for analysis. Information was expected back in a day or so.

"Who was the body?" I asked.

"Let's not talk details here at the breakfast table," Mother said.

Before I could ask another question Mother informed Joel and me to be ready after breakfast to go spend the day at Aunt Lynn's house. Mother and Sarah had planning and shopping to do. Great! Today being Saturday, I knew Uncle James was taking his family to the lake and Aunt Lynn would know all the latest on the body. They have a rug-rat Joel's age, so he would be out of the way. I couldn't wait to tell Beth what Aunt Dell had said about nubbins and such. After promising to behave like a lady, I grabbed Joel's hand and we raced to our rooms to get our swimsuits. *Jesus had forgiven me!*

Four.....growing up

My Father's side of the family, the Sanders, is the largest family in the county. Aunt Lynn is one of Father's four sisters (he has five brothers), all who have several children. Cousins abound and next of kin is never out of sight. My red hair and freckles are from Mother and Aunt Dell's side of the family.

After Father dropped us off at Aunt Lynn's, everyone loaded up and off to Lake Wayne we went. With it Saturday, the small beach area was filling up fast but our group found a good spot and settled in. Beth and I are excellent swimmers for our age (so we have been told), and we hit the water on the run. By eleven o'clock the place was packed and our friends, Joyce and Becky, had joined us. We found a spot at one end of the beach and commenced to grow up.

"That's what Aunt Dell told Sarah," I said, pretending to know what it all meant. "Keep his nubbin wore down. I seen Joel's, and it's a little thing."

"How's she going to do that?" Joyce asked. Joyce is the unenlightened one of our group and we are forever explaining things to her. The concept of someday wearing a training bra is beyond her grasp.

"I've seen Billy Martin rubbing Louise Applewhite's breasts one night while they were sitting on her front porch," Becky said. "They were kissing for at least an hour. He tried to put his hand up her dress but she wouldn't let him." This was old news but still exciting to talk about. The Applewhites live next door to Becky.

"If I ever have breasts and some boy tries to rub them, he's dead," Beth said with such force we all giggled.

"How does your sister keep his nubbin worn down?" Joyce asked again.

"By sleeping in the same bed with him and playing with it," I said.

"Gross!"

"It's called sharing each other's body," Beth said.

"Huh?" Joyce said.

We knew babies came from men and women sleeping together, but didn't have the foggiest idea how the mechanics worked. Beth had over-heard some six-graders saying babies came from a man sticking his thing into a woman, but that was crazy. I knew if a boy tried to stick me with any-thing, he was gonna bleed. Before I could bring up the subject, Aunt Lynn called for lunch and we ran to the picnic table.

While eating, Aunt Lynn answered all my questions about the dead body. The person killed was George Peden, a local mechanic who worked at Roger's Auto Repair. He had been stabbed once, with a long knife. "Whoever did the killing knew what they were doing," she said, "because the blade was thrust up through the liver and into the lungs." Now that was information!

"Has Father arrested anyone?" I asked.

"Lord, no, child," Aunt Lynn answered. "You live in the sheriff's house and know the least about what's going on. There are no clues, so they're checking Peden's friends for information. My money says brother has an unsolvable murder on his hands with re-election in three months."

After eating, my friends and I drifted over to the baseball field for a pick-up game. Several kids from school were there and Alton Welch overheard Beth and me talking about the body.

"You know who they're going to arrest, don't you?" he asked. "That crazy uncle of yours who's a killer."

Goose bumps covered my body and for a few seconds, I was speechless. Blue, Beth's older brother, stepped in and pushed Alton so hard he hit the ground.

"Shut your trap or fight," Blue said, his face angry and fists at ready. Although Alton was the same age and size as Blue, he got up and stomped off to the beach.

I didn't believe a word Alton had said, but my mind sent warning signals. Uncle Lomax had killed a person! He was a murderer! I felt sick in my stomach. Beth and I gathered around Blue.

"Do you think they suspect Uncle Lomax?" she asked.

"I don't know," he said. Blue is two years older than Beth and me, and he is my favorite boy cousin. His real name is Samuel but we call him Blue because he can't see all the colors.

Sides were selected and the game started with my team batting first. Sitting in the dugout, my mind was a whirlwind of confusion. Father surely doesn't think Uncle Lomax did it. What was bothering me was remembering how people reacted when Uncle Lomax first came home. If they think he did this, then the old talk, whispering, stares, and problems at home will come back.

Willie Johnson slid into third base with one leg high and kicked Buddy Leonard in the face. A fight immediately began and the other kids gathered around yelling and offering advice. Waiting his turn to bat, Blue stood at home plate watching the crowd at third base. He's the coolest guy I know. If Uncle Lomax is arrested for murder with the wedding about to happen… Mother will…Suddenly, my stomach felt queasy and I went around behind the dugout where I lost both hotdogs.

Five…..aunt dell

When Aunt Lynn drove up to our house, an unfamiliar car was parked out front. It had a state government tag on it and several tall antennas. In the back yard, I saw two men talking to Uncle Lomax. Slipping behind the hedges, I ran to the corner of his little house.

"You willing to take a lie detector test?" one of the men asked.

"I want to talk to my brother," Uncle Lomax said.

"Your brother is the one who called us in on the case," the second man said. "You got off from work at five o'clock that Thursday and never left this place? Who was the last person to see you that evening?"

After a moment Uncle Lomax said, "The two kids, Tracy and Joel. They were out in the garden with me until their mother called them in. Must have been after eight." *I was a witness!*

"Got any knives?" the first man asked.

"Just a pocket knife I use for carving," Uncle Lomax said and pulled in out of his pocket. One of the men took it and looked it over.

"The man you served time for killing was also carved up. No other knives in the house? What about a butcher knife?"

"All I have is the pocket knife."

That wasn't true! I had seen him in the garden with a large hunting knife!

"I think we need to continue this conversation at the sheriff's office," the first man said and, with one of them on each side of Uncle Lomax, they started towards the street. Father came off the back porch and met them in the yard. After several minutes of discussion, the two men left. Father and Uncle Lomax walked back to the shade tree and sat down.

"Lo, don't worry about this," Father said. "I'm digging into Peden's background and something will turn up. We've heard rumors he was into drugs and I've made contact with the police departments in Biloxi and Gulfport. Word is, he made trips there every weekend."

Uncle Lomax didn't say anything. After a moment, he looked over at where I was hiding. "Tee, you can come out now."

Knowing Father would be angry, I walked over to them. Father gave me his version of 'The Stare'. "I was on my way to the garden," I said.

"You run on into the house," he said. As I left, fear gripped my mind and I was feeling queasy again. They really think Uncle Lomax did it! He hadn't told the truth about the knife!

I called Beth and told her what had happened. All except the knife. She said her mother had been crying after they returned home from the lake. Beth said her father told them the news was all over town that Lomax Sanders was the only suspect in the killing. I hung up the phone and cried.

Later, when Father came into my room, he took one look at me and decided not to fuss about my overhearing the men talk. He took me in his arms and said everything was going to be all right. With Mother not at home, he then told me to take Joel and go to Aunt Dell's. He had business to see after.

"Here, have another cookie and don't worry about eating so close to supper," Aunt Dell said. "I'll tell your mother you're eating with me."

I was feeling better. Who wouldn't feel better at her house when treated so special? Aunt Dell is tall and slim, with red hair just like Mother and me. She smokes, keeps liquor in her home, and works part-time for an attorney over in Laurel. Her dog is named after a music guy named Axle Rose and, after a couple of drinks, she can tell you things by looking at your palm. Aunt Dell goes to church when she wants to and is of the opinion the pastor has too much education. Most of the ladies ignore her because they never know what she's going to say. I want to be just like her when I grow up.

"So, I know wedding talk fills your house, Tracy," she said. "Everyone getting excited and can't wait until the big day?"

"Guess so," I said. "Mother said I can have Sarah's room when she leaves."

"Never heard of getting married in late August. Makes for a hot honeymoon. Do you like this Bunns fellow she's marrying?"

I filed the hot honeymoon statement away for further consideration. "He's OK. He acts dorky but gives me gum sometimes. Aunt Dell, why do they think Uncle Lomax killed that Peden fellow?"

"Joel," Aunt Dell said, "here's another cookie and, why don't you take Axle outside?" Joel and the pooch left.

"Tracy, don't you worry one minute about your Uncle Lomax," she said taking a chair beside me at the kitchen table. "He didn't stab that Peden guy. It's just natural for people to suspect someone who's been in prison."

"But the highway patrol investigators came to our house," I said and told her about what I had heard, including the question and denial about the knife. "I've seen him with a big knife in the garden."

"Knives here, knives there, Tracy. Who's to say who has a certain knife?" She got up, went to a drawer, and pulled out a long knife. "Did it look like this one?"

"Yes ma'am." The knife had the same bone handle with a golden piece on the end and I was confused. How did this knife get in Aunt Dell's kitchen?

"I bet when Lomax told the law he didn't have another knife, he was telling the truth," she said. "And, if you tell the truth, you ain't guilty. Sooner or later the law, including your father, will have an original thought and know Lomax didn't kill that fellow. If your Uncle Charlie was still with us, he would set them all straight. Now, tell me which boy you like." When things are going badly, Aunt Dell has a way of making the sun shine.

Uncle Charlie, Aunt Dell's husband, had been a special uncle when he died in his sleep last Thanksgiving. Having no children, he treated all of us kids like royalty. There was always a smile and a hug and he took us on camping trips, fishing, the movies, and other good stuff.

At Christmas, I heard Uncle Leo say Uncle Charlie had died while climbing the mountain with Aunt Dell. That was puzzling because I had never heard anyone talk about mountain climbing, and it's hard to visualize Aunt Dell climbing anything. One day, when I told Aunt Dell what Uncle Leo said, she gave a big belly laugh. Later that evening, I asked questions at the supper table.

"Uncle Leo says Uncle Charlie died while climbing the mountain with Aunt Dell. Where did they go to find a mountain?" After I asked the question, Father took a deep interest in his pork chop and Mother gave him 'The Stare'.

"That's not Christian talk, Tracy," Mother finally said. "I wish you wouldn't listen to your father and your uncles when they are together." That's when I discovered Jesus had something to do with mountain climbing.

Six…..the wedding

The next day was Sunday and Mother was, as we say, very reserved. In church, people turned our way when we arrived and the conversation between the adults was strained. I thought they all needed to a talk with Aunt Dell. The pastor reminded us during his sermon to study the Bible; there would be a final exam someday. "Don't fail that one," he said. After church, Mother went to bed with a headache while Joel, Father, and I went to visit Uncle Leo.

Nothing happened that week until Thursday afternoon. It was five o'clock and Uncle Lomax and I were picking peas in the garden when we heard several cars drive up to the house. He told me to go inside; he had business with some men. Halfway across the yard I met the group, led by Father. From the expression on his face, I knew not to ask any questions. After they had passed, I ran behind the hedges to watch.

Uncle Lomax came out of the garden and the group gathered around him under the shade tree. When a deputy handcuffed him and they started to the cars, I ran out to protest. Father picked me up and carried me into the house, where Mother was in tears. After they had taken Uncle Lomax away, I became sick and lost my lunch on the kitchen floor. While cleaning up the mess, Mother gave me permission to go visit Aunt Dell. I needed some sunshine.

The news spread through town and beyond that someone had been arrested and charged with the killing of George Peden. That person was Lomax Sanders, a convicted murderer who had killed again.

With the wedding one week away, activity around the house became frantic. Mother and Sarah were on a mission and Joel and I knew to stay out of their way. Father was notified of the wedding decisions and costs. I overheard him tell Mother this marriage had better last or he wanted his money back. Any talk about Uncle Lomax was discouraged, so I saved my questions for Aunt Dell. Sarah was convinced a permanent blot had been placed on her life and marriage.

The week went by and we had the wedding rehearsal on Friday night, with dinner afterwards, at the First Baptist Church. As flower girl, I was introduced to the Bunns family and had to be on my best behavior. The rehearsal was boring because Beth couldn't be there; she was convicted and serving time for sassing a parent.

Aunt Dell was a big hit dressed in a tight-fitting, flowery dress and large hat, while reading the palms of the Bunns men. Later, at the rehearsal dinner, I sat next to Wayland Bunns, the groom's younger brother. He is three years older than me and had been a smart-aleck at the rehearsal. We ignored each other for most of the meal and then he asked me how old I was.

"Ten," I lied.

He looked me over. "You're kinda of skinny for a ten year old."

"Better'n being stupid," I shot back.

"Boys don't like red-headed beanpoles."

"Better'n having your backside for a last name," I said heatedly. I had heard joking remarks about Sarah marrying a Bunns. With the look he gave me, I knew I had scored a hit. *Pow! Bring it on brother!*

"At least I don't have a crazy aunt and my family doesn't go around murdering people," he said, his voice rising. People next to us stopped talking. Anger rushed through my body and I stood up.

"You're a bastard-butt!" I said, loud enough that the entire room drew quite and everyone turned to see what was happening. As Wayland started to rise, my bony fist caught him flush on the mouth, splattering blood like a ripe tomato hitting a brick wall. A Bunns lady with blood on her dress screamed, and then everyone started talking at the same time. I didn't see Wayland's left, and the next moment I was on the floor with my head ringing. Father appeared, picked me up, and led me out into the hall.

Whipped and in trouble forever, I am not a poplar member of my family. Sarah refuses to look at me or acknowledge my presence in any way. Mother asked her Sunday school class to pray for the family during what she calls 'my trying years'. Aunt Dell let me know she was proud I stood up for the family.

"Besides," she said, "both families have something special to remember about the wedding."

The wedding went off without a hitch, with me sitting between my parents on one side of the church and Wayland sitting between his parents on the other side. I had a big bruise on my face; he had a fat lip. A cousin was my replacement as flower girl and she did just fine. After the reception, Sarah and her new husband went to Gulf Shores in Alabama for their honeymoon. Aunt Dell was right; the last of August sure is hot for anything, including a honeymoon. And, my first public dirty word has come and gone. *Bastard-Butt! Go girl!*

Seven…..the trial

The new school year started the next Monday and word spread about my fight at the rehearsal dinner, plus the bruise was still on my face. For a couple of days, I was the star attraction of the fourth grade. Beth and I are again in the same class with Joyce and Becky. We also have the teacher we wanted, Miss Threadgill.

Everything about the new school year was going great except for Uncle Lomax. He was moved to the jail over in Hattiesburg where, after two weeks, a grand jury returned a murder indictment. From the discussions I overheard, everyone thought the evidence against him was weak. One Sunday afternoon, Father took us to see him at the jail and I carried a carving of a bird he had given me for his cell.

The next Saturday night I spent the night at Beth's house and Aunt Lynn gave me all the details about the upcoming trial.

"The evidence consists mainly of the fact Lomax and Peden were seen talking the week Peden was killed. Uncle Leo had one of his trucks in the repair shop where Peden worked and when it was finished, Peden drove it out to the construction site. There was an exchange of words between him and Lomax, but no one overheard what was said. Two other workers, who saw them talking, say the exchange was heated."

"Is that all?" I asked. Didn't sound like much.

"The argument and the fact he has no alibi from eight o'clock the night of the murder until five the next morning. They know Peden was killed shortly after midnight. Lomax is an easy target because he's a convicted murderer who has served prison time."

"The county DA is running for district judge," Uncle James said. "This is the only case he has and he intends to make the most out of it. The trial date is set for October 14th."

"The family has hired the best defense lawyer in south Mississippi, so I guess it's in God's hands now," Aunt Lynn said.

Later, Beth and I talked about springing Uncle Lomax from jail and making a run for it. We knew we couldn't do anything, but making up escape plans was better than doing nothing. Our best plan consisted of helicopters, bombs, and vicious dogs. It never occurred to us how Uncle Lomax would survive the attack on the jail.

The weeks went by and the whispers grew stronger as the trial grew closer, but none of the kids at school gave us Sanders a problem. My older cousins let it be known they wouldn't stand for any bad-mouthing. Things were also quiet around the house with the wedding over and Sarah gone. Mother refused to allow me to move into Sarah's room. Said my attitude needed improving. Father was busy running for re-election and Joel thought first grade was heaven.

The Sunday morning before the trial started on Monday, Father got up early and went to spend the day at the jail with Uncle Lomax. Mother was left to face the Sunday crowd at church with Joel and me. I could see she wasn't feeling well and didn't want to go, but get ready we did. As we were about to leave, Aunt Dell stormed in and took charge. A tall redhead in a bright red dress and white hat! At church, she spoke and shook hands with everyone, and you would've thought they were her best friends. The entire congregation knew she was in attendance that day. Mother was simply in the background and in a much better mood when we got home. Aunt Dell stayed for lunch and the sun did shine.

The next day the trial started. By Tuesday afternoon the news spread that Aunt Dell would testify for the defense. Great! If anyone can tell them Uncle Lomax didn't kill that fellow, it's Aunt Dell. Now, how do I get out of school and into the courtroom? After supper, Beth called to say Aunt Lynn had informed her the entire family would be in the courtroom tomorrow in support of Uncle Lomax. Could I come? I knew better than to ask Mother so I approached Father when we were alone.

"Can I go spend the night with Beth?" I asked. "Mother is upset and I don't want to do anything to disturb her. I could go to school and then come back home tomorrow afternoon."

"Sounds good," he said. "I'll call Lynn to make sure it's OK."

"I just talked to Beth, and she said Aunt Lynn told her to ask me to come over." Not exactly the truth, but close.

"OK, get your things. Your Mother is asleep; I'll tell her later."

Am I good or what? I could hardly contain my excitement as I raced upstairs to pack.

Aunt Lynn got us to the courthouse the next morning a full hour before the trial was to resume and joined several other family members in the rows behind the defense table. Blue pointed out that the Peden family would sit on the other side. After a while, Father, Uncle Lomax and his attorney, Andrew Farmer, came in. Uncle Lomax gave the family a wave. When Father saw me, he hesitated and then smiled. *Pow! I was going to be OK!*

When the jury was seated, the judge entered and we all stood. After several minutes, Aunt Dell was called to the witness stand to be sworn in. She was wearing a light green dress, matching shoes, a string of pearls and looked like a million bucks. The packed courtroom became quiet.

"Mrs. Thompson, you have come forward with information which pertains to the whereabouts of Lomax Sanders on the night of August 4th of this year," said lawyer Farmer. "It that correct?"

"It is correct," she answered.

"Please tell the court what this information is."

"On the night of August 4th, Lomax Sanders was at my home," Aunt Dell said. Immediately, there was a loud buzz throughout the courtroom. The judge banged his wooden hammer and ordered everyone to be quiet.

"Are you sure you have the correct date?" Farmer asked.

"Yes, because the next day I heard that the body of George Peden had been found. There is no doubt that Lomax was at my home the night of the murder." The buzz started back up and the judge used his hammer again.

"No further questions, your honor."

The prosecuting attorney, Mr. W.L. Simpson, sat momentarily at his table and then approached Aunt Dell. "Mrs. Thompson, if this is true, what was Mr. Sanders doing at your home the night in question?"

"Visiting." A few giggles could be heard. My mind was on full alert... what was Uncle Lomax doing at Aunt Dell's?

"Did anyone besides you see him at your home that night?"

"Not that I know of," Aunt Dell said.

"Had Lomax Sanders visited you before the night in question?"

"No."

"Has he visited your home after that night?"

"Yes."

"Tell me, Mrs. Thompson, how long has your husband been deceased?"

"Objection!" Lawyer Farmer jumped to his feet. "Your Honor, the death of this witness's spouse has nothing to do with this trial."

"Objection sustained," the judge said. "Next question."

Prosecutor Simpson thought for a moment and then asked, "What time did Lomax Sanders leave your home that night?"

"After five o'clock the next morning," Aunt Dell said. I heard gasps and the buzz started again. Uncle Lomax spent the night at Aunt Dell's! Did he sleep in the same room I do when I spend the night at her house? The wooden hammer went into action.

"A murderer, who spent sixteen years in prison, stayed all night at your house?" Mr. Simpson asked.

"Yes."

"Mrs. Thompson, do you have any proof of this?"

Aunt Dell thought for a moment. "Lomax has a tattoo on his left cheek."

Laughter spread throughout the courtroom and the judge was busy with his hammer. I looked at Uncle Lomax and knew he didn't have a tattoo on his face and... Wait... It's on his butt! Beth reached the same conclusion and we both giggled.

"Are you telling this court a naked, convicted murderer spent the night with you?" a frustrated Mr. Simpson asked.

"You ain't naked if you got a tattoo," Aunt Dell said.

Eight.....kinda cute

School is out for the Christmas holidays and Mother finally gave me permission to move into Sarah's bedroom. She waited until my ninth birthday before giving the OK. With the mid-year grades posted, Beth and I are once again at the top of our class. Father lost the sheriff's race and now works for Uncle Leo's construction company. The new sheriff has not arrested anyone for the murder of George Peden. Some folks think Uncle Lomax had something to do with the killing, but the jury said otherwise.

At Christmas dinner, Sarah and Richard announced that a baby will arrive in June. *I'm going to be an aunt!* After talking with Aunt Dell, Beth and I have figured out the details of this baby thing. I'm not sure I like that information...

The day after Christmas, we had another wedding. The weather was warm and it took place in our backyard, a simple affair for Aunt Dell and Uncle Lomax. She said it would be a few weeks before Beth and I could spend the night at their house. Darn!

Tommy Harper moved in down the street and he sits next to me in class. We ride bikes most afternoons and he is teaching me to throw a curve ball.

I think he's kinda cute.

The End

THIRTY-NINE HOURS

Lottie Boggan

SUNDAY-The day before
7:30 A.M.

Yesterday morning I had picked up our wedding photo that presided over a small table in the living room, and looked at it for the thousandth time. Was that really me? That glowing young woman in the arms of her handsome new husband? Where was the glow now? Three short years later.

In the beginning my mother had told everybody. "My Dears. It is a match made in heaven."

And to me she had said, "What a catch for you, Jean Ann. A young surgeon, and so good looking. Honey, you're going to be one rich, happy bride, and have a great life."

But to me it never felt right. I was never comfortable in that role. Not even in the beginning.

He was rough and demanding, and I was shy.

I studied Grant's face in the photograph. Had it been there all the time--- the anger, the attitude that he, the male, was always right? That he brooked no interference? No contradiction? Why hadn't I seen it then?

I set the picture back on the table, this time face down.

That was thirty-nine hours ago

*   *   *

SUNDAY
6:30 P.M.

It had all come down on me last evening. I had planned a special dinner and was right in the middle of cooking it: for an appetizer, a cheese ball rolled in dill weed; a special bottle of chilled red wine in a silver ice bucket; a marinating beef tenderloin; a wild rice casserole; and the makings of a Caesar salad. Candles ready to be lit, soft music on the stereo. Then, with the mood set, we might talk about a baby. If we got that far, in Grant's mind, I'm sure it would be a boy. That's what he'd want, and by God, that's what it'd be. Me, I wouldn't care. I just needed something to love.

The back door slammed while I was mixing up the cheese ball.

I raised my hands, thick with cream cheese and turned to him. I didn't like the way he looked. There was something threatening in his posture, a stance I'd come to dread. "Grant? It's just six thirty. You've never finished your hospital rounds this early. Is anything wrong?"

"You name it and it is." He fisted one hand and smashed it into the other one and then he swore a string of words under his breath, so colorful that it almost burned my ears to hear them.

Hoping to ease the tension, I put out my arms, but he gave a scornful laugh and backed away. "And don't touch me. You've always got something goopy in your hands, just like the damned O.R. nurses."

"I'm sorry," I said, as usual not quite sure what I was apologizing for, only wanting to keep the peace.

He looked around the kitchen, then snatched his stethoscope from around his neck and threw it on the counter. "Don't tell me you've asked company tonight? The last time we entertained it was a complete disaster!" He snorted in disgust. "I'm still embarrassed over that one."

Grant's usual discontent with me hung in the air like a familiar illness. He gave me a hard look then pointed to the wine cooler. "As far as I'm concerned you can pour that cheap Merlot down the drain. It's supposed to be served at room temperature. And after the day I've had, I need something stronger than wine."

"What's wrong?" I asked.

"Tell me what's not!" He glared, and even though I had no idea what had happened, a familiar flash of guilt washed over me. "The hospital administrator called me on the carpet over something that was none of my doing. The head O.R. nurse said I left for the doctor's lounge too soon and let an intern finish a routine surgery. The patient got in trouble, the intern couldn't handle it, and the patient almost died. After this hellacious day even a martini will hardly be strong enough."

He opened the refrigerator door.

My heart was already sinking before he turned to me.

"Where are the olives?"

"I forgot to buy them."

"My God," he yelled. "You don't have the brains that God gave a flea. I've gotta go somewhere and get myself together. To hell with it. I don't give a damn what happens. I can't stay here tonight."

The front door slammed. There was a racket in the garage, then a short while later the screech of tires as he sped down the drive in his Navigator. I heard a bumping noise and knew that he had hitched up his bass boat.

That was twenty-eight hours ago.

*   *   *

SUNDAY
10:30 P.M.

The downpour started after he left. He'll be home any minute, I kept telling myself. He'll have calmed down.

I waited as long as I could, and then started putting away our uncooked meal. I thought about the last time he took out his high powered bass boat. It had acted up, something about the motor. Grant had come home in a fit, grabbed me by the throat and slammed me against the wall like it was my fault. Was that the first time he hit me? I can't even remember. But I can remember that somehow, whatever had happened, I'm always the one to blame.

I crawled into bed by myself.

That was twenty-four hours ago

*　　*　　*

MONDAY-Today
7:30 A.M.

I tossed and turned all night. By early morning I still hadn't heard from Grant. Something bad's wrong. I felt it in my bones but if I called 911 and he was okay and found they were looking for him, he'd kill me. What if they put it on the news? "Prominent Local Doctor Missing?"

I was in a quandary about what to do, feeling that whatever decision I'd make would be the wrong one. At seven thirty-five when the phone rang I was sure it was Grant, but instead it was the anesthesiologist who would be scrubbing with him.

"Where's Grant ?" he asked. " He and I have an early case in about ten minutes and he hasn't shown up."

"He went out to test his boat motor late yesterday afternoon," I said. "And I haven't heard from him. I was hoping this was him calling just now."

There was a moment of silence. "Have you called the police?"

"Not yet."

"You'd better do it."

I hung up and dialed 911.

That was fifteen hours ago.

*　　*　　*

MONDAY
10:00 P.M.

When the doorbell rang, I was tempted not to answer it. At best a nosy reporter might be outside, at worst, the police with bad news. Then I thought better of it. I really had no choice. With my legs trembling from fear of what I might be facing, I got up from the kitchen table, turned on the back porch light and opened the door. A silver scarf of wind-driven rain whipped my face. It was so dark outside that at first I couldn't tell who stood in the black shadows, right beyond the glow of light from my kitchen window. Then I realized it was Dero.

I didn't know whether to be relieved or apprehensive, she had always affected my life, often in not too subtle ways. Although she had never been in our apartment, somehow I had known she would come tonight. She had been my best friend for years and sometimes it almost seemed as if we could read each other's minds. I beckoned, and she came into my kitchen, fast and hard, as if a heavy burst of wind had shoved her. Bracing herself on a counter she rubbed rainwater off her shoes and onto a green chenille floor mat.

"I brought these for you." A bouquet of white carnations was carelessly flung into the sink, much as if she were tossing a slow pitch soft ball. She dropped her wet trench coat across the glass-top kitchen table, hesitated a moment, then impulsively held out her arms, grasped my neck and held me close. She kissed my cheek. For just a moment when I felt the cold strength of her lips I wanted to lean against her, but as if sensing we shouldn't go there, she turned away even before I did. She reached for a chair, then hesitated. "This isn't his chair, is it? I don't want to take his place," she said with more than a hint of sarcasm in her voice.

When I said, "No," she pulled it out from under the table and sat down, spreading her legs, her blue slacks stretched tightly around them.

"I heard the news bulletin on the radio. I thought you might need me. Old friends and all of that." She took a deep breath. "Where's your mom? I thought she'd be with you."

"She does relish the dramatic," I said, "and I don't need her theatrics tonight."

"You said it, I didn't," Dero shot back at me.

"I asked her not to come, I told her I was better off by myself," I said. "But somehow I knew you'd be here. Your being with me makes me feel better."

"I wasn't sure whether you wanted company or not, but we've always been there for each other." She nodded her head, as if she were already agreeing to something neither of us could name or understand. Maybe, without us saying it, we were beginning again where we had left off.

When we were teenagers we were inseparable. Our mothers were afraid they were raising a couple of queer girls, but they just didn't understand and we laughed behind their backs. Dero and I liked to lie for each other, sleep together and tell secrets. It was just the two of us, locked in our own safe world. For a long time nobody else could come in--especially boys.

Dero had a beautiful face, delicate bone structure, but where she was concerned, her beauty was almost a senseless thing. Totally indifferent, she cared nothing for it one way or the other. For starters, she was tall, too tall for the boys, and to make matters worse she had a throaty voice that would probably have turned males on if she could have been sawed off about five inches. None of them wanted to go out with a medium-sized Amazon though, and in so many ways her size and her voice had shaped her, had made her what she was. You could tell by the frantic way Dero acted around boys that she knew she was a lost cause where they were concerned. When I first started dating, I wouldn't go unless my date could find somebody for her too. That ended when my mother sent me away to college in another state. In my mother's mind, I think she tried to head off what she saw as a possible family scandal looming on the horizon.

With me in one state, and Dero in another we drifted apart. We remained friends, but after that it was never the same. Shortly after graduation I met Grant, thought I was in love, and we got married.

*   *   *

Back in our home state, before my husband and I returned so he could set up his medical practice, Dero made a life and name for herself, cultivating her voice and brains. She became known as talented and artsy. I guess she has sung at more weddings than anybody in town. She sang a soul-touching *Ave Maria* at mine.

In the last few years our encounters had been infrequent and guarded, so I looked at her closely for the first time in months. Her clipped black hair had faded slightly, gray was invading. She looked older, but somehow a little more regal than the last time I had seen her. And now we were together.

"How are you?" She studied me with her slate gray eyes.

"Right at this moment, I'm not feeling so good."

"As always, you look like a million dollars to me." She ran the palm of her hands across the table top.

For a few, tension filled moments we sat and looked at each other. Finally, to give both of us something to do, I reached across the table, touched her hand and asked if she wanted some coffee.

She nodded. I got up and went to the stove and turned the gas burner up to high. When the water boiled I poured it into a cup, mixed it with instant, then put in two heaping spoonfuls of sugar--sweet, the way I knew she liked, with a lot of cream. "I know it's not good for you," I said.

"So are a lot of other things we do," she answered. "On a scale of one to ten, it's a minus."

I was nervous. She was here. He wasn't and I didn't know if he ever would be again.

"Men," I said.

"Not all. Just some men," she answered.

My hands trembling, I spilled coffee on the floor. "I'd better get this up." After I handed Dero the cup, I bent over and wiped up the coffee with a damp dishtowel. "Grant thinks I'm clumsy and messy." I halfway laughed. "He'd be mad. He doesn't suffer fools well."

"He?" With a question in her voice, she emphasized the word. "He, doesn't suffer fools well?"

When I raised up, I saw she watched me, hard.

"On a weekend like this. That river's an icy no-mans land," she said. " And with small craft warnings he goes out in a boat. Alone." She shook her head. "That's foolish. You don't have him trained very well."

"Training about anything is not an option in our house."

She shrugged her shoulders. Slowly she sipped her coffee, puckering her lips, blowing the hot steam away. "That's begging for trouble. God, what in the world possessed him? You'd think any fool would know better." She leaned her head back.

"You don't know him like I do," I said. "He's like a lot of surgeons. A control freak. He thinks he's a law unto himself."

"Life doesn't work that way. Even I, the non-medical, renegade girlfriend know better than to challenge the gods and go out in this kind of weather." She put her coffee down, got up and went over to the sink.

"I guess you heard it on the news," I said. "He didn't come home. That's why I notified the authorities. He's been missing since last night. It's windy and cold, and the rivers up." Even to myself it sounded as I were laying the groundwork and preparing myself for something tragic.

Dero stretched across the sink, raised the blind a little and looked out, I guess to check and see if it was still raining, because it was pitch black and there was nothing else to see. She must have thought she needed to reassure me, because she turned around. "Yes, but he can take care of himself." Her eyes gave away a flash of anger. "Men usually can."

She picked up the bouquet of flowers she had brought in, opened the cabinet beneath the sink, and dropped them into the garbage. "They were already shriveling around the edges. These must have been half dead to begin with. It was a courtesy thing, and it gave me something to hold on to when I came in here." She went back to the table, hitched her slacks at the knees and slipped back into her chair. "You always did know how to please me." She picked up her coffee and took a long drink, "You do fix a good cup of coffee.

"It's just instant," I reminded her. "But I remember how you like it."

Bending forward, she ran her fingers far down into the pocket of her tight slacks, feeling for a cigarette. She found them and held the pack up to me, but I shook my head.

"For the most part, I've given it up."

She gave me an amused smile. "There's nothing worse or more self-righteous and boring than a reformed sinner."

"Oh, I still do a little back-sliding," I said, even though it wasn't true.

Pulling her lighter out, she flipped it several times, but the flint didn't catch.

"I gave the police and the Sheriff's department our unlisted number," I said. "They'll let me know if they hear anything. Or find anything." Saying that seemed to place him back in time and I felt like I was going to cry. I didn't want her to see me do that. Although I knew I'd have to open the windows and air the room out before Grant got home, I got up to find some matches. Opening a drawer, I rumbled through it, found a book and tossed them to her. She caught them easily and lit her cigarette.

Dero looked embarrassed, like she wanted to say something but didn't know how so she drew deeply on her cigarette and blew out a veil of smoke.

We sat and waited. Finally she slid down in her chair, stretching her legs in front of her. "Sorry I haven't called or been by. Seems like I'm in a rut, just like everybody else. That's not much of an excuse, but it's the truth."

"That's okay. We've been busy." I tried to laugh, but even to me it sounded forced. "Moving back home. Starting a medical practice. Since he's a surgeon, you could call 'adjusting' the operative word so to speak." I looked down at my hands. "And with all of that going on, we haven't had too much time either."

There was so much I wanted to say and now that I had the chance the right words just wouldn't come. "It's silly, but you know, he's always been jealous of you." I looked to see how she would take what I'd said, hoping it wouldn't offend her.

"He called me 'the smart giraffe with a case of laryngitis,'" she said, "And thought it was funny."

"I didn't," I said.

Her face gave away nothing of what she was thinking, but her words were different. "I could have told you; he wouldn't understand about us." She straightened and the chair grated on the floor. "I knew he never liked me. Or approved of my lifestyle." She raised her voice and tilted her chin when she said this.

My old protective mode with Dero kicked in, I wanted to comfort her. I wanted to go and try to make it all right between us, but when I started to get up, she shook her head and motioned me back with her hand.

"I don't care what he thinks, Dero. As far as you're concerned, I've made it plain. That subject's off limits."

"There was a time when you were my best friend. More than that." She picked up a spoon and slowly stirred her coffee, her dove gray eyes thoughtful as she watched the dark liquid twirling around the spoon. "I thought my world was safe with you. Our world. Then one day I turned around and you were an ROTC sponsor, marching in parades, riding in convertibles. And I, your admirer, stood by myself on the sidewalk. But that still didn't end our friendship. Your mother and mine finally took care of that. And, I'm sure you were ready for a change and played your part in it too." She laughed bitterly, laying the spoon down. "Oh, those horrible days. What a fool I was. When you left it showed all over my face how hurt I was." She leaned back in her chair as if she had a weight on her shoulders. "Everybody laughed. Even people I counted as friends. I was frantic. Couldn't help myself. But that was a long time ago. The past is dead and I've come a long way since then."

She puffed out a large smoke ring and watched it fade.

"I'm sorry. He won't let us have an ashtray in the house." I pushed a saucer to her. "Use this."

"You and I have both moved on and built another life, but I've never stopped missing you. Our friendship," she said. She took a long, last drag off her cigarette and crushed it into the saucer. "It left a void in my life."

"I never meant to hurt you."

"I know." Dero got up quickly like she was going to leave, but instead she came and stood by me, cupping her hand on my head. I remembered how it was. I wanted her to stroke my hair, so I could turn my head up and down against her hand which I knew was firm yet gentle, but even before I could do it, as if sensing this was off limits, she moved away, whispering, "It's been so goddamn lonesome."

She went over to the sink, poured out the remainder of her coffee and ran some water into the cup. When she turned back to me, her teary eyes were almost iridescent, like morning fog melting in the sunshine. "Are you happy?"

The question in her voice, almost as if she wanted to ask a favor of me and didn't quite know how, made my heart ache and my throat feel tight. "I guess. I want to be. I try. A lot of the time I feel like I'm dressed in someone else's clothes and only going through the motions of what I'm supposed to do."

"It shouldn't be that way." She bit her bottom lip and shook her head.

"Oh, Dero." I needed to make her understand. "Just like everything and everybody, we got bogged down in everyday routines. He likes to work hard and play hard. He has goals. I guess he loves me." When I said this I felt like I was cheating on him, and for some reason I couldn't understand, I wanted to explain. "He likes to sleep with me, if that means anything."

There was a moment of quiet, and then she laughed. "Okay. But where do you fit into the picture? Sounds like big I, little you, to me."

"Most of the time with Grant, it's like I'm living with a stranger." When I said this I felt as if I'd crossed a line. Things may change, I thought, but I'm not sure that they'll ever be any better.

A funny look crossed Dero's face as if she expected me to say something more. She folded her hands against her chest, almost as if she were praying.

When I didn't say anything else, she stood and stretched, arching her back, pushing her thin breast bone up. "If you want, we could turn the TV or radio on. We're just sitting here like a couple of damn Sphinxes, waiting for the other shoe to drop. You'd probably hear something before the station will, but it'll help pass the time."

I shook my head. "Don't turn it on. I'll step outside and see what the weather's doing. It's almost eleven and we're supposed to have a break in this storm before midnight."

I got up, opened the door, went down the steps and stood in the yard. The storm had let up a little. It was intermittent now, thin streams of rain slapped my face, like an old sewing machine, with its pedal pumping up and down and pushing out spurts of filmy material. Cold water puddled around my feet, seeping into the seams of my tennis shoes. Soaked weeds waved in standing water, looking like a dead person's hair. For a moment I listened to the rainfall and couldn't help wondering if Grant could hear it too. Somewhere I had a husband who might be face down floating in a whirlpool of river water.

I went back into the kitchen, scraping our warped door as I pulled it to. The kitchen was empty but a light came from our bedroom. I slipped off my wet shoes and walked bare-footed down the narrow hallway. Dero stood by my dresser. "I wanted to look for something. I hope it was okay." She held up a large, green brocaded jewelry box.

I sank down on the bed. Dero sat beside me and put the box between us. She opened several small drawers, one after the other, pushing necklaces, earrings and pins around with her fingers.

"After all these years." She pulled out a gold charm bracelet tangled in with the other jewelry and shook it loose.

"Do you remember?" she asked. "We both swore we'd never let ourselves grow up and get old; we'd never grow hair under our arms, and we'd never walk on shaky high heels that made your seat stick out. We would do something about it."

"I remember," I said. "You and I, we lit candles and shaved. We draped towels over our heads, trying to look like nuns. Sacreligous girl played holy sisters and prayed. Surely God would point his finger down and do what we wanted. But God, nature, or whatever you want to call it, let time have its way."

Dero looked at me and rubbed the gold with her fingers, making the bracelet jingle. I reached out my hand. She dropped the cool circlet into it. A single gold disc covered with a thin piece of glass hung from the links. I turned it over and read the familiar inscription.

"True friends forever.

Happy 13th, Love, Dero."

"I had saved my allowance for weeks to buy it for you. We pricked our fingers with a needle, pressed them together, and let our blood mix. It's still here, under this glass covering."

She gripped the side of the bed with her hands. "I can't believe you kept this." She reached for my other hand and held it. "It's not too late for us, you know." Her face was soft, and she pressed my hand gently. "I wish you'd come and see my place. I think you'd like it. It's really nice. Much better than what I had when we were growing up."

Pain had honed and made my senses sharper and although it almost hurt to breathe, for the first time in a long while, I felt alive.

I squeezed the bracelet tight and looked at Dero. There was the same shadowy look of hope I had seen in Grant's eyes before I finally gave in and we slept together.

"Let's don't have secrets," she said. "I can read you like a book. What happened?"

"We had a fight. He told me he couldn't stay here."

"Did he threaten to do anything to himself?" She cut straight to my secret fears.

"Not in so many words. But I didn't tell the police or the sheriff everything. I just said he went out to test his new boat motor. The truth was, Grant said he was going to the river and he didn't care what happened."

A helpless feeling of frustration and anger had me close to tears. "Bottom line, I think he loves himself too much to do anything. For his sake, I hope so. But, even if he was just trying to scare, or punish me, it's freezing and the river's at flood stage. He likes to run that boat wide open."

"Would you feel better if we went out to the dam?" she asked.

"No."

"It's your call. It always has been." Dero reached for my arm. She snapped the bracelet on my wrist and hooked the safety catch. "It still fits." She leaned forward and gently brushed hair away from my forehead, and then she sat back. "You always did have tiny bones."

Neither of us moved. Minutes inched along, as if we were honor bound to stay at the wake of a distant relative, waiting for the proper amount of time to pass so we could take our leave.

She rose suddenly. "I guess it's time for me to go." Dero put my jewelry box back in the drawer and left our bedroom.

The phone rang. With a shiver, I got to my feet, reached for the phone, and leaned against the wall.

"We found a capsized boat," the sheriff said. "It doesn't look good but there are dozens of sand bars and finger islands in that part of the river. I've got the police helicopter searching. I want you to know, we'll do everything possible to find your husband. Such a fine doctor. A fine young man, with a bright future ahead of him."

My teeth chattered so violently it was hard to get the words out. "Let me give you a cell phone number where I can be reached." With trembling hands, I hung up the phone, picked up my makeup bag and grabbed a change of clothes.

I closed the back door, put my key in the lock and turned it.

The storm had passed. The night was a black velvet evening cape, sprinkled with rhinestone stars and fastened with a moon-pearl clasp.

Dero waited at the bottom of the steps.

MONDAY
10:30 P.M.

Our time had come.

YANKEE FATHER

Carlene Singleton

1947

"We can't even move," Charlotte said tearfully. "We can't pay the rent we already owe."

Her young husband, Johnny, swallowed the last of his allotment of coffee for that morning and glared down at the cheap formica table.

It was a miserable way to start the day, and Charlotte had hoped their baby, Carrie, would sleep until Johnny went job hunting. Carrie was about two years old with fair skin, blue eyes and light brown ringlets like her mother. She was also awake.

Charlotte changed the baby's clothes and took her back to the table, where she opened her sweater and wrapped it around Carrie to warm her.

"Well, we sure as hell have got to do something," Johnny said. "I'm not begging him for more time again." His hand on the table was curled into a fist.

In New York he could have worked at menial labor on the docks. But he was in Mississippi, where the war had brought him for flight school when he was barely eighteen, and where he had met and married Charlotte before he shipped out for England. In Mississippi there was white work and black work. He was white, so manual labor was closed to him. Charlotte's family tolerated him for her sake and Carrie's, but to them as well as to everyone else, he was Irish, Catholic, but worst of all--a yankee. He couldn't have been more unwanted in the South if he had tried.

Charlotte opened her mouth to speak, but Johnny leaned toward her and all but growled, "Don't even say it. We're not asking your family for anything else. I can take care of my own goddamn family."

His voice frightened Carrie and she began to cry. Charlotte's heart jumped too, at the tone and the language. She wasn't used to the harsh language Johnny had brought south with him. Southern men didn't swear in front of women the way he did.

"Carrie, sit next to Daddy and I'll fix your cereal," Charlotte said, wanting to change the focus of the conversation. She sat her next to Johnny. But Carrie stood up. She wanted to go with her mother.

"Siddown, kid," Johnny said, turning his head toward her but not looking at her.

His thick brows were drawn together. His face was darkly shaded with beard stubble that ran up into thick black hair. His lack of attention toward her, his deep voice and angry expression frightened her. She didn't move.

"Do you want a lickin'?" He turned again and this time looked up at her.

Carry didn't understand lickin', and didn't know if she wanted one or not. Johnny grabbed her arm and jerked her down onto the seat. "Stay there," he said, not looking at her again.

Johnny hadn't expected to become a father at twenty and he had wanted a boy. He didn't know anything about girls. Carrie's diapers, ruffled dresses and bows were a mystery to him. He could barely grasp her shoe laces to tie her little shoes. He also had no idea how to affect a soft voice when he spoke to her or how to play with her.

*   *   *

Out on the streets, Johnny found an abandoned newspaper in a cafe and marked every possibility. As he walked along one of the main streets of Jackson with the wind in his face, he was shivering and it infuriated him. It's spring, for Chrissake, and I'm cold—in Mississippi. There's snow on the ground up home. He knew he was cold from lack of food and it scared him. He had experienced hunger when he was a child in the depression, living in the slums of New York. People were so poor there that long ago it had been nicknamed, "Hell's Kitchen." It was the specter that haunted him now— that his wife and child might end up in such a place.

*   *   *

After Johnny left to look for work, Charlotte spent her days reading and smoking her small ration of cigarettes. She had been a spoiled and rebellious sixteen-year-old when she met Johnny. She told him she was eighteen, so he wouldn't think she was a kid. Carrie was left to amuse herself. She looked at the pictures in the Little Golden Books her grandmother had brought her, and watched out the window as people passed by in the street below.

*   *   *

When Carrie got hungry again, Charlotte emptied the remaining baby cereal into the bowl, tapping the box to get every flake. She poured the last of the milk into her bottle with enough warm water to fill it. She gave her all the baby food that was left, hoping Carrie would nap longer. The baby would go hungry again, but at least today Charlotte prayed she wouldn't cry from hunger pains all afternoon.

*   *   *

After futile hours of walking, Johnny hit the door of a drug store so hard the waitress behind the counter looked up, startled.

"Water, no ice," he said, snatching a chair out from a table, twirling it around and sitting in it backwards. He took the piece of newspaper from his pocket and lit one of his few remaining cigarettes. Well, I've been turned down by most of the good businesses in this burg. Now I guess I have to beg for work at some of the crappiest.

As he puffed on his cigarette his thoughts turned to Charlotte and the baby they hadn't expected. Childhood mumps was supposed to have left him sterile, so his plans never included kids. Charlotte had been thrilled he couldn't have children. Now he was the father of a little girl, and Charlotte wanted to stay near her mother to help with the baby.

On the outside, the former Army-Air-Corp lieutenant looked confident and calm, an attitude he had learned to affect at briefings before flying his Thunderbolt over Germany just a couple of years before. But on the inside, the scared and angry kid in him was as deflated as a torn balloon.

He closed his eyes and saw the woods outside Tarrytown, New York, where he had hunted before he dropped out of school to enlist. He could smell the winter air of the woods and the moisture of the snow. It seemed if he opened his eyes he would be there--before the war. No dead buddies, no wife and baby, no walking the streets of Jackson, Mississippi, begging for work. Back then he had planned a wonderful life in the wilderness of Alaska, and when he married Charlotte, she couldn't wait to go with him. Their war letters were full of plans of living in the wilderness and the house they would build there. As soon as he came home from the war, they would be off to Alaska. But Charlotte had gotten pregnant right before he shipped out for England. When he came home, Carrie had been born, and Alaska had been out of the question. A little more fatigue and he wouldn't have been able to blink back the tears.

*   *   *

Two hours later Johnny erupted from a hotel like he'd been shot from a gun. He had taken all the rejection he could stand for one day. The people in Jackson don't want to hear a yankee accent, eh? Shit! I didn't fight them in the Civil War. Everywhere I turn, I'm not good enough. I'm a yankee, I'm Catholic, I'm Irish, I didn't kill enough Krauts in the war, my eyes are too brown today to put hazel on the application.

Staying in Mississippi so Charlotte and Carrie could be near Charlotte's family was turning out to be a far greater sacrifice than he had expected.

*   *   *

Johnny came back to the room furious. He cursed Jackson for being so small and backward. He cursed the men who turned him away for his yankee accent. He cursed the ones who wanted him to have experience. "What the fucking hell is an ex-fighter pilot supposed to do? I couldn't finish high school and go fight the Gerrys at the same time. Now nobody will even give me a chance to show'em what else I can do. Somebody start another damned war," he added under his breath. He furiously scrubbed his hands with a tiny piece of soap.

*   *   *

As her father raged, Carrie crawled to the farthest corner of the room. She lay down quietly, holding her books against her chest and curled up into a tiny ball, with her back to Johnny and Charlotte.

"Johnny, please, don't use that language around Carrie. I don't want her hearing those words. I know you're mad and frustrated," she pressed her fist against her mouth to stifle the tears, "So am I." And I'm terrified, she thought. I never dreamed we could end up still in Jackson and stone broke.

"Yeah . . . I know," he said wearily. He stood by the sink, drying his hands on an old dishtowel.

*   *   *

Later Johnny left and came back with somethings Charlotte called Krystals. Carrie wasn't hungry just then and refused to eat one. They smelled funny.

*   *   *

After Charlotte put her to bed, Carrie's tummy started to hurt again. She cried, and reached up toward the cabinet where the baby food was kept, but there wasn't any.

"Don't start that," Charlotte said. "We told you to eat when we did. There's nothing left. Lie down and go to sleep."

Carrie's stomach burned. She cried harder. Charlotte shouted at her, spanked her, laid her back down repeatedly. Even Johnny said, "Go to sleep," from across the room. Carrie cried even louder. Charlotte jerked her to her feet and shook her. "You stop that goddamn crying, or you're going to get the spanking of your life," she screamed.

Johnny jumped up and ran to catch Charlotte's arm. "Let go, you'll hurt her," he said.

"I want to hurt her! You're not here every day, listening to her whining and crying for something to eat. I'm sick to death of it," Charlotte said, angrily pulling away from him. "We should be in Alaska right now!" She snatched the almost empty cigarette pack from the table and went out, slamming the door. Johnny could hear her stomping down the stairs, leaving him alone with Carrie.

*   *   *

Carrie's eyes widened in fear when he reached for her, and he saw it. He lifted her and gently dried her face with a cloth diaper. Her body shook with sobs, but she stopped crying.

"Poor kid," he said softly. "I don't know why in hell God gave a son-of a bitch like me a little girl. He wiped her nose again. "I've been so damned mad I couldn't take care of you and your mother. I haven't been thinking about anything but getting a job."

He sat down and held her on his knee. "I feel guilty. And I never thought about how you felt. You've got an empty gnawing gut—I know how that feels." He cuddled her against his chest.

She breathed a sobbing sigh and was still.

" Well, no kid of mine is going to sleep hungry, if I have to steal your food."

He took Carrie to the top of the stairs and called Charlotte. "I'm going out," he said.

She ran up the stairs. "Where are you going?"

"To find her something to eat. Don't spank her or yell at her while I'm gone. It's not her fault she doesn't get three squares a day like a kid should It's mine."

*   *   *

When Johnny came back, Carrie lay in her crib sucking a pacifier. The pains had stopped and she was almost asleep. He had a small paper sack. Inside was a little bag of candy corn. He opened it and handed it to her.

"It's not what you need kid," he said, " but it'll make you feel full."

She rolled over toward him, shoving the candy into her mouth two pieces at a time, her eyes fixed on his.

Returning her gaze, he suddenly realized she wasn't a little stranger. She was part of him. She was his parents' only grandchild. He had been seeing her almost as a member of Charlotte's family, not his. She was tiny and female, but she was still a child; and God had made him her father. Something inside him relaxed, and his face softened. He smiled as his little girl closed her eyes, happy with what he had been able to provide.

ANTICS

Marion Barnwell

I was planting my silver corn and staking the tomato plants in the side lot when he roared up, hopped over the door of his Cadillac convertible. Here comes trouble, I thought.

The scarecrow I'd ordered off the internet had come in the day's mail. I had already dug me a hole and stuck him in, congratulating myself on getting a jump on the birds. My garden is a solace. Plant squash seed and you get squash. Tomato seed and you get a tomato. With people, it's a crap shoot.

I dusted myself off and took another look at the man who would turn our lives upside down over the next few days. The same breeze drying and cooling my sweat-drenched limbs seemed to annoy him. He was trying to keep it from messing up his tie and ruffling his coiffed salt and pepper hair. He made a call on his cell phone, snapped it shut, grabbed a cooler from the backseat, and stood back a minute to admire his car. He's mighty proud of it—or what it represents—seven juicy dealerships across the South.

I headed to the front porch to greet him. "Dewey, my man," he said, slapping me on the back a little too energetically. I caught him when he stumbled over the step that needs bracing. I should never have agreed to buy this old house for Louise. She'd been born in it and so had Rip. We'd all three lived our entire lives right here in Midnight, Mississippi.

The house is an old Victorian, historic now. The upkeep is outta sight. I might have afforded seven Cadillac dealerships myself if I hadn't bought out Rip's part of the house. Every day I wake up and say, "Well, Mr. House, what can I do for you today?"

We'd planned on filling it up with children, but we only had the one. Louise might've been different if she'd had more. Sally's never been much of a challenge. She's easy-going, like me.

I stood at the door while Rip lifted his sister off her feet and swung her around. "What'd you bring us?" she asked, pointing at the cooler. He lifted the lid, fished out a quart of oysters and a bottle of champagne.

"Oh, goody, what're we celebrating?" Her voice had already climbed to giddy. The two of them always start out so hopeful.

"Anything you like. The full moon, the summer solstice or . . . the new dealership I just acquired in Atlanta." Louise squealed. I showed polite interest, but his false modesty didn't hold any truck with me.

He busied himself uncorking the champagne. He didn't bother to check his watch and repeat the tired old line about it being five o'clock somewhere. He knew it was useless trying to be clever in a place where drinking is an art form and justifying it is pure poetry.

Louise can't hold her liquor, though, never could. Goes straight to her head and makes her mean. For these thirty years I've been married to her, I've pointed out this cold fact to both of them. But here he goes, popping the cork at three in the afternoon. We toasted to his success.

"Come on, Dewey," said Louise when the bottle was empty, "let's fix a feast for the Prodigal Son—or brother--as the case may be." She marched off to the kitchen, where I knew she'd flutter around uselessly from pan to pot while I put something together. I thawed the beans and corn I put up last year and fried up a mess a catfish I'd caught myself and frozen.

"Y'all remember the last time I came for a visit, the toilet wouldn't flush," said Rip, settling in at the dinner table.

We looked at each other. Louise had discovered the toilet threatening to overflow just before he'd arrived. She thought it was funny. Relished the idea of Mr. Bigshot having to plunge. But I'd taken pity and sneaked in after him every time, knowing how he'd take it out on Louise if I didn't.

"You weren't supposed to know about that," she said.

We finished supper and took our cigarettes and glasses of gin to the porch. "Remember that time Harley and I stirred up that ole bee hive?" Rip began. Harley was their brother who died. He'd been blown up by a terrorist bomb in Barcelona eighteen years ago. He'd worked for the CIA. He was twenty-eight when he died.

"Remember?" he repeated. We told him we did.

"All my idea," said Rip.

"Sure it was," said Louise, laughing, knowing nothing had ever been his idea.

I'd loved Harley too. If I ever got a word in edgewise, I could have told Harley stories starting before we started school. Like the time he picked every flower blooming in our yard and presented them to his mother.

"You ever know a bird dog to tree a hive of bees?" Rip asked Harley, our spaniel, scratching him under the chin. That's right. Harley. Louise named him that despite my objections. "No?" Rip went on. "Well, that's what our dog Splasher did that warm June day. Treed them bees. If he hadn't barked at 'em, me and your namesake might never have known they were up there.

"Harley talked me into going up first. I shimmied up that ole tree, thinking about nothing but tasting the honey on Mama's biscuits. First sting and I came down a lot faster than I went up. Streaked across the pasture, Harley fast behind me, the bees hot behind him. I still feel bad about Harley getting most of the stings. 'Specially with it being my idea."

"He did make you go up first," Louise pointed out.

"Now, Honey," I said.

"How 'bout the time I caught the big one?" Rip asked.

"Tell," I said.

"Oh, for Heaven's sake, that's enough," said Louise. She got out another cigarette and I stood to light it.

"Tell us about your new girlfriend, or something. Iris, isn't it?" Rip shrugged.

"Hellfire, Rip. I know that look. Means you've dumped her already, haven't you?"

"Shut up, Louise." He got that determined look, resting his elbows on his knees and staring out at the gathering dark. Now he was telling it for himself. "Harley'd just turned eleven, and I was still ten, and it was the first time Daddy let us fish by ourselves out on the Quiver River. I got ready to cast and rared back with my pole. It snagged on something. I tugged on the line, and Harley let out a yell. I turned around. Then I followed the line with my eyes right up to the back of Harley's shoulder. I'd caught a big one, all right!" I laughed in spite of myself even though that one had worn thin as a penny run over by a train.

"Then Harley spotted the car stuck in the mud," said Louise not able to resist goading him. I swear.

"It was ME," said Rip. "I was the one who spotted it."

"Whatever," said Louise.

"Spotted it a mile off," said Rip. "So then Harley starts yelling to the folks. Yelling and waving with that ole hook glinting in the sun and dancing on his shoulder. And the closer we get, the more I'm thinking it can't be, not in a million years."

"But it is," said Louise, swinging her foot.

"Yep. Dr. Harrison himself," said Rip. "Him and his wife and all four children jumping and hollering like monkeys."

"Imagine," said Louise.

"So we bounce through the ruts they made in the pasture and pull up alongside. Doc tells us they're stuck and we tell him we can see that."

"You're in luck, Doc Harrison," Louise mimicked, beating Rip to the punch line. "We got a chain, if you got a scalpel."

We all lit up again. She's just jealous. Part of it is those seven—no, eight—Cadillac dealerships. But mostly, it's the time he got with Harley, and her a girl and four years older.

The evening wore on. A drowsiness crept into Rip's voice and the stories wore down like popcorn when it's about to finish popping. Louise was the first to turn in, then Rip. Usually, by this time, they're arguing over the make of Harley's first b.b. gun or whether he had Mrs. Pigott in First Grade or Miss Murphy. I knew better than to hope for anything.

I climbed the stairs, wondering for the upteenth time what I'd done to be inflicted with these two. I buttoned my pajamas and climbed into bed. I'm a simple man. I work at a hardware store, an old-fashioned one with real people who work there and can help you find what you need. Want a rake, we'll find you one.

Last time Rip came, I woke up one morning and they'd both disappeared. I'd left them sitting on the porch drinking gin, and when I got up, they were gone.

I went outside to look for them and heard a bunch of hollering from the direction of the playground two blocks away. I got over there quick as I could, arrived about the same time as Jimmy Jay. Jimmy Jay's an old high school buddy and a cop.

It had been raining for three days. And there they were, slugging it out on the playground and covered in mud. He shoved her and she kicked him where the sun don't shine. Every dog in town was barking. Jimmy Jay threw them in the back of his squad car and took 'em to police headquarters. I had to pay their fine for disturbing the peace. Shoulda kept 'em in jail, my opinion.

One time Louise stole Rip's precious Cadillac and took his credit card. She took off in the middle of the night, high-tailed it to the coast, and went on a spending spree. When Rip got wind of it, he sold her five-year-old Buick to the junk man for four hundred dollars and pocketed it. Told her it was shock payment.

But this time, after the champagne and then the gin, I woke up and looked at the clock saying four a.m. For a minute, I was fool enough to think nothing had happened. I can still recall how good it felt to wallow in the thought that they'd finally grown up, their antics over with. But then I reached over and realized there was no Louise, only air where her body should have been. I stumbled downstairs, threw open the front door. She wasn't on the porch.

I hurried back upstairs, flung open the door to Rip's room and was mightily relieved to find him in bed, snoring away. I went down to the porch, sat on the stoop, and lit up. Sometimes I felt like I was married to the both of them. Make that all three.

In the middle of dinner Sally called from her home in Eugene, Oregon. I asked her where she was so I could picture it. In her kitchen, she told me. I tried to picture her there and told her about Rip's visit. She told me to remember my blood pressure and not let them get to me. Just before we said goodbye, she said, "Daddy, you're too nice," and I hung up the phone thinking how nice is not a word I care to be remembered by.

I thought about Louise out there somewhere cooking up something, anything to get to Rip, to let him know the spirit of Harley is in her every bit as much as it's in him. The dog hauled himself off the doormat and plopped down at my feet, waiting to be scratched. I scratched him awhile and mashed out my cigarette.

I could go after her like I always did, I thought. Or I could do something different. I walked over to my garden and kicked a rock. The scare-crow, shimmering in the moonlight, gave me a ghostly grin.

About the time the sun showed up, she did too. She was walking along on the other side of the fence. From where I sat, I could only see her from the waist up. She was looking all perky and casual, normal even, except she was either talking to herself or somebody I couldn't see. A dwarf wouldn't surprise me. She came on through the gate, and I saw she was leading a goat. "Hey, Dewey," she said. "This is Fred."

She's got this thing about animals, or so she says. Once, she borrowed Earnest Nelson's horse and rode it right into our living room. I swear. If she likes animals so much, why can't she watch a squirrel gather nuts and be satisfied?

Rip tried not to let on, but I could tell he thought the goat was a big fat hoot. Didn't take that goat half an hour to discover my garden and start nibbling on the tender leaves of my tomato plants. "That's it," I said.

I strode off to the store and told Johnny—he's my assistant manager--he'd be in charge for awhile. Told him it was high time he learned to run the place. Then I walked around the block to see Miriam at the travel agency. She's a straight shooter like me, somebody I can understand. "Miriam," I told her, "get me on a train to the west coast."

"Yessir, Mister Dewey. Northern route or Southern?"

"Whichever's quicker."

"You got it, Mister Dewey."

*   *   *

Next morning when I didn't come down to breakfast, Louise came to see about me for a change. "Dewey, what on earth are you doing?" she asked.

"What's it look like? I'm packing my grip." I squeezed the suitcase together, fastened the locks.

"Where are you going?" she asked, her voice rising.

"I'm going on a trip. Now listen. While I'm gone, you'll have a lot to do. First, you'll need to make a choice between me and the goat. After that, you'll have to decide if it's me or Rip."

I saw her cranking up to argue with me and put a hand up to stop her. "You don't have to decide right now. Just think about it while I'm gone."

She looked at me like I'd just poured a bucket of water over her head. "Well, I swear," she said.

*   *   *

Before I knew it, I was studying gardens, trees, and crops through a train window, traveling along the Northern route all the way to Seattle with a stopover in Eugene, Oregon, where I'd finally get to see Sally in her kitchen.

For awhile, I held onto the satisfying feeling and told myself it was well worth the loss of one tomato crop. What I didn't predict was how my last sight of them would play out over and over in my mind.

As I crossed the foyer with my suitcase, I glanced into the parlor. They were sitting in the two wingbacks, facing each other and holding onto each other's outstretched hands. Holding on for dear life, looked like. And crying. That's what took me awhile. They were crying. Talking and sobbing and crying. Grieving for their dead brother, a grieving I could've told them was long overdue.

About the time Mr. Amtrak crossed the Oregon state line, I felt something zigzagging through my body like lightning, a zig of happy and a zag of sad. Happy for them, but sad for myself, my own shortcomings, and I'm not talking about envying those seven, no eight, Cadillac dealerships. I'm talking about being the one in the way. Me, with my stupid, infernal, interfering, dadblamed, high-handed peacemaking.

GOSHEN

Peggy Gilmer-Piasecki

The old man sat, rocking back and forth, the floorboards of the porch squeaking rhythmically. Abruptly he rocked forward, stopping the chair in mid-motion, and declared resolutely, "When I die, I want to be taken to Goshen." Then, having made his wishes known to anybody, or nobody at all, he released the chair and allowed it to begin rocking once again.

The old lady never heard a word.

"Yessiree," he said, "when I die, I want to be taken to Goshen. I surely don't want to face eternity a'layin' in a grave alongside Madam or none of her hard-shell kin."

The old lady leaned forward and through puckered, practiced lips, let fly a snuff-stained projectile catching a near-by yard bird off guard and sending her scurrying for cover into the tall grass a few feet distant.

The old man was slight, with brown, leathery, skin criss-crossed in a dozen directions by laugh lines. His bright eyes were alive, their mischief barely concealed by the wire-rimmed spectacles he wore. His once sandy hair was thin, and his daily uniform was a striped shirt buttoned all the way to the top with galluses holding up his trousers. On his feet he wore gaiters.

The old lady was gray all over. Her gray hair was pulled back severely and twisted into a bun at the nape of her neck. Her facial expression matched the severity of her hairstyle. She may have owned one gray dress, or a dozen. It didn't matter. They always looked the same. High collars, long sleeves, and shapeless skirts from under which protruded old ladies' comforts worn over thick cotton stockings, and which one might expect, but never know for certain, were rolled down at the knee. Completing her garb was a white bib apron with a pocket, just large enough to hold her snuffbox.

Her ample lap provided a resting place for the Holy Bible, laying, perpetually unopened, but always at the ready.

When it wasn't in her mouth, her black, gum snuff brush was waiting for her on a small near-by table.

The old man said, "Yessiree, eternal peace. I won't have to share my society no more with Madam. I will have me a nice quiet resting place right by myself up at Goshen."

The old lady raised up, and the Brown Leghorn, remembering her recent lesson, started to run. But instead of targeting the chicken, she cupped her ear with her hand and said to the old man, "Did you say something?"

To which the old man replied, "Not a word, my love. Not a word."

The chairs fell back into their familiar rhythm and the only sound heard for a half mile was a blue jay across the road in the ancient white oak tree.

The porch ran the full length of the old frame house, and upon it, in addition to the two old people in their rocking chairs, were the snuff-brush table, a swing, and a wash stand upon which stood a cedar bucket half-full of well water. A gourd dipper hung on the wall alongside a broken mirror and a fertilizer sack towel. If a speck of dust, growing larger, appeared on the distant horizon, it meant a car was coming, and it would have to be company because the red dirt road ended at their mailbox.

"The Good Lord knows," the old man continued," I ain't been a saint, but I'll be hanged if any man ought to have to abide all that religion. All them 'thou-shalt-not-this' and 'thou-shalt-not-that' goin' on for eternity would slam wear a body out, saint or not."

"What did you say?" the old lady asked, and this time she deliberately took aim at a white chicken with a droopy tail.

"I never said a word," he said, adding, "You old biddy."

"I hope she outlives me," he thought out loud, "so she can see me get taken to Goshen."

" I know you are a'swearin' over there, you old heathen, and you are a'goin' to be called upon to given an account for your soul," she warned.

He smiled to himself remembering when her judgment had once been tempered with a little mercy. After she'd delivered those ominous, obligatory warnings she would sometimes allow that she hoped he would find redemption before he died so they could go to Heaven together.

Lately he wasn't so sure he even wanted to go to Heaven if he had to go with her. The first step would be just not to get buried in that confounded hard-shell cemetery. And he had a plan to avoid it. He just needed somebody he could trust to see he got taken to Goshen. That's where Mud Cat came in.

Mud Cat was his eldest grandson, and as wild a one as ever there was. The old lady said regarding Mud Cat that the apple didn't fall far from the tree, just skipped one generation, in fact. The old man said Mud Cat was his favorite grandson. And as much as the old lady didn't want to admit it, she had a soft spot in her heart for Mud Cat too. When he came by every day to fetch in the firewood and draw fresh well water and feed the chickens, she slightly inclined her head toward him to receive the peck of a kiss he always put on her wrinkled old cheek.

The truth of the matter, Mud Cat reminded her of the old man way years back when she first knew him and held out such hope for him. Every now and again still he rode through her mind on that fine white horse, looking just like he did that Sunday morning at May Meeting so many years ago. Back then, pulling the horse up to a fast stop, jumping off and bowing from the waist, tipping that brand new straw hat to her as she stood looking out from behind her Ma in wonder. In that instant it was more than abundantly clear to her that he had been predestined to be an Elder in the Sojourner Primitive Baptist Church.

Madam had told him over and over again that the Doctrine of Predestination was what set her one true church apart from the likes of the Methodists. He had tried untold times to reason with her and explain his position, which was: If it was predestined that he would go to Hell, then what would be the harm in him having a little bit of fun since it wouldn't matter anyway? And if he was predestined to go to Heaven, then it would just happen with no particular effort on his part. A person just couldn't reason with Madam about something that would make so much sense to most everybody else, he thought.

For her part, the old lady dreaded the sound of the final trumpet when judgment would be meted out to sinners and His chosen ones alike. She was going to have to give an account of why she went against her Ma and her Pa and married just such a scoundrel. God must surely know that her heart had been pure, and that she had believed up until just a few years ago that all it would take to bring him into the fold, was just the guidance and prayers of a good, Godly woman. In the dark of night and the light of day she pondered what her answer would be.

The old man was thinking that he probably could not count on any act of Divine Intervention, and would just have to depend on Mud Cat.

To the unlikely union of the old lady, who had once been young, and the old man, who still was, had been born numerous children. Hezekiah, Nehemiah, Obediah, and Jeremiah, were interspersed with Ruth, Esther, Dorcas, and Aquilla. God knows, the old man was a fool about all of his children, and it seems loved each new one more than the one before. But even he would have been a hypocrite if he hadn't owned that he was a bit relieved when fertility waned and he did not have to face the prospect of explaining the one named Lamentations.

A speck of dust appeared, moving very quickly and growing larger and larger until the bright red of Mud Cat's pickup truck came around the curve at a high rate of speed and sent the whole flock of chickens flying every-which-way.

*   *   *

Seasons turned into other seasons. Years turned into other years. Presidents were elected. Kings were crowned. Wars were fought. Soil eroded making smooth again what had once been furrowed. Kudzu crept upon the sleeping land, possessing entire communities, and obliterating any vestige of wood or mortar. The wind blew away the final notes of the sounds of laughter or weeping. Troubles disappeared, and triumphs were forgotten. The old folks died. Their children died. Their children's children died.

Then on a windy March day, more than half a century later, a silver-haired child linked by DNA and doubts, and guided by nothing more than Rand-McNally and some very old memories, set out to find Goshen. After several hours of driving, missing roads, backtracking, and trying other roads, Goshen came into view. A walk of the cemetery revealed no familiar name, and just as the owner of the small, disappointed, soul was about to leave, a flash of white came from a distant, deserted corner.

Underneath an old, spreading oak tree, which in summer would generously give its shade and in winter a blanket of its leaves, stood a grave stone bearing the name of the old man, and the inscription, "At Rest." By its side, a second, obviously newer, stone duplicated the name, with the addition of the words, "Mud Cat," and the announcement that he, too, was "Also at Rest."

THINGS THAT GO BUMP

Bill Patrick

It was almost midnight and my eyelids were so heavy I could hardly keep them open. In a pre-sleep stupor I was just reaching for the arms of Morpheus when the most god-awful rattling, clacking, clattering and clanging racket jarred me back from the half-conscious state into which I had begun to plummet.

Without reason, without remembrance, without realization of circumstance, my innate sixth sense and the inherent desire for survival that had kept me alive through one war—excuse me, I meant one 'police action'—and would suffice to do so through another yet to come—this one to be fought under the auspices of a 'conflict', as opposed to a war—launched me to my feet and had me clawing for the door and the outside and whatever freedom and safety might lie there. Jimmie, the relief caller and I collided in the anti-room door jam but I had a height and weight advantage which, impelled by my bulk and momentum, shot me past him as I inadvertently gave him a push, unintentionally propelling him back into the room.

Somehow, between that anteroom door and the double doors exiting to the front porch, he flew around me like a quarterback scrambling for his life behind the line of scrimmage who, all of a sudden spots a minuscule hole in the defensive line and dives through, turning what had been a sure loss into an unexpected gain. He was turning around on the sidewalk as I crashed through that final bastion separating me from the catastrophe about to take place within.

Without slowing I reached the spot where he had halted, quickly turning to gaze back into the black abyss shielding the cacophonous diatribe that was pouring forth from that area that had once been the reception room.

It all started several hours earlier—at 2:45 to be exact—when I checked by the Caller's office after completing my daylight shift on the Shed job, where we had spent the day switching out cars on the incoming passenger trains. The caller, Joe Wright, said, "Soapy, you know the Yardmaster's brother died this morning. The Brotherhood of Locomotive Firemen and Enginemen is asking for volunteers to stay at the funeral home and sit with the body in four-hour stretches through the night hours. I took the liberty of volunteering you and Skinny for a shift."

Much like today, in the fifties when someone died, friends gathered 'round in support—with one major difference.

Back then the coffin remained open in the mortuary viewing room from the time of its initial placement until it was removed for the service. This entailed family and friends sitting at the funeral home overnight— either to keep company with, or to keep watch over the deceased. I was never quite sure which.

Such was the case in '56, shortly after I began working on the railroad.

Tonight I was paired with Jimmie Lang, the relief caller. We were assigned the witching hour. At about a quarter after eleven, Jimmie picked me up in his forty-nine Caddie ragtop. We made a quick stop at "Pop" Bailey's on Mill Street to fill our thermoses with fresh coffee and off we went on our grand adventure.

Jim parked on High Street across from the funeral home and we went inside. We were relieving Red Miller and Scrappy Roberts who, for some strange reason seemed somewhat antsy and rather anxious to get out of Dodge. After only a cursory greeting they disappeared quicker than the Artful Dodger.

We went in to view the decedent and then returned to the waiting area. Jimmie took the easy chair while I settled in on the sofa.

It had been a long day and we were both about to collapse, so in spite of the uncomfortable accommodations the sandman was kind, his visit immediate, and the soporific state of dreamland speedily spread throughout the gloaming much like the cloud of death made its way throughout Egypt in Cecil B. De Mille's newly released colossal film extravaganza. It glommed on to its next pair of victims with the same results expected of an anesthetist administering ether in an operating room. I immediately relaxed, closed

my eyes and was about to enter the twilight zone, when in the merest instant I was transported back to a foxhole on a mountainside outside the vil-
lage of Ha-ga-ri near the Chosen Reservoir once again hearing the blaring
bugles and clanging cymbals announcing the coming of the screaming Red
Chinese hoards as they crossed the Yalu into North Korea.

I was completely outside before I was fully awake and returned to reality.

On the sidewalk, the fresh night air exuded a quietude beyond belief
while serving a more noble purpose, that of helping to clear the cobwebs
from our heads—until a moment later when we heard the penetrating albeit, distinct chiming of a grandfather clock.

As the light dawned, so did reality and we both began that uncontrolla-
ble fortuitous laughter that erupts from the psyche from time to time, usually
following a traumatic experience of some type. The clock was one of those
monstrosities with pulleys, levers, hinges and ball bearings that dropped
down several levels with loud clunking sounds.

Some things do change. No one sits with a corpse these days.

Some things never change and will always remain the same. When we
came out at daylight, both the wheels were missing from the curbside of
Jimmy's '49 Caddie parked across the Street.

PRETTY BOY

David Creel

The dazzling lights of Times Square flicker on into the rainy night. I sit so close to the forty-second floor window that my breath upon the cold December glass fogs up again and again. Wiping it away with my pajama sleeve, I smile and think to myself that the view from the top ain't so bad, admiring the skyline of Manhattan with all the gleaming skyscrapers towering into the night reflecting the colors of Broadway's neon bulbs below while taxi cabs buzz through the streets flanked on either side by sidewalks of people the size of ants. "Ants," I whisper to myself as I can't help remembering Dykes Chapel Road so many miles back in my hometown and my memory. I was a long way from the branches of Mawmaw Belle's Sycamore tree where a little boy like me would wrap my bare toes around the knotty limbs and dangle above the ant beds underneath, invincible, untouchable, then and now as I sip my hot chocolate brought up a few minutes ago by the butler at the Righa Royal Hotel. Staring into the dark New York night makes me wish it could be as glitzy and glamorous as I felt while a child in rural Mississippi.

The truth is, there ain't never been a stage anywhere as magical as the one atop that old torn up freezer in the neighbor's junk pile. I burst onto it early in life with my best friend Tracey and the world as my audience. Proud, noble, and magnificent, I felt while I sang into an old stick found near the storm cellar. It did not take much to impress, just the star quality stance that was well rehearsed, maybe even worthy of Dick Clark from *American Bandstand*. That day would be no different than most days when I stood high on my tiptoes until I could see way past the cows in Daddy's pasture, way past the pond, beyond the fence even to the imaginary stands where all the fans sat cheering me. In the front row near the tire swing just off center from the stage were usually the neighborhood kids, a few mutts and, of course, the paparazzi, camera men and a slew of celebrities as vibrant as my imagination would allow. Like that movie queen from long ago, I was "ready for my close-up." A dazzling performer, I was deliberately posed with left hand on one hip, palms flat, fingers lifted just like I had seen all the other stars on the big console television set on Saturdays. It was almost showtime, but from down the dirt road came the background noise of men laughing. In the distance followed the words, "pretty boy," the sound of a man's rough voice deliberately strained into a high pitch, stopping me in my tracks. The spotlight immediately dimmed, crowds cheering turned back to corn stalks and indifferent cattle, and my star went out a little each and every time I heard those two words. Chronicling my childhood of barefoot dreams, adolescent longing, and grown-up fairytales helps to erase the tainted moments, only to draw them again, this time coloring outside the lines.

Climbing over my mama's crisp black pants to nestle myself comfortably between her and my daddy in our blue and white pickup truck, I was tickled pink that Saturday had finally come and everyone knew what that meant. Not just any Saturday, but *the* Saturday. All those weeks of scribbling circles around just about everything between pages 119 and 167 in the *Sears Christmas Wish Book* had not been wasted, because with that tattered and torn toy book on her lap, my mama reached down into her navy blue purse and whirled out three pieces of Juicy Fruit gum on our way into the big city. The first piece was always for my mama, the second she passed to me with a wink and then the third to my brother Tony who chose to stand up most of the way there, asking my daddy questions about most everything under the sun. As I tore open the paper wrapper of my gum, sticking it to my nose first to smell the sweet and familiar aroma, then slowly peeling away the silver foil, my little eyes gleamed at the very notion that we were on our way to town. Unlike my brother who always just ripped away the paper like a savage animal, stuck the whole piece in his mouth and crammed the wrapper in his pocket, my way was more civilized indeed. Without losing the dialogue she was carrying on with my daddy, my mama knew to hold out her hand to gather my Juicy Fruit wrapper so that I could call for it later when I was done chewing. Yes, predictable as I was, my mama was always two, maybe three steps ahead of me. After a few stops, one of which was for my daddy to yell at the neighbor's cows to get back behind the fence and another at Mr. Coty's Country Store for him to pump gasoline and us boys to scramble through the aisles for something, anything, to toss on Mr. Coty's counter that my mama might consider as worthy as her ice cold bottle of Nehi Peach, we bumped along the winding country roads that would soon turn into busy city streets.

Following closely behind my mama's pants and taking turns looking up at the lights shining through her reddish brown hair, then back down to the shiny black pumps peeping from underneath the hem of her bell-bottom slacks, we hurriedly walked toward the toy department. Unable to contain his excitement, my brother ran ahead to the aisle with great big plastic trucks, soldier figurines standing at attention and such with Daddy towering above as Tony pointed to "the big twuck" as he called it. Without further ado, the salesperson wheeled a ladder around at Daddy's instruction to bring down not one, but two "big twucks." Holding this abomination in my little arms and looking up at my happy parents making "ooh and ahh" sounds down at me, it was there in the Sears toy department that I lost my marbles, every one of them, and threw the truck down with more than hint of drama. Running from aisle to aisle in my frantic search for what had been on page 123, the thing that had laid torn out and folded up again and again under my pillow, where was it? Betsy Wetsy, where are you?

As I searched high and low, far and in between My Little Ponies and Rainbow Brite, shuffling past Strawberry Shortcake and all her friends with reckless abandon, it was on aisle nine that my eyes met the big blue baby doll eyes of my dreams. I embraced Betsy Wetsy, box and all. Hours later, back home on the yellow carpets of my bedroom that Mama always called gold even though they were the very same color as my crayon clearly marked yellow, it was over those plush, velvety floors that my brother would crawl from room to room driving his big twuck. Much smaller than him with his long, lanky legs, I was never more than a rock's throw behind him as he made those big twuck sounds so easily. It was the "eeeerrrrkkkking" sounds to mimic tires squealing as he spun around a closet door or backed up into a dresser drawer that impressed me most.

The sound of my mama and daddy whispering in the next room

seemed to be growing louder with every turn of the wheels on my brother's truck, and while we made our way across the linoleum of the kitchen floors the loud whispers turned into yelling that muffled the sounds of the evening news anchor, the one with incredibly big hair, so unnatural I thought. "It's just a doll, just a toy," my mama said as my daddy could now be seen rolling his eyes and sipping his coffee in that way which indicated to us that he was not pleased. " Folks will call him a sissy!" Daddy countered, while my brother and I crawled down the flagstone steps which my daddy happily told every guest that he had laid himself with his own bare hands. "Folks already call him a sissy," my mama said quietly, matter-of-factly. "But this sissy is ours." As we rolled the big truck around the tips of my daddy's old worn cowboy boots, he lifted one higher than the other and smiled lovingly down at us. The sounds of the truck engines stopped. My brother looked around at me as we both jumped up, grabbing hold of Daddy's boots in the way we loved to do and pulling hard. It was a contest, a game of wills. Who would get the first boot off? Of course, Daddy could always humor himself by sinking his heel down into the sole to make it more challenging for us to earn that dollar bill promised to the winner. As usual my brother would give up early in the game, and as I vigorously straddled the boot with tiny fingers wrapped around those dirty heels, I would not relent until my breathless victory. "That's daddy's little man, yep, that's my little man!" were the words that kept me going until the last boot fell off onto the floor beside the wood piled near the roaring fire. Standing straight up, pulling my faded Winnie the Pooh jeans up and tightening my belt, I was proud as I crawled over, lifted the little plastic door of my brother's big twuck trailer just enough to pull Betsy Wetsy out from her chauffeured ride slowly, as not to mess up her hair, then spun around and with a huge squeal of delight said, "Betsy Wetsy needs to go potty, Daddy!"

One must understand that my daddy was the eldest son of thirteen siblings raised deep in the heart of the country. Dirt roads carried barefoot little boys like him alongside rusted barbed wire fences, across wooden cattle gaps and into dusty rows of pea patches from dawn until dusk and then to the fabled out house. Tales abound of my daddy's daddy keeping a close watch for the first one to look up, dare sit down or much less ask for a drink of water, for fear of a whipping. If strong men were broken in and made even stronger by tough love and a merciless whipping now and again, then my daddy was bound to be as strong as iron. With jet black hair, usually combed straight back with a little plastic comb that he kept in his shirt pocket, dark piercing eyes that spoke volumes without even a sound and a tall, slender frame like that of Elvis Presley, I used to think in those Sunday matinees with hula dancers and such, that my handsome daddy looked like the king of rock and roll. Dark, tanned skin was a sign of long days in the sun hoeing in his own garden or walking the green pastures contemplating acres and hillsides filled with cows. A hard life he had been given with little time as a child to play, much less with a doll, but everyone on Dykes Chapel Road said my daddy had "done good for himself" and his family. By all local standards, he had become a fairly wealthy and very successful man.

"Hmmmph," he would mumble with a nod of his head from side to side while Betsy Wetsy and I got along well that winter. My early years growing up in Richton, Mississippi, thirty plus years ago are flavored with moments, colorful moments that stand still in my grown up memory today. As small town America goes, my little town was right up there with the best of them. As luck would have it some pieces of the puzzle that complete the story of my life are lost, forgotten or just buried deeper than I can reach, but like small flecks of light from one of those bright sparklers on some Fourth of July of my recollection, images come and stay for awhile in my mind and heart. The bitter cold wind cuts through me like ice, and I find very little warmth in my Louis Vuitton scarf. Winters in New York are not the winters of the South with the occasional Christmas day in short sleeves, never mind the gloves, scarves and wool sweaters wrapped under the tree that many years were not even needed. I miss those temperamental, moody Southern days, but as I peer into the holiday windows of Saks Fifth Avenue on this freezing night, New York warms me up inside. The lines form around city blocks that seem a mile long with crowds of out-of-towners and even locals clad in holiday attire just to get a glimpse of sparkling life-sized toy soldiers, glittering nutcrackers and dazzling little drummer boys on parade. Outside the glass windows a child and a child at heart stop for a moment, transfixed by the fantasy, the magic of it all. I stand on my tiptoes, grabbing my scarf and sinking down into it a bit more while my ears become numb. I have stood in this line for an hour and a half, but now I can stretch high enough above the elderly Asian man and his grandson in front of me, just enough to get a glimpse of a giant music box with a real life ballerina twirling inside it. My heart skips a beat.

When I shut my eyes all those innocent times come alive once again like my Cousin Tammy's little white jewelry box from my childhood a thousand miles ago. It sat perfectly still on the dressing vanity of her lavishly decorated bedroom when we were small. When my Aunt Trucine distracted Tammy from our play for some secret mother/daughter purpose, I confess before God and all the disciples that I bounced off Tammy's yellow ruffled canopy bed, turned the little box on its side to wind the dickens out of it, only to open it and fall totally under the magical spell of a tiny ballerina that danced. Twirling and twirling to the melody that must have been made by little angels that lived inside the heaven of that white box, just as mesmerizing today are the colorful moments twirling into my adult thoughts as if I tilt myself and give me a good winding. Turning away from the windows of Saks to walk through the crowds of Rockefeller Plaza in Manhattan, making my way back to my hotel, I notice a fragile little girl all bundled up in her Christmas coat clinging to her doll. I think to myself that I can't quite explain the love affair I had for beautiful dolls as a little boy, but it did all begin with Betsy Wetsy and I can recall numerous occasions in the Sears Department Store not just crying, but wailing big puppy dog tears for a stuffed Winnie the Pooh that sat high above the smaller, less impressive ones. It was the giant yellow honey bear with a bee on his nose that had me unglued in front of mama, my Aunt Avis and all the crowded shoppers in the store. A stuffed animal no less and little boys just could not have a bedroom full of dolls and stuffed animals, Aunt Avis told my mama. No sirree! Mama had already given in with the blond haired, blue-eyed plastic baby doll that peed and pooed, but her patience was growing thin. Of course, not being the kid who would ever leave empty handed I settled for the smaller, less impressive Winnie the Pooh doll and gave the big Pooh of my dreams a little over the shoulder wave farewell, wiping a tear off my cheek and grabbing my mama's hand tighter.

Mama knew the small stuffed Pooh would just grow old and end up in the toy box behind my bedroom door with all my other abandoned things— George the stuffed bulldog with plastic eyes that always creeped me out, more rabbits than any child should have (probably leftover from Easters) and other less important "little boy" paraphernalia. But I surprised her. Winnie the Pooh required so much attention, first, a blanket for bedtime and then all the Nestle chocolate mix was poured out of its aluminum can to make a sufficient vessel for Pooh's food and water. There was even talk of my mama making Pooh some little clothes, but after a long time with that little yellow fuzzy bear it just disappeared, vanished. Mama had strong suspicions the neighbor's dog was as enamored of my bear as I was and she threatened to kill that mutt, kill it dead. Of course, she chose the more practical and humane approach and drove to town to buy the big Pooh instead.

I only wish my mama was here with me in my New York City because I know what we would do. She and I would stroll down the bustling streets to the Disney store and stand for hours in the toy department, and I just might buy her a stuffed animal or two. Mama always loved stuffed animals, too— cats, dogs, bears, Easter rabbits, and God love her for it. I can remember waking up on the lower bunk bed as a little boy and arranging all my stuffed friends ever so neatly. Yes, my daddy insisted on bunk beds for my brother Tony and me, and they must have been on sale because even my teenage brothers John and Richard had bunk beds. Imagine being the high school quarterback, making out with Wanda Sue who my mama had deemed the town slut and having to sleep on the top bunk. I would wake up early in the morning, slip out of bed and across the dew wet grass of our yard and over the gravel that led me up my Aunt Paulette's driveway to their front door. It was there as I stood banging on the door waiting to get inside and tell my friend Misty Ann all about the dream I had last night that I looked down to discover I was wearing nothing but my underwear. With nowhere to hide, the horror of it all was staring me in the face as Misty Ann's daddy swung the screened door open, looked out at me and pointed down at my trembling little knees which by now were freezing, or maybe the nerves were the cause of the trembling. "Boy, what are you doing up this early? And where are your pants?" my Uncle James Arthur screeched. With nothing much to do but take the honorable approach, I stood up tall (at least three feet tall) and looked down at my little pastel colored undies, then back up at this big old blond headed man who I never really liked, just never did, and matter of factly confessed that I was unaware of the time of morning, but would he please tell Misty Ann I will be back later to play. Without further ado I got the hell out of there. "Don't come back in your panties, son!" that old fart yelled as he laughed. When I got up the driveway and completely sure I was out of sight I slowed down a bit, turned in his direction and shot him the bird, not just once but twice. My brother John taught me this invaluable skill that I have used well into adulthood. That was the last time I put on pastel colored undies without a fight. A little boy just could not be caught out in public with pastel colored undies, no, not ever.

Misty Ann was my next door neighbor and the adopted daughter of my mama's brother, the one I never liked. The whole adoption thing was quite hush-hush in the community, and I would later find out it was something of a scandal. Misty Ann had the life a little boy like me dreamed of with the bedroom to die for, literally. Jesus, just take me now if I could wake up in a Strawberry Shortcake ruffled canopy bed with matching pillows. Even the wallpaper was Strawberry Shortcake and for her birthday she got a lamp to match. Misty Ann had dolls, even all of the cousins like Apple Dumplin' and Huckleberry Pie, and the hours we spent coloring in the pages of our Strawberry Shortcake coloring books, my, oh my. I loved Misty Ann for no other reason but that when the bedroom door was closed and it was just the two of us, we were sisters for life. It was also inside the sanctity of Misty Ann's bedroom that a little country boy like me would be introduced to his first kiss, as sinful as my mama would think it to be. Yes, indeed it was there in Strawberry Shortcake world that I had my first, uninterrupted foolin' around with Misty Ann's giant Barbie. Well, it was just the head, but lord have mercy that Barbie was the love of my life. Soon I would realize that I did not want to despoil her. I wanted to be her. All the boys, and there were many of them whenever you combine my three older brothers, Misty's three older brothers and the neighbors boys from down the road, could be heard from the Strawberry Shortcake motif curtain-clad windows of my friend's room as I curled up somewhere near the closet which held all of that little girl's shoes. Since her mama, my Aunt Paulette, was a born again Pentecostal saint among all other saints who had come before, most of the shoes were "church shoes," black shiny patent, white with tiny bows, all of them scuffed from kicking the pews or chasing the boys through the gravel rocks behind the sacred walls of Mount Olive United Pentecostal Church. Sometimes when Misty was not paying too close attention to the likes of me, sometimes, just for a second or two, I would slip my dirty little toes into one of those glamorous shoes. Ah, the soft plush cushion underneath as I squeezed every toe deep down into the shoe imagining how it must feel to prance onto a hard linoleum floor or skip down a sidewalk. "Clikkety clak, clikkety clak," I would mumble under my breath while Misty used both hands to tie yet another one of those big fluffy hair ribbons around her ponytails. As I ran my tiny fingertips along the narrow, slender ankle straps finessing my foot almost far enough into those little heels of heaven, almost got it, before the sound of heavy footsteps growing louder outside the door scared me back to my senses. Only seconds before one of Misty Ann's big brothers barged into the sanctity of our space, the shoes flew back into the closet, the closet that held the giant Barbie head with all her blond locks of curls, turquoise blue eyelids painted with the true perfection of an artistic genius. I got both eyes lined, meticulously drawn on and up deliberately to make everyone stop and stare at Barbie's presence. Well, except Misty Ann because she just shrugged her shoulders and rolled her eyes across the room at me as I fell deeper in love with that Barbie head each day after school, weekends and occasionally whenever my mama was in the next room having my Aunt Paulette tease her brown hair. I would sneak into the refuge of Misty Ann's dark room and stare up at the big brown box high up on the top shelf of the closet with deep desire in my heart.

Aunt Paulette pulled, teased, stretched and pulled some more on Mama's hair until she looked like something out of that movie I wasn't allowed to watch but did anyway, *The Exorcist.* I have to give it to Aunt Paulette. Nobody performed on stage better than her with two, three or maybe even four women sitting in admiration, most Pentecostal and each eagerly awaiting her time on the kitchen barstool or on the piano bench for a hairdo that defied gravity, enough hairspray to kill a full grown horse and a picture perfect beehive worthy of Misty Ann's mama's favorite quote, "The higher the hair, the closer to heaven." In New York it's always fun to gaze up into the posh salon windows off Park Avenue sighting busy stylists at Oscar Blandi, Frederic Fekkai or some colorful salon in China Town beside a bakery and maybe a tattoo parlor. But back then all of us kids would just make fun of those funny looking old women with strange hairdos as they scooped up pursefuls of Martha Washington chocolate candies and waited for their husbands to collect them, all except for my mama who always drove her own car, a midnight blue Oldsmobile with plush seats and an FM radio complete with eight-track stereo and Fats Domino recordings. It was an abomination to all the high and mighty church matriarchs who deemed my mama a pants-wearing, independent woman of sin, but the only thing I wondered is why Mama put herself through the judgment each and every Saturday night before Sunday at Aunt Paulette's house of style when all she ever did was march straight home and wash it out. In her honest opinion, and it was honest, it should be a sin to make somebody's hair look, as my mama put it, "like a perfect pile a shit." Of course, she went through this ritual of teasing, being prayed for and washing it out at home and doing it herself, only this time less poofy, for years and years to spare Aunt Paulette's feelings. "Heaven help us all," my daddy would say as he took one look after another at Mama week after week with the beehives from hell.

Moving fast forward from my independent mama and my daddy who was much kinder than by rights he ought to have been, I look again at the rain pressing hard against my Manhattan hotel window. And I remember the very moment that my mama drove me to the small town post office to receive the gift my daddy had sent me from far away where he worked in the oil fields of Alaska. When I opened it, there before me was a beautiful Eskimo doll, yes, a doll, dressed in perfect native attire. To this day, I keep it on a shelf in our bedroom to remind me. Maybe it reminds me of all the girls I have loved. As a child there were Vernon Renee, Misty Ann and Tracey Annette who kept my attention all through kindergarten and even into adulthood with their Southern antics, girly dreams and midnight giggles. Or maybe it was the earlier girls like Betsey, Barbie, Rainbow Brite and Smurfette who heightened my love affair with fantasy. Whether it was all those girls or not, it was most definitely the first girl I ever fell in love with that put a little Christmas light inside me from Mississippi to New York, or even my imagination. And that was my mama. Finally, I remember the day she was lying in the hospital getting ready to be rolled in for open heart surgery. Mama introduced us all to her surgeon just before the anesthesia was administered. As my partner, the love of my life, stood there with my daddy, my three brothers, the Pentecostal preacher, and me, my mama simply said, "This is my husband, and these are my five sons." And I think that maybe being a "pretty boy" is not so bad after all.

HAPPINESS

Sue Stock

Mrs. Biggers rode her bicycle to the Mattie Hampton library every Monday morning at eleven. This particular morning there had been an early rain storm that left the sky clear and the streets wet, with pothole puddles. A wire basket clamped on the handle bars held the two books she was returning: *How to Win at Black Jack* and *Forever Amber.*

Mrs. Biggers, nee Imogene Salter, had never gambled but she planned to go to the casino this very evening and she intended to win. Moreover, for 37 years she had been married to Thomas Biggers, whose interests lay more in banking and deer hunting than in sex, leaving her satisfaction up to her.

Forever Amber, a very erotic book, had proved an antidote to adultery. The bicycle she rode had belonged to her daughter, Clara, who had gotten it from Santa Claus when she was twelve. Clara was now 36, mother of two and divorced. The bicycle was steadily rolling along, needing only a dash of axel grease on its chains once in a while. Ah so, Mrs. Biggers.

As she rode, she sang softly to her self, "Give me land, lotsa land and the starry skies above, don't fence me in…" Her voice rose on the last words, and passers by turned their heads. Unfazed, she sang louder and pedaled faster: "Let me ride through the open country that I love…" She pedaled blissfully down the street, her loose gray air fanned out behind her, her age-spotted arms akimbo, until she arrived at the library and parked her bike outside the square, single-story building. An outpost of the municipal library down town, it had changed neither outside nor inside since it was built forty years earlier. Laura McKenzie stood by the door and wisely did not offer to help her up the steps, having seen her disembark from her bicycle quite agilely.

Somehow, Mrs. Biggers's happiness followed her into the room, any room. Grace Wilson at the front desk looked up and smiled, solemn Laura McKenzie walked with a jaunty step to the reference desk, gave a backward look and nod to Mrs. Biggers. The air seemed lighter, seemed almost to buzz with excitement about nothing anyone could have named. Marjorie Phelps, age eight, jumped up from her seat at the reading table and held out her arms. Mrs. Biggers herself seemed to glow, as if being here in this place with these people was the most wonderful thing on earth.

Grace Wilson's pleasure at seeing Mrs. Biggers was disturbed by a thought. How could Mrs. Biggers be so lively and happy when Mr. Biggers had died only a year ago? She should have been, well, not still grieving, perhaps, but more …. somber? Less like a free spirit, riding around on her bicycle, singing. Checking out books that young people read whose future would certainly turn out poorly. Ms Wilson shook her head and sighed as Mrs. Biggers approached the front desk.

"Grace, dear, how are you?" Mrs. Biggers leaned across the high desk. "I've brought you a little token." She reached into the cloth bag that hung from her shoulder and produced a box wrapped in gold paper with a narrow gold ribbon. "You do so much for us, managing this library and helping all of us who love to use it. We owe you." Grace Wilson ducked her head in embarrassment and fumbled with the ribbon. She looked up at Mrs. Biggers in amazed surprised when she opened it, then caught her breath. It was almost a gasp. There in the tissues was a pair of pearl earrings.

"Why, Mrs. Biggers!"

"Why, indeed. I never wear them and they would look lovely on you. That's all there is to it," she replied brusquely, turning sideways, adjusting her glasses. "I'd like to check out *Lolita* by that Russian man, Nabokov. I'm sorry I have not mastered your computer and you no longer have the card catalog." This was the only break with the past in the building.

"I'm sorry, I'm sorry," mumbled Grace, half genuflecting. "Of course we don't expect our senior citizens to use the computer to find their books and check them out. Let me get it for you. Just wait here."

"That won't be necessary," proclaimed Mrs Biggers. "I will fetch it myself. I am well acquainted with the stacks."

Mrs. Biggers's seraphic glow considerably dimmed, she moved softly across the room and down the stairs into the stacks. She always wore tennis shoes to the library and secretly deplored the boots and high heels favored by the younger women readers. So noisy. Men, who came mostly on weekends, generally wore sneakers or moccasins.

When the book was found, Mrs. Biggers sat at one of the little desks offered in the bowels of the stacks and read it. It was two o'clock when she rose with a satisfied sigh and turned to discover that behind her, unnoticed until now, sat a young man concentrating on a very thick book. He raised his eyes to meet hers, slammed the book shut, and smiled. "I've been waiting for you," he whispered, and put his index finger to his lips.

"For me?" Mrs. Biggers whispered back, slightly alarmed. She was a reader of mysteries as well as game and sex books.

"I–want–that–book!" he said with narrowed eyes, and rose to a height of over six feet. "Now!" He reached for *Lolita* and Mrs. Biggers clutched it to her bosom. He put his hands on his hips and spoke sternly. "I reserved that book at the electronic check out. Why are you keeping it to yourself?"

Mrs. Biggers was about to apologize, then quickly changed her mind, tossed back her hair, lifted her chin to look up at him, and asked, "Do I know you, young man?"

"No, Mrs. Biggers, but I know you."

Their conversation was getting beyond the whispering stage. Mrs. Biggers countered with, "I shall call on Grace Wilson to reprimand you for loud talking!" she threatened. Then she realized what he had just said. "What do you mean, you know me?"

"We should get out of here," he said, putting his finger to his lips again. "You're getting much too noisy."

Mrs. Biggers drew herself up to her full five feet five and blinked in disbelief but could not think of a word to say.

"Come on, Madam." He stepped around her desk, took her elbow with a firm grip, and led her down the aisle to the stairs, her copy of *Lolita* under one arm, her large cloth purse dangling from the other, the one by which he was herding her. To what end? she wondered. Having realized with relief that he was not going to produce a hunting knife from the pages of his large book and slit her throat in the seclusion of the stacks, she now feared he was kidnapping her, although her more sensible self knew this was an absurd notion. What would he do with her? Hold her for ransom? Fat lot of good that would do him. Ha. As these thoughts were racing through her mind, he was pushing her up the steps in front of him, his hand on her back. When they had reached the top, where Grace Wilson's tall check-out desk was in view, he took her hand, swinging it as if they were a pair of fifth graders walking home from school together as they approached Grace Wilson and the front door. Mrs. Biggers was prepared to scream out to Grace if he pushed her toward the door, but that turned out to be unnecessary.

"Walter! Where have you found Mrs. Biggers?"

"Why, in the stacks, Mum. Where would you expect her to be?"

Confused, Mrs. Biggers looked from one to the other and was silent.

"But she was gone such a long time. I was terribly worried. Oh, Mrs. Biggers, I sent Walter to find you. I hope you don't mind. But Walter," she added accusingly, "You were gone a long time, too. I was worried to death about both of you."

"I can explain, dear mother o' mine." (Walter liked to mimic an Irish brogue when he was cheerful.) "Mrs. Biggers here, the party of the first part, was so intensely occupied with reading one of the kind of books she is partial to, that it seemed a shame to disengage her. That she was reading the book which I had reserved properly by electronic means was further cause for my forbearance."

"Oh, shove it, Walter. Your pretentious vocabulary is ridiculous. And besides you aren't making any sense." She addressed Mrs. Biggers. "Mrs. Biggers has this impossible boy been pestering you?"

"Tell her the truth, Mrs. Biggers – may I call you Imogene?—you love being pestered by a good looking man like me. Don't you, now! Not for nothing was I named for Sir Walter Scott. I know a romantic when I see one. Besides, I know what kind of books you read!"

"Walter!" cried Grace Wilson.

But he had turned to Mrs. Biggers, who was enjoying this banter between mother and son now that she'd gotten the gist of it. "Imogene, never believe that a librarian can be trusted. She has told all and I am enchanted. Will you go for a ride with me in my limousine?"

"You are making fun of me, young man. And I do not find it amusing," said Mrs. Biggers, gravely.

"No, indeed. You know, Imogene, Mrs. Biggers, it would give me great pleasure if you would take a ride with me in my ancient Chevy convertible. I promise to bring you home safely. Will you do me the honor?"

Mrs. Biggers could hardly refuse. She was very fond of Grace Wilson and she found her rather foolish young son engaging. Besides, it had been a good many years since she had ridden in a convertible.

"Will the top be down?" That's all she asked, and followed him out to the parking lot. Before he opened the car door for her, he asked, "Have you brought *Lolita*?"

"I have," she said, and pulled it out of her large purse. "You checked it out, and here it is."

Satisfied, Walter helped her onto the red leather seat of his 1985 red Chevy convertible and zoomed out of the parking lot onto Main Street extended, Mrs. Biggers's hair streaming behind, her face uplifted to the wind. They rode to the Indian Mounds in Winterville and looked at arrowheads. They rode to Merigold and looked at pottery.

"It's tea time," said Walter. "Would you like to stop here and have a cuppa?"

"No, I would not," said Mrs. Biggers. "Tea time, my foot. I'm starving and I want a double martini. Or two."

He made a quick u-turn, drove back to town and stopped at Shapley's where they each ordered steaks, medium rare, Mrs. Biggers her martini and Walter a beer. Mrs. Biggers produced a credit card for their bill. Surely now she would ask to be taken home to her apartment, Walter thought.

"Well, my friend," said Mrs. Biggers, "It's just the right time of night to head to the casinos. I have a sure fire way to win at black jack and I'd like to teach you."

Walter groaned. "No, Mrs. Biggers. No. No."

"You are not out with one of your teen age girls that you can spend the next few hours making out with. It's too early to call it a night. Besides, you owe me."

"Owe you! What for? Dinner? Thank you very much but I have chauffeured you all over the country, let you finish reading my book, and now it's gambling you want and I don't have the money. No, no, and no. I'm taking you home."

"Very well, just drop me off at the library, it's open till nine. I can check out another book. Maybe Henry Miller's, although it's rather a bore. I like D.H. Lawrence much better. Have you read *Women in Love*? It's erotic but subtlely so."

"Mrs. Biggers, I will gladly drop you off at the library. I am not interested in sexy books. I read how-to books."

"Really," said Mrs. Biggers with aroused interest.

Walter bit his bottom lip and hurried to reply, " Not how-to have sex, if that's what you're thinking."

"Actually that is what I was thinking and I thought that would be a very instructive kind of book for a young man. But never mind. You refuse to go to the casino so I shall have to find my own way there. I know where the shuttle picks up."

"All right, dammit. I'll take you and let you out and you can get a shuttle to bring you home. I hope you win."

Mrs. Biggers was visibly happy with this turn of events; she beamed at him, she patted his driving arm, she rummaged in her purse for her wallet.

"I have an extra hundred here. It's yours if you want to join me."

"No, thanks. I wish you luck." He pulled up to the top of the hill that led down to the river boat casinos, brightly lit below, and carefully drove down to the entrance to the Lucky Lady. "Is this where you want to get off?" he asked.

"This will do fine. If I don't win here in an hour I'll try another one."

"Mrs. Biggers, Imogene, I want to tell you something." He cut the motor and turned to face her. "I think you are the most interesting woman I have ever met. You seem like a very happy person. But I'm curious. Do you ever do things for others? I mean, you seem to get a lot of pleasure out of life, but do you, like, do good works? It may be out of line for me to ask, but I want to know you better."

Imogene Biggers was silent. At last she said, very softly, "You are asking me to tell you things about myself that I don't talk about. I'm not proud of these things, because they are not about me."

"What does that mean, they are not about you?"

"It means that there are wonderful people in this world who do remarkable things with no expectation of reward. I have met many of them and they have done unto me, to paraphrase scripture. I live in constant gratitude for the goodness of people, some of whom I do not know at all, but who have made my life better, even possible. What I have done for others, as you ask, is to listen, to appreciate, to do unto the least of these so far as my energy and pocket book can go. In my earlier years, I supported various projects – Habitat for Humanity. Stew Pot. Shoestring. Animal Rescue. Amnesty International. Alzheimers Research. Some with cash, some with hands-on work. But I truly believe that what we can do to make this world a better place is to be happy ourselves, to love others as we love ourselves, to wish them happiness."

"Well," said Walter, "I'm not sure I totally agree with your philosophy. But I will tell you, you have given me a very happy day."

Mrs. Biggers had a lucky night. She enjoyed the excitement, the challenge, the randomness of her luck. Her hundred dollars brought her five hundred and she quit the tables, cashed in, caught a shuttle bus, and when she got to her apartment, wrote a check to the Animal Rescue League, although she had never had a dog or a cat.

THE SOLOISTS

Anne Evans

The two high school senior girls sat side by side in the rehearsal chairs, each, Mrs. Locke knew, consumed with bitter and private thoughts about her. Heather sat with one leg crossed over the other at the knee. She kicked her elevated foot in rhythm with the snap of her gum.

"Heather," Mrs. Locke said, "No gum at practice."

Heather flipped her tussled blonde curls and huffed. She marched to the front of the room. Without bothering to wrap it in a tissue, she spit out her gum so that it clung to the side of the metal wastebasket like a slug. She swished back to her seat. Mrs. Locke frowned at her tan legs that were bare to the ankles. She had rolled her socks down so low that they plunged into her penny loafers, a minor uniform infringement of the kind Mrs. Locke usually let pass in order to avoid a battle.

"Roll up your socks," she said today.

Heather pouted and mewed, but eventually rolled up her socks with her pink tipped fingers.

The other girl, Madeline, sat tall and straight in the metal folding chair – a rigid foil to Heather's elaborate fidgeting. Her ankles and toes kissed. Her white socks met neatly at her knees. Her long neck arched slightly forward. She ignored Heather's performance and appeared to study her own thoughts as if they were concrete beings standing before her.

At one time in their childhood Mrs. Locke recalled, Madeline had been as pretty and happy as Heather. When they were nine, Mrs. Locke had first heard the clarity and timber of their voices above the rest of the third graders in the Christmas pageant. She had them sing a duet, "What Child is This?" and it brought down the house. Back then Madeline was still bony thin, but her hair was a pleasing reddish brown and her big green eyes were soft. She was queen of the playground, too, because she invented the most fun games. Each day recess transformed into a new and brilliant world: Madeline handed out roles to play and all the children eagerly acted out whodunit style mysteries, mafia jailbreaks, pirate shipwrecks, acorn battles between cowboys and Indians, and damsel-in-distress rescues. Madeline always cast Heather as the damsel.

But as a teenager Madeline had grown quiet, and, well, Mrs. Locke hated to say it, but quite frankly, ugly. It was as if the girl were purposely sabotaging the features God had given her. Such a shame, like burying your talents. She wore thick, black gunk on her pretty eyes, which she covered up with black square framed glasses – men's glasses – that Mrs. Locke suspected, she didn't even need to see the board. She had dyed her lovely hair jet black and lopped it off in the most scraggly of manners. Bangs half an inch long dusted her forehead, while the back shot out in sharp and jagged angles.

Both girls wore their St. Elizabeth's uniforms, but when Mrs. Locke ran into them outside of school she was often aghast at their clothes. Heather barely wore anything at all: décolleté tops and short miniskirts with make-up fit for a porn star. Madeline wore jeans and t-shirts. The only time Mrs. Locke saw her in something like a dress, she wore a floor length red Japanese kimono with combat boots peeking out beneath.

But now, Mrs. Locke thought as she arranged the music on the piano, she had them exactly where she wanted them. The two songbirds were going to do her bidding, whether they liked it or not. Mrs. Locke had taught music at St. Elizabeth's for thirty years, and never in her service did she have two voices like Heather's and Madeline's. It was to her chagrin that neither girl had the desire to fully develop her talent. Heather didn't find choir "cool" since Jr. High and stopped taking the class as one of her required arts classes, choosing theatre instead. Madeline continued to take choir for the A, but her sullen attitude – she didn't really like singing, she explained. She didn't choose to be good – it showed through in her performances time and again, even though she had the best voice. It was a bothersome slap in the face to Mrs. Locke who knew the potential beauty each girl held tucked in the back of her vocal chords. But now, after some luck (and yes, a little manipulation, Mrs. Locke must admit) they would put on the best school

concert ever. Once they wowed the parents and won the state championship, Sr. Fatima, the principle, would have to put up the money for them
to go to Nationals and expand the choir budget overall. Mrs. Locke often
imagined herself standing onstage with her back to the hot lights and audience in St. Louis, where this year's competition would be held. She heard
the rustling of the people in their seats as they quieted down under her lifted
arms; felt the tight anticipation in her muscles; and saw the eyes of the choir
locked on hers, waiting for her cue. In the vision her self-consciousness
about her middle-aged (OK – late middle-aged, she must admit) plumpness
disappears, no flab shakes from her underarms as she directs the singers, her
hair is styled and sprayed in place, the gray temples shining favorably in the
spotlight.

"Girls," Mrs. Locke said, returning to the choir room, "stand up and
begin your scales."

The girls dutifully stood up without making eye-contact with each
other nor Mrs. Locke. Heather coughed loudly, as if she had a frog in her
throat. Madeline stared at a thought on the wall behind Mrs. Locke's left
shoulder.

"You know, Mrs. Locke, I think I'm getting sick. I probably shouldn't
practice today," Heather said.

"I'll be the judge of that," Mrs. Locke said. "Key of G." She played a
G chord on the piano and lifted her hand. "The M&M song."

Both girls hummed and sang the words to the scale that they had practiced ever since beginning their school life at St. Elizabeth's, "My mom
made me mash my M&M's." They sang this line over and over with every
note in the scale.

After scales Mrs. Locke handed them sheets of music to the first re-
quirement of the state competition: classical music. Her fingers tingled with
excitement as she did so. She had picked out these songs specifically for the
girls' voices: Heather's lofty soprano for *Ave Maria* and Madeline's earthy
alto for *Panis Angelicus*.

"We'll begin with *Ave Maria*." She sang the first verse to give them the
tune, singing each of their parts separately. Then she raised her hand to
command them.

Their voices filled the room like the wind. Such power! Such grace! It was even better than she had anticipated and today was only the first day! And she knew it could only get better – especially Madeline, who was holding back on purpose just to spite her – whispering next to Heather's rich lifting tone. And Heather, Mrs. Locke knew, was secretly enjoying herself even though it wasn't cool.

At the end of the practice Mrs. Locke hummed and smiled to herself as she gathered her purse and umbrella. This concert was just what those girls needed. She could see it in the shine of Heather's blue eyes, the way her body swayed and her chest and abdomen relinquished to her voice. Once Heather knew how good she was, how much joy her singing brought to others, then she'd quit seeking affirmation from the boys at school with her body. She'd feel good about herself and keep her legs closed tight. Madeline would take longer to crack open, but Mrs. Locke believed the power of singing would melt her eventually. You just couldn't sing such beautiful music and not feel anything. Not feel, well, better....like a child of God.

*   *   *

The next day at practice Madeline was still singing from her throat, not her gut. They were starting a new song to fit the Broadway category of the program, and Mrs. Locke had picked out "You'll Never Walk Alone" for Madeline. She spent extra time with her, while Heather lay on four rehearsal chairs pushed together, her arms dangling at her sides.

"I think it sounds better this way," Madeline said.

"It doesn't. You have much more power if you use your diaphragm. Now let's do some breathing exercises."

"I have plenty of power in my throat," Madeline said.

"You wish you knew how to use your throat," Heather said suggestively from her bed of chairs. Both Mrs. Locke and Madeline ignored her.

"Quit being so difficult," Mrs. Locke addressed Madeline. "You're a smart girl. You've been studying music long enough to know the difference, and you're going to sing this song right, from your diaphragm and with emotion."

Madeline rolled her eyes. "This song has no emotion," she said.

Mrs. Locke in all of her years teaching music had never wanted to slap a student as badly as she did right then. Her hands sizzled and flicked at her sides. She turned away from the girl, a flush in her cheeks. She took a long deep breath, holding it in her chest, feeling it bang against the sides of her own diaphragm. She exhaled and turned around.

"Now, you listen to me, carefully, because I'm only going to say this once," she said calmly. "It is important that you excel in this concert, and to excel you have to follow my direction to a T." She formed a T with her hands. "And do you know why?"

"No, but I'm sure you're about to tell me," Madeline said, staring defiantly through her ugly black glasses at Mrs. Locke.

A slow smile crept up Mrs. Locke's face, because she knew she had her now. Getting Heather had been chance, a boon from above, but Madeline was work, and work always felt more satisfactory than luck. "Because," she took a step closer and looked up at the tall, morbid girl, whom she knew harbored ambitions higher than her own. Madeline wanted out of this town, out of her little life. She wanted to be some important thinker or artist type, and the way she planned to do it was to go to some hot shot college in some Eastern city. She made no secret of why she strove for straight A's; ran all of the newspaper and literary staff; entered and won all of the essay contests; and last, but certainly not least, since Madeline could never make it in school politics or as an athlete, sang in the choir, excelled as a soloist, won awards. But choir was a class, too.

"If you do not perform to the expectations I have of you, you will fail."

Madeline's eyes flashed beneath the glasses, but she made no other move.

"Is this a threat?"

"Is it?" Mrs. Locke fisted her hands on her hips.

"You can get fired for something like this."

"No, I can't. That's what a grade is, dear. You are graded on your performance in other classes, why would you not expect the same in choir? Just because you've always gotten A's before?"

"Everyone knows how well I sing."

"Do they?"

Heather sat up and stared at them.

"Heather heard you," Madeline said. "She's a witness."

"Yes, well, Heather knows a lot about witnesses, don't you Heather?"

Heather looked from Madeline to Mrs. Locke. She shrugged and slumped back in the chair.

"What? Are you blackmailing her too?"

"Heather and I have an understanding."

"Heather?" Madeline asked – a desperate move on her part. Mrs. Locke knew she would never try to form an alliance with the likes of Heather, unless she had no other card to play.

Heather rolled her eyes over Madeline, and then Mrs. Locke, as if savoring their rapt attention. "You two are just alike," she said.

"What does that mean?" Madeline asked.

"Can't you just sing like you know how to sing? Why are you being such a bitch?"

"Heather! Language! I'll not have that talk in the choir room," Mrs. Locke said.

Heather blew a bubble that covered her nose, popped it, and sucked it between her lips. Mrs. Locke ignored the bubble. The girls were divided. Neither had any weight without the other. The show would go on.

Madeline slung her eyes from Heather to Mrs. Locke. A queer smile crossed her lips. "Play the music," she said.

*   *   *

The next day the girls were equals at practice. One voice matched the other, voices so luminous and rich they shook the thickly sprayed hair on Mrs. Locke's head. She fought hard to conceal her delight. If the girls knew the inkling of their power, they would surely not give their all the next time, she thought. And so she directed them with her hands, pushing them to new heights, all the while biting back the emotion that threatened her eyes and throat.

As the weeks of practice went on and the teenagers sang their dutiful little hearts out, Mrs. Locke rediscovered her old fondness for them as children. She remembered their eagerness and shyness before her. The way they giggled at her jokes. How on the first day Heather hit a miraculous and clear high C, Madeline had given her a hug. When was the last time Madeline had hugged anyone? She wondered. It saddened her that the girl had turned so angry from such a loving, imaginative child. Sometimes that's what happened to overly smart people. Mrs. Locke had seen it many times before. Her own brother, who was one of the most gifted people she knew, had fallen down the tubes of alcohol and depression. Her most talented friend in high school, voted wittiest as well as most-likely-to-succeed, had developed the most bitter and caustic sense of humor by mid- life that Mrs. Locke couldn't stand to go to lunch with her anymore. Where had the joy gone that used to fill these people? Why had their talent gone so completely awry? The mystery saddened her, and she shook her head to shake it away.

She had a chance now, however, to give these girls a sense of beauty, a chance to believe in themselves and something good in the world. She didn't feel bad about manipulating them. It seemed that God had put Mrs. Locke in the position of stumbling upon Heather and that rascal of a boy, Nick Dickson – the one they called Nick Dick – in a compromising position in the choir loft after school. At the time she couldn't believe her eyes, the very private place that boy had his mouth – and in a church! Stunned, she didn't know what to do until Heather, zipping up her pants and scrambling to her feet had pleaded, "Oh, please, Mrs. Locke, please don't turn us in to Sr. Fatima! I promise I'll do anything you ask."

Now it seemed ordained. God wanted Heather back in the fold and Mrs. Locke was the vehicle of delivery. And if he wanted Heather, then he certainly wanted Madeline, too. If she could get them to see what joy they could bring to themselves and others through their talents, perhaps they would never slide into the abyss. As Mrs. Locke mulled over these thoughts, she was seized by an inner panic. Her well-developed diaphragm expanded and contracted at an alarming rate, her heart plunged and mounted in her chest. It occurred to her in a flash that these girls were perhaps very much in trouble – already at the edge of the abyss, just a second away from teen-pregnancy or teen-suicide, and that she, Mrs. Locke, was the only person standing between them and certain doom. The gravity of the responsibility squeezed her soul.

"Oh, Lord," she prayed, "Give me the strength to persevere in this task."

She felt an impulse to run to the phone and tell each of them what a special, talented, wonderful girl she was. Tell them that things would be better in a few years. That high school was just a flash in the pan. Tell Heather that she didn't need boys to like her to like herself. Tell Madeline that … well, what would she tell Madeline? What comfort could she give a stone? She'd tell her she loved her. Yes, that was it. Love could melt the rocks of a mountain.

Mrs. Locke stood in her kitchen and looked out the window. She knew she wouldn't run to the phone and do such a rash thing. But she resolved to be gentler with the girls. To compliment them and encourage them. To be a pillar of support. Mrs. Locke hugged her arms across her chest. She stirred the vegetables on the stove and opened the oven door to check on her chicken breast. In the dark cavern the single breast, pale and limp, baked in its own juices. She shut the heavy door with a squeak and a slam. She turned back to the window. A pall of loneliness fell upon her like a shawl. She allowed herself to think of Ed, her husband who had died five years ago. She would like to tell Ed about the girls, about the preparation for the concert. She wanted him to be there to see what a lovely performance she would conduct, the state championship trophy they would win, and then, quite possibly, the national! She thought to call her daughter, but it was 8pm, bedtime for the baby, and her daughter had scolded her many times about how they had to keep a tight ritual at bedtime or else the baby wouldn't fall asleep, and they'd be fighting her all night. Any little disturbance, especially a phone call from Grandma, would disrupt the whole system. And so, Mrs. Locke stared out the window and waited for her chicken to cook.

*   *   *

The last week of practice, Mrs. Locke cheered the girls on. "You're doing wonderfully, splendid. You're going to knock their socks off."

The girls, if they were excited, didn't show it. Madeline now sang from her gut, but remained stoical throughout practice. Heather radiated confidence, but shrugged off the compliments. Besides practicing their solos and duets alone, this last week they also practiced the entire show with the choir.

After the group practice, Mrs. Locke took the girls aside and said, "Did you see how your peers watched you? How they admired you? How they enjoyed your singing? You have gifts. You should be very proud of yourselves for working so hard to develop them."

"Nick Dick seemed to like it," Heather said.

Madeline laughed, and the girls exchanged smiles like covert comrades.

Mrs. Locke flushed bright red. Something had changed between the girls. "You want them to respect you," she sputtered. "You demand it from them and they will."

"Oh, come on, Mrs. Locke. I just want to have some fun. It's no big deal."

Mrs. Locke ignored Heather and turned to Madeline. She refused to give up this chance to teach them something about themselves, the power they held. "Madeline, did you see how you moved them? How rapt they were at the glory of your voice?"

"Yes ma'am, I certainly did." She said, but without any heart.

"All right, get some sleep. Only two days till the state competition!" She reached out to them and gave them an awkward hug. Heather patted her back limply, but Madeline remained as stiff as a board.

As she gathered her music and purse, she thought she heard Madeline say from the doorway, "did you see their rapt attention at the glory of your ass?"

Mrs. Locke's ears burned as their laughter spilled into the hallway.

* * *

The night of the performance, Mrs. Locke gave the choir a pep talk. She told them what marvelous progress they had made, congratulated them on how hard they had worked, and told them they were going to do a fabulous job.

"Remember," she said, "tonight the judges from the state competition will be here. Let's show them who's best!"

Privately she gave each of the girls a silver bracelet made of treble clefs encircling each other like snakes. She had enclosed a note to each of them that read, "You are a very special soloist."

The performance began with a zippy number the students sang as they entered from opposite sides of the auditorium. Mrs. Locke had jazzed up their entrance with a little choreography. She caught Heather's eye – who beamed with the joy of performance, and then Madeline's – who looked, unusually, strangely timid. Was the girl scared? Could it be? She gave Madeline her most trusting, confident look. You can do it, she mouthed, as panic thrust in her chest – how could she have missed that Madeline had stage fright? Immediately she shook the thought away, dismissing it as her own imagination.

The first three group numbers went off without a hitch. The auditorium swelled with the lush young voices, the smiles and the bright eyes. Then Heather sauntered up to the microphone for her number, "Ave Maria," which was even more beautiful than the day before in practice. Mrs. Locke swelled with pride and pleasure. There were two more group numbers and then Madeline's song.

At the podium, Madeline's eyes, due to uniform standards of the show, seemed naked without their customary black eyeliner and black framed glasses. She stood in front of the microphone, but her stiffness that had always registered as defiance to Mrs. Locke now appeared to be fear. Mrs. Locke felt like kicking herself for not working on Madeline's stage presence. She hadn't even recognized that it might be a problem!

Madeline stood, as tall and thin as a carrot, her wild hair brushed flat to her head, her long limbs pressed close to her sides. She swayed slightly and Mrs. Locke gasped, thinking she might faint in the lights. But Madeline recovered, righted herself, and took the microphone in her skinny fingers. She nodded at Mrs. Locke, who in turn nodded at the pianist. The music began.

Madeline walked to the edge of the stage, microphone in hand. She took a deep breath and began to sing. The first note squeaked out. Mrs. Locke cringed. It was as if Madeline were messing up on purpose. The words trickled out, light and thin, like a flourless white sauce. The soft A of "Panis Angelicus" came out so flat so that it sounded like the English word "panties" instead of the Latin "Panis." The little witch! How ungrateful! After all she'd done for her, just to show her up. But then, a different fear gripped her: what if it wasn't on purpose? How could it be after all the afternoons of practice? All the glory in the choir room? Mrs. Locke wanted to call time out. Begin again. But this wasn't practice. This was the real thing. She tried to think of something she could do to help the girl as she stumbled over the words. But it was useless, she was on her own.

Eventually, though, the song picked up. About halfway through Madeline found her voice and turned it around. A remarkable feat after the disturbing beginning, but no where near award winning. She'd have no trophy to add to her college application.

At intermission, Mrs. Locke rushed backstage. One look at Madeline told Mrs. Locke she'd done it on purpose. The girls whispered in the corner as if they were planning something. Aghast, Mrs. Locke marched over to break it up. Seeing her, both girls looked down.

"I'm sorry, Mrs. Locke, my performance was awful wasn't it?" Madeline said.

"Yes, it was," she said, barely able to contain her fury.

"I got scared up there. I'll do better next time."

"Suit yourself," Mrs. Locke said sharply. But doubt had crept into her conviction that the girl was sabotaging her performance, and so she said the only thing she could say. "You sing from your heart and you'll do as well as you want. I can't make you do it." She turned to Heather. "A fabulous job, young lady. I expect a blue ribbon from that performance." Heather beamed.

The last song of the night was Madeline's solo, "You'll Never Walk Alone." Mrs. Locke cringed as Madeline approached the microphone. But when the girl opened her mouth, the most glorious sound soared into the rafters. She sang like some banshee, a fury and loneliness in her range mixed with – could it be? – Mrs. Locke shut her eyes in concentration – yes it was – love. She'd done it! She'd reached inside and sang from her heart! She sang it as if she was the only one who could. The thin lanky body shook all over until the last note, when she sang her own breath out. She never cut off the note, but instead held it until the blue climbed up her neck, nose, cheeks, ears, and forehead.

The audience sucked in a collective breath. In the naked quiet Mrs. Locke felt her own diaphragm tighten in pain. She gasped for air and fell forward just as Madeline fell to the floor. The microphone echoed a dull thunk as it hit the stage. People rushed by Mrs. Locke, a high heel crunched her hand, and the auditorium was filled with shouts of "Help her! Somebody get a doctor!"

The pianist performed mouth to mouth resuscitation on the girl, while Mrs. Locke struggled to pull herself to her knees. She felt as if she had fallen from a precipice into a dark and cloudy abyss, and was scratching at its clay edges to pull herself free. She rested her chin on the stage and watched as Madeline, coughing back to life, under the eager vigil of the audience, stole the show.

In the stifling heat, Mrs. Locke fought for breath. Gradually the crowd sighed and began to disperse. Cool air rushed across Mrs. Locke's face. Her chest loosened as the air flushed through her lungs. Her diaphragm heaved with life. What was it she had witnessed? What was it she herself had experienced? She wondered, rising to a standing position.

She watched as Madeline sat up wearily. The girl's naked eyes fluttered against the hot spotlight. She lifted her thin hand to shield them. Mrs. Locke smiled as she looked upon the young girl in awe.

HERESY

John Tucker

Hattiesburg, Mississippi. August, 1998.

Saturday night, we all went to Tal's to see Call Me Mommy and the Side Effects, a punk rock double bill, knowing that we'd get shitfaced, stay up all night and go to church the next morning. We'd been planning it for two months.

We were headed downtown in my ugly-ass beige Plymouth Acclaim. Terry, Oliver, and Billy were in the backseat. Micki was in the front passenger seat and I was driving. After leaving the club, we would go to Terry's apartment and change into clothes more appropriate for church. But for now we were dressed like the miscreants we really were. Terry had on a black T-shirt, baggy grey shorts and combat boots. His sandy blonde hair was gelled vertical. Oliver was wearing a Porn Star shirt with the sleeves ripped off. Billy had the fifties greaser look going, as usual, with a white T-shirt, tight jeans and boots. Micki's hair was dyed burgundy and cut so short that it was wire-stiff, and her ears and nose were pierced with lots of silver. She was wearing a T-shirt that said, "Haven't I ignored you somewhere before?" At five foot two and maybe ninety-five pounds, she was obnoxiously adorable, like a little metallic porcupine. We'd been pretty close for a while. People used to think we were a couple, but it was never like that. She had an earnest, childlike smile that made it seem like everything was right with the world for her. But I knew she'd had a pretty rough childhood. She hadn't told me details; just that her stepfather was a mean sonofabitch, and she resented her mother for putting up with him. She said she would never have kids herself because of the way she grew up. Billy was her current boyfriend; that's how we knew him. I had met Micki years ago, when we were both in a bar we had gotten into with fake IDs. We were both drunk, and I was really shitfaced. I walked up to her, staggering a bit, and said, "I'm not drunk. I walk this way to confuse snipers." She laughed, and we started talking. We had been friends ever since.

"They don't pass around rattlesnakes, do they?" Billy said. "I'm not holding any damned rattlesnakes."

"You wimp!" Oliver said. He clung to the whole anarchist hellraiser philosophy like it was a talisman, always boasting that he wouldn't live to be thirty. He was one of those hyperactive short guys that's always getting heckled.

"No they don't handle snakes," Terry said. "They just jump around and go nuts, kinda like we do in the mosh-pits, but without the music. It's gonna be like a grudge match. On the other team's field! And they won't even know it's a game!" He was talking really fast, already getting excited. It had been his idea. He'd heard about the ramshackle Pentecostal church about four miles out of town, and had gone there one Sunday in June to watch. We had to see it, he told us, and it had gradually developed into a bona fide scheme. "It's a plot, it's a plan, it's a scheme, it's a scam," as he liked to say. He'd gone back recently and told the preacher he had some friends who wanted to get saved. The plan was to "infiltrate, imitate, and escalate," as Terry put it. We were going to see how much bizarre behavior we could get away with while supposedly under the influence of the Holy Spirit.

"Terry, let me try some of that shit you're drinking," Oliver said. Terry handed him the jug, full of a bright yellow mixture of Everclear and pineapple juice. Oliver took a swig, and stifled a grimace. "How much of this is juice?" he asked.

"About half," Terry said.

Terry was the most voracious drinker I had ever seen. He was also the most reckless and unpredictable of us. His energy was more negative, more rooted in anger. Hanging out with him was like walking down a street littered with downed power lines. Not long ago he called Rite Aid's toll-free number to scream at customer service because the pharmacist had given him generic Valium when he'd asked for the brand. They hung up on him twice, and the third time he yelled, "Look motherfucker, you're paying for these calls, and I've got nothing better to do than keep calling all day until I feel better! I don't care what the pharmacists say, generic Valiums aren't as good! Now do you want to give me a sincere apology, or just keep dragging this out?" He got an apology. And everyone he told the story to thought it was hysterical, especially considering it was a forged prescription in the first place. But Micki and I were at his apartment when he did it, and he wasn't doing it for fun. His face was deep red, and he was screaming so loud that spit was flying. Sometimes Terry was frightening, but that was part of his appeal. For better or worse, he made things happen.

When I thought about why all of us were friends, and what we had in common, it seemed like it wasn't so much the things we liked, but the things we rejected.

We got to the club around ten, and had to park a block away because there were so many cars. We all took a pull from Terry's jug before going in. Tal's was cramped and smoke-hazy, but it was cozy that way. Little white or neon green triangles, the corners of torn-down flyers, were scotch-taped all over the rough wood-paneled walls. The flyers for tonight's bands had been up for awhile, and were already stained to an eggshell color from cigarette smoke. Most of the familiar deviants had turned out. Call Me Mommy always drew a good crowd. They were from Louisiana, but had a following here. Both Micki and Terry knew the singer. The Side Effects were opening for them; they were local.

"This is a freakshow," Terry said. "A total fucking freakshow!" He was talking too loud, and heads were turning. He headed straight for the bar. Micki and I walked over to the wall, next to the cigarette machine. Billy loped after us, staying a few feet away, silent and sullen. I could tell it bothered him that Micki and I were always sticking together.

"It's gonna be a long night, before we even get to the main event," I said to her. "Are you sure you're up for it?"

"I'll have to be. I don't want to just hear about it. I mean, this has the potential to become local folklore. Maybe we can score some crystal meth to keep us awake."

I scanned the crowd. "That girl Erin usually has some. But I don't see her."

"Billy," Micki said, "Keep an eye out for Erin. Or that guy Sam; he would know where she's at. You remember Sam? That big ugly dude?"

"Yeah," Billy said.

The Side Effects had taken the stage, and were tuning up.

"I guess I'll get a beer before they start," Micki said. "Billy, let's get some beers." They started toward the bar. "Are you coming with us, Slate?" she said, looking back at me. "Or you want us to bring you one?"

"Yeah, thanks," I said.

Micki had been calling me "Slate" almost as long as I'd known her. When I asked her why, she said, "Because you're so hard to read. Your face is like a blank slate, and I never know what you're thinking."

"Really?" I'd said, thinking that sounded cool.

"No, it's like when they call bald guys 'Curly'."

"Oh, so you mean I'm really easy to read?"

She had only smiled in response. That had been about three years ago. And ever since, whenever she called me "Slate," it made me a little uncomfortable. Like she knew just what was going on in my head.

The Side Effects had a pretty good set. The crowd got livelier, and we were getting drunk. While Call Me Mommy was setting up, Terry went out to my car and smuggled in two half-pint bottles filled with his yellow concoction. He passed one of them around.

"Why didn't you bring those in in the first place?" Oliver asked.

"Because we have to pace ourselves," Terry said.

Billy had located Erin. She was a very pretty girl, though in a conventional way. Tall and thin, long blonde hair, and her bones had all the right angles. She said she didn't have any crystal, but she did have some Ritalin, and said she'd sell them for four bucks apiece. Terry haggled her down to two-fifty, and we pooled our money and bought a dozen.

"Four bucks apiece," Terry said as she was walking away. "She tried to rip us off. The bitch!" He purposely said this last part loud enough for her to hear. She turned around and glared at him. He gave her a sarcastic, closed-lipped smile, and she walked off. We each took one of the pills, and Micki put the rest in her purse for later.

Then the singer of Call Me Mommy greeted the crowd, signaling that they were ready. Many local fans cheered. Some of them started chanting, "Mom-my! Mom-my! Mom-my!" We all moved closer to the stage. "Sean!" Micki yelled, waving at the singer. He smiled just a bit and nodded toward us. He was tall and vulpine, with very short yellow hair. They opened with a song called "Versus the University," that we all recognized. They were louder, faster, and better than any of the local bands, and soon everyone was dancing and bouncing around. Drinks were spilled as people bumped into each other. It was like being inside a pinball machine. Terry passed around the bottles until they were both empty. I kept an eye on Micki. She was a good dancer, and I liked to watch her. Oliver became more and more obnoxious, getting into playful shoving matches with other moshers. About halfway through the set he started tackling Terry and me, with this enormous grin on his face, like he always did on a really good night. It got irritating, but he did it with such exuberance and earnest affection that we just tolerated it. We pushed him back and forth between us, shouting things like "Okay, enough, Oliver, get him now!" I was drinking white Russians, and between being tackled by Oliver and bumping into people, I kept spilling them, then going back to the bar to get more, spending more than I could afford. But so what? This is what it's all about, I told myself. These could be the best times of my life.

The music seemed to get better the more I drank. I tried to get as close to the speakers as I could, but it was the most crowded next to them. I finally maneuvered my way next to one of them and let the music pound through me, feeling the vibrations with my entire body. I looked back at the crowd and watched it undulate like a small storm-tossed ocean. After a few minutes I looked over and Micki was right next to me. She smiled at me, and I smiled back. We stayed there, listening to the music until it stopped and the lights came on. My ears were ringing. It was two o'clock and people started leaving. The singer was having a drink at the bar, and Terry and Micki went over to talk to him. Billy and I went outside, where it wasn't as hot. I offered him a cigarette; he took it. Still, we didn't talk. I wanted to like the guy, but I just couldn't stand the thought of him being with Micki. Once she had tried to explain to me why she was with one dull, boring guy after another. She said she didn't like sleeping with guys she cared about. I told her I thought that was a lousy way to go about things. She said she didn't care.

After about ten minutes, Terry, Micki and Oliver came out.

"We have some new recruits," Terry said. "Sean and the drummer are coming. And Erin; she's driving them. She's drooling for Sean, so I can probably get her to give up some more pills. They're going to get some different clothes and meet us at my apartment."

We got into my car and headed to Terry's.

We had all brought different clothes to change into, but Oliver had merely brought a different T-shirt. Terry bitched at him.

"Well, it has sleeves," Oliver said.

"Oliver, you stupid little shit. If you want to be a real troublemaker, you've got to learn to disguise yourself," Terry said, and tossed him a white Arrow shirt.

Micki had bought a dress for the occasion, because she hadn't owned one. It was long and black, with long, clingy sleeves.

Terry had a suit jacket that he would use to smuggle in one of his bottles.

After changing, we took out our various piercings and brushed our hair.

"Micki, what are you gonna do about your hair?" Oliver asked.

She looked at him blankly.

"He's right, Micki," Terry said. "I don't think you can pass. It's hardly a natural color. Besides, they think it's a sin for women to cut their hair."

No-one spoke for a few seconds.

"We can shave your head," Terry said. "Make you look like a cancer patient."

She thought abut it, then shrugged. "Okay. That might be cool, actually. I've always wondered what I would look like without hair, anyway."

Oh shit, I thought. Micki, don't do that.

"Yeah, a cancer kid, and you can pretend to get healed!" Terry said.

Oliver laughed.

We went into the bathroom and Terry got some electric shears from a drawer. "Are you sure?" he asked her.

"Yeah, why not?"

I cringed and turned away. I walked out into the hall, but could still hear the damned buzzing. When I went back into the bathroom, Micki was bald, and appraising herself in the mirror. "Cool," she said.

"Well," Terry said, "You've still got eyebrows. Chemo patients lose their eyebrows too, I think."

"No, I don't think so," I said.

"Yeah, they do," Terry said.

"Fuck it, I'll shave them off too," Micki said. "I've never really liked my eyebrows. I could draw on ones I like later."

"Micki," I said, "You're drunk. I don't think I've ever seen you this drunk. You'll regret it."

"It's not a big deal," she said.

"Really, lighten up," Terry said.

I couldn't believe Billy wasn't saying anything. He should be pissed at Terry. Billy was totally worthless, I decided. Dead weight. I turned away again, and cautiously turned back around when the buzzing stopped.

"Not bad," Terry said. "But you've still got eyelashes."

"No-one's touching her eyelashes!" I said, louder than I meant too.

She smiled at me. "Calm down, Slate. I'm not that drunk."

"You look perfect," Terry said. "You could be a twelve-year old girl."

We took the rest of the pills and sat in the living room, waiting for the others. Terry put on a CD. It was "The Downward Spiral," by Nine Inch Nails, cacophonous, angry industrial music. He started singing along to one of his favorite songs, "Heresy." "God is dead! And no-one cares! If there is a hell, I'll see you there!" I watched Micki stare into space. She was drinking aggressively, with a grim determination that made me uneasy for her.

The sun was just coming up when Erin and Sean and whatshisface the drummer finally got there, but it was still too early to leave.

Sean convinced Erin to surrender the rest of her pills. She dumped them out on the coffee table, next to the stack of Bibles we'd gotten to complete our disguises. We crushed the pills into powder and snorted it. Terry would spit on his thumb and suck it up his nose after doing a line; he said it helped with absorption. Oliver decided to do it too.

Then Erin asked Terry for a spoon. He went and got her one, and she took out a needle and some heroin from her purse, and started cooking it. Seeing this felt awkward, because none of the rest of us ever did that. We watched her digging around with the needle under the skin of her arm, trying to find a vein that had grown calloused and illusive, with this look of intense concentration, while blood slowly ran and dripped. It reminded me of someone cleaning out an ear with a cue-tip. She noticed us watching and looked up momentarily. "It doesn't hurt," she said.

I sat there listening to the music, which now seemed more somber and plaintive than angry. I heard the singer whispering under the clamor of music, almost as if he wasn't sure he wanted to be heard. I heard him say, "Maybe I don't have a choice. And maybe that is all I have, and maybe this is a cry for help." I started to think that maybe something was wrong with all of this. I couldn't really get to the root of it, though. It was the same feeling of wrongness that I'd always had, that I'd never been able to figure out. And I knew by now that I never would figure it out, so I just kept drinking. I was afraid that what we were going to do might turn out really badly.

Before leaving, we all gargled with mouthwash to cover the smell of alcohol.

Terry gave me directions from the backseat while I drove. Erin followed us. The Ritalin had mostly cancelled out the debilitating effects of the alcohol, so driving wasn't too dangerous. I just felt kind of disconnected from everything. The buildings and trees and signs were passing me by, and I was merely watching it all unfold. The church was in the rural area north of town. It was a simple, white, wood building at the end of a dirt road in the woods. There were about eight cars there already, all older models, most of them dusty and run-down with cracks in the windshields. There was a small group of people standing around the front of the church. The women all wore long dresses, with hair hanging down to their asses. The men wore dark pants and white shirts. Most of them were middle-aged or older, and there were a few children, but I didn't see anyone who looked close to our age.

"Man, these people are hard-core," Oliver said.

"I thought they all wore fancy dark jackets," Billy said.

"Maybe these people are different," Micki said.

"It's probably just too hot for them to wear jackets," Terry said as I pulled to a stop. Erin parked beside us, and we all got out. The sun was higher now, and it was going to be another hot day.

"We've still got about fifteen minutes before the service starts," Terry said. "I'm going to go talk to the preacher." He smoothed his hair back and walked toward the group, looking for all the world like an honest, well-behaved young man. We stayed back and hovered around our cars.

The preacher was a heavyset man, a redhead, middle-aged, with a stern brow and deepset, accusing eyes. Fuck you, you self-righteous prick, I thought. Like you're so much better than us. He glanced at us and nodded as he listened to Terry, who was probably telling him that Micki was dying of cancer. The idea bothered me now, and I wondered why it hadn't before.

Other cars were pulling up now. Oliver and Sean and the drummer guy were making jokes about the people who were arriving.

"Damn, that woman's ugly," Sean was saying. "She's so ugly, they'd make fun of her on the island of Dr. Moreau."

Oliver and Whatshisname the drummer laughed. Erin smiled appreciatively at Sean. Billy obviously didn't get it. Micki wasn't listening. I took her aside and whispered, "Are you sure you want to do this?"

"What? Do you think I'd turn back now?"

"Well, no, of course not. You just seem kind of – I don't know, glum."

"I'm fine, Slate. It'll be fun."

A young woman had just arrived, and she was leading a toddler, a little boy, by the hand. She had dressed him in the same kind of clothes as the men. The starched white shirt was too big, and the collar reached almost to his ears. His black shoes shined with fresh polish.

"Look at that kid," I said. "He seems really young to bring to church."

"He's adorable," she said quietly, like she was thinking out loud.

"You almost sound like you want to have one of your own."

"That might not be so bad," she said.

"I thought you said you'd never have kids, because of your stepfather, and all that . . ."

"I can't ever have kids. Because of my stepfather."

It took a few seconds for me to understand. If he did something to her when she was really young . . .

"You don't mean . . ." I said.

"Yeah, I do. Yeah, he did."

I just stared at her. She looked even smaller without hair. Her eyes looked even bigger without eyebrows. I realized that I'd never touched her, except by accident. Right then I wondered what it might be like to do it on purpose. The only thing that allowed me to resist the urge was that I just didn't dare. Sometimes the possibility of something is too valuable to risk losing.

Micki. Little porcupine. You seem so naked without your spines.

Then a pickup truck pulled up, with these two big, beefy farmboy types in it. I watched them get out. They were both wearing overalls, and both of them were over six feet, with big rough hands that looked like they could snap raw corncobs in half.

Terry came back up to where the rest of us were waiting. "It's on," he said, grinning.

"Terry, look," I said. "Maybe this is a bad idea. We could end up getting into serious trouble. I mean, look at those two guys," I gestured toward the young men who'd just arrived. "They could probably beat the hell out of us."

"Hey, come on, have a little faith," he said, tauntingly.

"That word is not in my vocabulary."

"Well, isn't that why you're here? Wasn't it you who said that if God were in His right mind, why did He decide that believing without seeing is the ultimate virtue? Admit it; you're angry. At this place, and all places like it. Just like me; just like the rest of us. Don't try to pull some responsible, older-brother shit now."

"Really," Oliver said. "You do act that way sometimes, man."

"Come on," Terry said, leading the way in. "Let's make some shit happen."

The church was one big room, with no air-conditioning. It was already hot. A woman opened the windows as people filed into the pews. Our group sat toward the back, on the left side of the center aisle. The farmboys sat right behind us. The preacher walked slowly to the front, smiling and nodding to a few of the regulars along the way. After everyone was settled and the room got quiet, the preacher cleared his throat and began.

"I'd like to welcome everyone back on this lovely morning of our holy seventh day. I hope you've all been well, and have used your time away in service of our Lord and savior . . ."

The air was heavy and stale; it was crowded and the pews were too close to each other. I should have borrowed some deodorant from Terry before we left.

"And I'd like to welcome those who are here for the first time. I hope you find today's service to be rewarding and enlightening . . ."

We all exchanged glances and tried not to smirk too visibly.

"I'd like to begin by reading from second Corinthians. If you'll open your Bibles to chapter ten, verse ten . . ."

I opened one of the Bibles that Oliver had stolen from the Comfort Inn where his mom worked, pretending to look for the appropriate page. Micki opened the one that she and Billy were sharing. On the other side of me, Erin looked on with Sean. She was already leaning on his shoulder, the shameless slut.

The little boy was sitting on his mother's lap a couple of rows down, examining a bookmark. Micki kept glancing at him.

The preacher's voice was low and booming. It was stuffy as hell in there and I was already sweating from my brow. He droned on, and pages turned. Dammit, hurry up and get to the theatrics, I thought.

"And that, brothers and sisters, is the point I've been trying to make." His voice was getting louder now. "The promises of God are yes and Amen! But you must believe them to receive them. If you don't believe, you won't receive! Do you believe the promises of God?"

"Yes we do!" a woman in the front said.

"Amen!" someone in the back said.

"We have angels watching over us! For he shall give his angels charge over thee, to keep thee in all thy ways, lest thou dash thy foot against a stone! Psalm ninety-one eleven! What have we to fear if we have angels watching over us?"

"Not a thing!" someone said.

"Ye have not been given the spirit of bondage again to fear, but ye have received the Spirit of adoption, whereby we cry Abba, Father! Romans eight fifteen! We have been adopted by God!"

"Hallelujah!" a woman said.

"I will not leave you comfortless: I will come to you. John fourteen eighteen. The Spirit is with us always. Thou shalt call, and the Lord shall answer; thou shalt cry, and he shall say, Here I am! Isaiah fifty-eight nine!"

"Praise God!" someone said.

"At destruction and famine thou shalt laugh; neither shalt thou be afraid of the beasts of the earth. Job five twenty-two! When thou liest down, thou shalt not be afraid; yea, thou shalt lie down, and thy sleep shall be sweet! Proverbs three twenty-four! God watches over us even in our sleep!"

More voices of approval from the crowd.

"We must always obey the Holy Spirit! Those who are led by the Spirit of God shall be called the children of God! Romans eight fourteen! If the Spirit moves you to surrender your last penny, then surrender it!"

"Yes Lord!" Someone said.

"Surrender!" someone else said.

"Surrender to God!" the preacher said, pointing at the speaker. More voices of eager assent followed.

"If the Spirit moves you to raise your hands to heaven, then raise them!"

More hallelujahs and yes lords.

"Raise them!" the preacher yelled, pointing to a woman in the front. She promptly stood and raised her arms. Here we go, I thought.

"I feel it!" she shouted. "I feel the Spirit!" Loud voices of approval came from all around now. The little boy started crying.

The preacher continued. "If the Spirit moves you to stand and shout, then stand and shout!"

Terry stood up and yelled, "I feel it! I feel it too!"

"Hallelujah, brother!" The preacher said, pointing at him.

"Hallelujah!" several voices repeated.

Then Oliver sprang up and said, "I feel it too!"

"Yes, brother!" the preacher said, pointing to him. "I believe the Spirit of God is in this church today! Who else believes?"

Two others near the front stood up and answered.

"Yesss!" the preacher said. "And if the Spirit tells you to stand and sing, then in the name of Jesus, stand and sing!"

Taking the cue, Sean stood up and started singing "Amazing grace," loud as fuck, gravelly-voiced, breaking the words into too many syllables and punctuating the verses with rapid gibberish, pretending to speak in tongues, and we could almost hear the guitars exploding in sync, growling at fever-pitch, amped through huge, bad speakers. We all got up and started slinging ourselves around, and the rest of the church's faithful rose and joined us, screaming about the power and the glory. I couldn't believe it. They actually thought we were sincere.

Things escalated quickly. People were yelling, swaying, spinning, and falling down as though unconscious. Whatshisname the drummer was running in place on a pew, feet pounding the wood loud and fast enough to wake all of Dublin's dead. Oliver was skipping and leapfrogging up and down the leftmost aisle, intermittently stopping to see if anyone was watching him. Terry was over in the back corner, stomping his feet and gulping from his bottle. Micki was dancing smoothly and elegantly, her long black dress swishing to and fro, arms moving in a graceful serpentine motion. The heat was tremendous; the noise was deafening. I could see the little boy wailing. His mother had supposedly fainted. In fact she was on her second fainting spell. The farmboys were rocking back and forth, smiling and watching.

"I believe revival is in this place!" the preacher shouted.

And I absolutely couldn't believe it. I had been wrong to doubt Terry.

I danced closer to the front, toward the preacher, strutting right by his bare-bones podium. As I did, he glanced at me. Up close, his eyes looked different. They were grayish-blue, the lower lids drooping at the edges, making him look weary and sad.

"Save me preacher!" I yelled.

"Call to Jesus and you will be saved!" he told me.

"Yes! Yes!" I said, and swiveled my hips like Elvis.

I turned around and saw Micki. She had stopped dancing, and was just standing there, staring at the bawling kid. His mother was turning in faster and faster circles, her long hair flying as she spun into another swoon. And there she went, collapsing again. He was terrified. Micki slowly started to walk toward him, arms outstretched. But her strange appearance only frightened him more, and he screamed even louder. She stopped abruptly

251

and withdrew her hands, as though she'd heard a curt voice telling her she wasn't allowed. Her face turned forlorn, like it might crumble down the front of her dress. And I knew that all this had been a mistake.

Micki, you can't have children. Because your stepfather-Jesus, Micki.

Terry pranced up to her, taking her arm and shouting, "C'mon Micki! Come get healed! Come on!" She shrugged off his hand and shook her head.

"Come on Micki!"

"Terry!" I yelled, "Just leave her alone!"

He looked at me contemptuously, and rolled his eyes in exasperation. He took a swig from his bottle, then sauntered past me, toward the front.

I don't know how many people saw what happened next, other than Micki and me. Terry walked right up to the preacher, spit a mouthful of that nasty yellow shit right in his face, and screamed, "Praise Jesus!" Then he smiled this wicked smile and broke into his silliest dance. It looked kind of like off-balance jumping jacks.

In the back row, the farmboys started laughing. I heard one of them say, "I like that guy! He's crazy!" We had been planning this scheme to come in here and make fun of everyone for several weeks, and apparently these two came in here and did it every Sunday.

The preacher stepped back and wiped his face, eyes wide with shock. I watched his surprise slowly turn to livid rage as he understood. I waited for him to begin choking Terry to death. His eyes moved across the room, taking in everything: his congregation, their heads thrown back and their arms waving in paroxysms of joy, and us in our conservative camouflage, making fun of them all. Micki watched. I waited. Everyone else was yelling and dancing and sweating. It was so hot in there.

Then the preacher said, "Yes, praise Jesus . . .praise Jesus!" His voice got louder with effort, trembling a little, but not with jubilation. He was mad at all of us, mad as hell, but he was just swallowing it, because he didn't want his congregation to know what was really happening. And I suddenly respected him, because that's what he was most concerned with. He wanted to protect them.

I thought about the difference between us and them, and I realized what my friends and I had in common. It wasn't what we'd rejected, so much as what we felt rejected by. It was all the promises we didn't believe.

And why had coming here and doing this been so important to us? Were we trying to make some kind of statement? If so, what was it? I remembered what Erin had said back at Terry's, while she was bleeding all over herself. "It doesn't hurt." Maybe that was what we were trying to say, to them, and to ourselves.

We don't believe you, don't believe there's a reason for everything, that it all works out for the best, that all the wrongs will be made right. We don't believe it because we can't.

And it doesn't hurt.

Micki sat down in the pew, her mouth open in silence, helpless to do anything but keep watching. I should have known better than to bring her here. Small and skinny with her bald head, she really did look like a child who was sick, and would never get well. Maybe because that's what she really was. I wanted to tell her I was sorry. But for what exactly? For how much of this? For how much of everything? I didn't know where or how to start, so I just turned and walked toward the doors at the back of the church, feeling ugly and dirty. I needed to stand outside for a minute, alone, before coming back in to get her.

And God shall wipe away all tears from their eyes;-Revelation 21:4

ABOUT THE WRITERS

MARION BARNWELL, who retired from teaching English at Delta State University in 2003, edited *A Place Called Mississippi (University Press, 1997)* which won a Special Achievement Award from the Mississippi Institute of Arts and Letters in 1998. She co-authored, with Patti Carr Black, *Touring Literary Mississippi* (University Press, 2002). She has written many articles, short stories, and a play. She was co-founder and editor of *Tapestry*, a faculty literary magazine at Delta State University, and was also co-founder, co-editor, and contributor to *On the Way Home*, a collection of stories published by Ruby Shoes Press in 1996.

PATTI CARR BLACK, former director of the Old Capitol Museum in Jackson, received the Governor's Award in 2003 for her contributions to the arts, and the MS Institute of Arts and Letters award for non-fiction in 1999 for her book ART IN MISSISSIPPI. She is the founder of Edge Press which published EUDORA WELTY'S WORLD; WORDS ON NATURE. A native of Sumner, a graduate of MS University for Women and Emory University, Black lives in Jackson.

LOTTIE BRENT BOGGAN, Jackson resident and author of a memoir, *Come Up Churning and Keep Your Buckets High*, is a long time travel writer for The NorthSide Sun. She has won many awards for her fiction as well as her non-fiction. Lottie says, "When I write, without meaning to, I go back to the places where memory begins. As a child I heard the voices of older people around the dinner table, on a porch swing, as they told family stories or their own tales."

DAVID CREEL, a native of Richton, Mississippi, is a distinguished local journalist, having served as the beauty, fashion and style columnist for The Clarion-Ledger and VIP Jackson magazine. David's writing career began as *"The Makeover Guy"* for the Northside Sun, and he has also been published in *Premiere Bride* and *Mississippi Baby and Child*. David is the editor of the state's first magazine dedicated exclusively to fashion, beauty, and style which is appropriately entitled *Beautiful With David* and the new online version of the magazine debuted in September 2008 at www.beautifulmagazine.org. A frequent guest lecturer at Millsaps College, the producer/host of a local radio talk show, Unzipped on WLEZ-FM 103.7, and former owner of two successful salons this southern boy is living his dream. David and his partner, Dr. Chris Gilmer, call Jackson home along with their four dogs Sophia, Lillian, Stella and Naomi.

ANNE EVANS was born and raised in Jackson, Ms. She graduated from the University of Notre Dame in 1995 then moved to Oakland, CA where she worked as the volunteer coordinator for the Center for AIDS Services. Anne continued her education at the University of Mississippi where she earned her M.A. in Southern Studies and George Mason University where she earned her M.F.A. in Fiction Writing. She taught composition at Ole Miss and creative writing at Tougaloo College and is currently a visiting professor in creative writing at Metropolitan State College of Denver. She has written two novels and numerous short stories and poems. Anne has also appeared in the anthology, *Fireflies in Fruit Jars.*

JOHN FLOYD is the author of more than 700 short stories and fillers in some 200 different publications. This year his stories have appeared in (among others) *The Strand Magazine, Woman's World*, and *Alfred Hitchcock's Mystery Magazine*. John won the 2007 Derringer Award for short mystery fiction and has published two books, *Rainbow's End and Other Stories* (2006), and *Midnight* (2008).

PAT FLOYD was born and raised in Simpson county, Mississippi and now makes his home in Clinton. His stories have appeared the 2007 anthology Fireflies In Fruit Jars and in the 2008 Winners' Circle sponsored by the Arts Council of Clinton. Pat also won first place in the 2007 Winners Circle that was judged by the author Carolyn Haines. Yarns and lies are his passion.

SARAH FRANCES HARDY worked as a fine artist showing in galleries throughout the Southeast as well as in New York before writing children's books. She worked with Steve Wynn, casino mogul and renowned art collector, creating artwork for his casino on the Mississippi Gulf Coast. Over the last few years, she has refocused her creative energy toward writing and illustrating books, and she is a member of SCBWI. Recently, Sarah won an honorable mention in the adult fiction category of the *Writer's Digest* annual writing competition. She graduated from Davidson College and the University of Mississippi School of Law.

PHILIP L. LEVIN, president of the 90-member Gulf Coast Writers Association, markets his best-selling suspense thriller *Inheritance, Chinese children's fable, Consuto and the Rain God,* and the GCWA anthology, *Teacakes and Afternoon Tales* from the website www.gcwriters.org. Not having learned his lesson from Katrina, he's back on the beach, continuing his "other job" as an E.R. Doc at the Memorial Hospital of Gulfport.

RICKEY R. MALLORY is a native Mississippian. She has published 9 romantic suspense novels for Harlequin Intrigue and 5 paranormal romances for Ima Jinn Books. Her backlist and upcoming books can be seen at www.rrmallory.com http://www.untimateagents.com Rickey credits her love of books to her mother who taught her that books are precious and should be treated with loving respect. Her grandfather and her father were both steeped in the southern tradition of oral history, and could hold an audience spellbound with their storytelling skills. She aspires to be as good a storyteller as her father.

CHARLINE R. McCORD, a resident of Clinton, Mississippi, was born in Hattiesburg and grew up in Laurel, Mississippi, and Jackson, Tennessee. She holds a Ph.D. in English from the University of Southern Mississippi and bachelor's and master's degrees in English from Mississippi College, where she won the Bellamann Award for Creative Writing and edited the literary magazine. She has co-edited a series of books with Judy Tucker – *Christmas Stories from the South's Best Writers*, *Growing Up in Mississippi*, *A Dixie Christmas*, *Christmas in the South*, *A Very Southern Christmas*, and *Christmas Stories from Mississippi*.

MARY DAYLE McCORMICK grew up in the Mississippi Delta. She received her Bachelor and Master of Fine Arts degrees from Louisiana Tech University. She and husband Hugh live in Greenville where they own an independent bookstore, McCormick Book Inn. She writes feature articles and book reviews as well as short fiction. Mary Dayle says, "I try to sink so far into my words that the reader forgets about me and enters my story. If the magic works, it's just the reader and the characters forming their own relationships."

MELANIE NOTO is a multi-published author of romantic suspense under the pen name of Melanie Atkins. She is an editor for an online publishing company. Writing, Melanie says, is more than an escape—it's a way of life. She grew up in the deep South listening to tall tales, reading about far away places, and penning fascinating stories about her cats. Now she writes gripping stories of love, suspense, and mystery with the help of her latest feline muse. You can find out more about Melanie and her books at www.melanieatkins.com

BILL PATRICK is a native Jacksonian who took a 27-year hiatus to see the world, courtesy of Uncle Sam. Before returning home he stopped by the west coast and completed his postgraduate studies. His avocations are food and travel and he has written extensively about both.

PEGGY GILMER-PIASECKI is a mother and grandmother. She has had a long career as an administrative professional and enjoys reading, writing, gardening, and sewing as an art form. She and her husband, Ed, live in Jackson and enjoy taking short or long car trips together, exploring out-of-the-way places. Her writings include poetry, short stories, a children's book, and at present she is working on a novel.

RICHELLE PUTNAM is an editor/reviewer for *Sotto Voce* magazine. She is enrolled in the Gotham Writers Fiction Certificate Program and has completed three Institute of Children's Literature courses, the Advanced Writing Program of Open College for the Arts, and Gotham Writers Playwriting and Advanced Poetry Courses. Her work has been published in *Flashquake, The Copperfield Review, Common Ties, Cayuse Press, Writer's Journal, and A Cup of Comfort for Mothers and Daughters.* Her literature for children has been published on the Institute of Children's Literature's website, Gotta Write Network, *Writing Korner,* and Wee Ones, and in print publications, such as, *Boy's Quest, Appleseeds,* and *Hopscotch Magazine for Girls.* She is Founder and President of Mississippi Writers Guild and is on the Literary Arts Artist Roster for the State of Mississippi.

DOROTHY SHAWHAN is the author of the novel, *Lizzie,* and is co-author with Dr. Martha Swain of the biography *Lucy Somerville Howorth: New Deal Lawyer, Politician, and Feminist From the South.* She is professor of English and Chair Emerita at Delta State University where she taught for 25 years and chaired the Division of Languages and Literature for 14. She holds the B.A. Degree from Mississippi University for Woman, the M.A. from Louisiana State University, and the M.F.A. from George Mason University. She lives and writes in Cleveland, Mississippi.

CARLENE SINGLETON is a native of Jackson, Mississippi. Over the span of twenty-six years, while a wife and mother, she fostered over forty babies, some of whom were severely handicapped. She is known for her work in Child Advocacy. On the founding board of the MS Council for Public Policy and adoption Ministries of MS, she was also on the Board of Right to Life of Jackson, where she wrote and produced radio ads. Her book, *We Carry Gold*, about her foster babies, was her first writing effort. Encouragement from other writers led her to pick up writing again.

SUE STOCK spent twelve years at school in Crystal Springs, then went off to college in Lynchburg, Virginia, where she wrote for the literary magazine and the newspaper. After graduating from college, she worked a year for a newspaper. She has written short stories, poems, and a novel, and continues to find great pleasure in the writing of others.

JOHN MICHAEL TUCKER, born in Fairfax, Virginia, received degrees in English and Psychology at University of Southern Mississippi and did post graduate work at Mississippi College. His short story *Heresy* won 1st place in a national colligate fiction. His poetry has been published in *Emerald Coast Review* and his story "Lunatic Fringe" took first place in Tupelo's Gum Tree Festival.

JUDY TUCKER is an independent editor and playwright. She was awarded a Literary Arts Fellowship by the Mississippi Arts Commission in 2007. *Growing Up in Mississippi* compiled and edited by Tucker and Charline McCord will come out in spring of 2008 and their fifth anthology of Christmas stories will be out in fall of the same year. She and Lottie Boggan have collaborated on, *On the Sleeping Porch, Fireflies in Fruit Jars,* and on this book.

 **JACQUELINE F. WHEELOCK**, born and reared on the Mississippi Gulf Coast, received the Bachelor of Science and Master of Education from Southern University in Baton Rouge and her Master of Library Science degree from University of Southern Mississippi. She won the Zora Neale Hurston-Bessie Head Fiction Award at the Gwendolyn Brooks Writers' Conference. She was an award winner in the William Faulkner Awards for Short Fiction in 2003. "Christmas Lights" was selected for inclusion in the *Christmas Stories from Mississippi.* She and husband Donald live in Madison.

 **RUTH WHITE** has a passion for her native South with its rich settings, diverse characters, and treasure of stories handed down through the generations. The daughter of an educator, she also pursued teaching literature at the high school level until she turned to writing as fulfillment of a lifelong goal. RC White has two novels appearing in 2008, *Ascension at Antioch* and *Devil's Trace.* When not writing, she loves spending time at her farm, where she and her husband have worked to create a wild-life habitat.